Robbie Cameron

DEDIC

To Mary McHugh
the love of my life...
the mother of my children

✝✝✝

THE REFERENDUM FOR
SCOTLAND'S INDEPENDENCE
18 September 2014

Wha for SCOTLAND's king and law,
Freedom's sword will strongly draw,
FREE-MAN stand, or FREE-MAN fa'
Let him follow me.
—Robert Burns

iii

D. N. Curran

ACKNOWLEDGMENTS

My thanks to Carol Zimmerman
(The von Raesfeld Agency)
Without her editing assistance,
this book would never have been published.

My thanks to Dorothy Hardy
She has brought Robbie Cameron to life.

Prologue

As I take pen to paper, I began my life in Western Scotland in the year of our lord 1730. I'm Scottish by birth, British by decree, and a Highlander by the grace of God Almighty. My father was a groom for the clan chief, Cameron. We were more fortunate than most as my father was employed by the great man, so we always had a roof over our heads and food on the table.

Cameron of Lochiel was like a king of sorts. All members of his clan paid homage to him, and were bound by his rules. To disobey his wishes meant a man became an outcast. On this particular day the men of the clan were gathered in the main hall of the castle.

It was a grand sight, the smooth sandstone walls of the interior were covered with rich tapestries depicting the history of the clan battles down through the generations. Tall, arched windows were glazed with gaily colored glass set in lead astragals.

In the center of the ornate paneled wall facing east, was a great stone fireplace, so big that a stone bench was built into both sides of the hearth. When the flames died down after the ceremonial supper was over, there was a warm place where a man and his guests could sit and partake of a dram in comfort while the clan piper entertained them.

Being a superstitious lot, the Scots always built their homes facing east and preferably on a raised area with a view over water, so many of the great homes and castles were built in this fashion.

The windows looked out onto a large expanse of grass bordered with trees and shrubs beyond which were the gardens which supplied the clan's vegetables. The loch (or "lake" as the English refer to an inland water) was the set piece of the view. Beyond that, high snow-capped mountain peaks dominated the skyline.

Rumors and folklore spoke of a secret passage that could be entered from the rear of the fireplace by merely pushing on the heavy wrought iron bracket holding a huge cauldron blackened by the smoke of many fires over hundreds of years. Some said it led down to the loch shore where a small row boat, complete with sail, was always ready lest the chief have a need to flee from invaders.

In my time the invaders were the English, but before that the Norsemen were an invading force, who raped and pillaged over hundreds of years. All that remained of that time in Scotland's history were small areas, particularly near the ocean, where inhabitants had names like Anderson, Medhus, and other Danish names.

I was one of the last to arrive as the chief strode into the room dressed in black silk britches and a long coat with matching cloth buttons, topped off with a high collar, which gave shelter from the cold blasts of wind that came howling in from the North Sea.

Chief Cameron walked well for a man his age, but always with the help of a cane. My father told me by merely turning the gold crest on the handle in a clockwise direction, the man could pull out a long slender sword if the occasion warranted such an act of desperation. With his long wig of shiny black ringlets, he was a man to be admired.

Tommy Spear, the young man standing next to me, whispered in my ear. "Robbie lad, me and Willie Urquhart are planning to leave this very night for the Carolinas."

"Have ye asked permission of the Chief, Tommy?"

"We'll not be doing that, Robbie. That's one of the reasons we're going lad. We're weary of following orders and never getting ahead. We're told by them that have been that the Carolinas are a place where a man can make something of himself and not be worrying if he has an idea for self-enrichment that can get him branded as a trouble maker. After a couple of years in servitude, we'll be free to start a new life as free men."

"How I envy you, Tommy. My cousin James has been gone five years now. He writes that many men in his position have taken Indian maidens as wives. You remember Jimmy? He made such a decision and now is happily married with his own land and three sons to help him carve out his new life as a landowner. The tribe welcomed him to marry the daughter of their chief. He could never have achieved this if he'd stay in Argyll.

"Really?" Tommy said. "Man, to think I might succeed like Jimmy, wouldn't that be something?" he chuckled, giving me a friendly dig in the ribs.

I myself had often lain in the barn on the sweet smelling hay, dreaming of going to the colonies. It was my favorite pastime after I'd done my chores which consisted of seeing to the horses and making sure the cattle were fed and watered. At times I would be asked to do a bit of milking, but normally that was done by the young maidens of the clan who weren't already spoken for.

Father Toomey, our priest, would often talk to me about the situation in our land. He was only too happy to have someone who listened and asked questions. He was an historian at heart and my showing interest in all things endeared me to him. Of course, his primary task was to teach the Bible, which besides giving us an understanding of God, also taught us to read. Reading a page of the Bible every night soon enabled me to become an avid reader, especially when a letter would arrive from James, my wealthy cousin.

My father would gather us 'round the fire after our evening meal. "Robbie, lad." He'd call me over after having taking his place by the fireside in his favorite chair and my mother having set a glass of his best homemade purchine by his side. While the young ones from various families sat at his feet in anticipation, he'd put on his spectacles, take out the letter from James, and when everyone was quiet, he'd hand it to me.

"Read out Cousin James' letter, lad, and tell us all how he's faring."

First I cleared my throat and looked around to make sure I had everyone's attention. "James writes he is prospering beyond his wildest dreams and wishes we could come over and join him."

I'd then tell of all his many deeds of daring in that far off land of America, inhabited by men whose skin was red and the many opportunities for those willing and able to take a chance.

"I can well imagine, Robbie. James has found wealth and happiness. God only knows there's not much to be happy about living in Scotland under the rule of the English."

Father Toomey would often call for me in the evening when my chores were finished and we'd spend time by the Chief's river fishing for trout as he'd talk of politics. He'd tell of how the Chiefs walked a very fine line between insurrection and obeying the king's laws, which mostly amounted to more taxes.

"English laws don't sit well with unruly Scots, do they, Father?"

"How well you might ask, Robbie, especially for those of us who are of the Highlands, not like those folk in the south, the Sassenachs. As you well know, Robbie, in Gaelic that's not-so-nice term for those brothers who choose to accommodate the English and their laws.

"Hence there's a certain amount of friction between the Highlanders and those who live in the lower half of Scotland. The chiefs are always arguing amongst themselves how to treat their English rulers and their army that we nicknamed 'Redcoats.'

"Some do favor peace at all costs with the English king and there's talk of them forming regiments to fight for the Crown. This means when their young men join the army they no longer have to be fed and clothed, making it less of a burden on the clan—not to mention the money the men send home to wives and mothers from time to time."

"Father, why is it that money seems to be at the root of all our problems?"

"Ah, Robbie, it's been like this from time immemorial. Why, even in the Bible we read about brother against brother and I don't see it being any different in our time. I'm sad to say, it was thirty pieces of silver that was the cause of Christ's crucifixion. Yes, Robbie, it is the root of all evil."

"Do you think it will ever change, Father?"

"I fear not, Robbie, as long as the English hold the purse strings. I don't see it happening any time soon."

* * *

So those were the days I spent hoping for a chance to make my fortune, which would make my life a better one than that of my family. That's why I was shocked to hear a man talk about young Prince Charles, son of our banished King James.

As I stood in the village square, a young man of obvious means summoned all the common folk to a meeting. He was dressed in clothes worn only by gentlemen with his silk pantaloons and his broad-brimmed hat with a pheasant feather stuck in it at a jaunty angle. He was a sight to behold with his sword and two finely crafted French pistols stuck in his broad red sash.

He took a scroll from his pocket and began to read as the sleeves of his fancy silk shirt billowed in the breeze.

"Men and women of Argyll, Charles Stuart, our rightful king is coming to Scotland to claim his Scottish throne from the English monarch, Wee German Georgie, as we Highlanders refer to him." His voice hardened. "It's not a view held by many in the lowlands though. They favor peace at all costs."

One man in the crowd yelled at the top of his lungs. "Where are you from, sir? Are you a spokesman for our liege?"

The messenger climbed up on a stone stoop, swept his hat off his head, waved it in air and shouted, "Aye, I'm from the court of the Bonnie Prince himself."

The crowd cheered. Some starting singing songs now outlawed by the Crown. It was said if a man was caught with his clan tartan worn around him or if he sang such songs, the penalty was death by hanging.

After the meeting, the men went into the inn to drown their sorrows and talk treason. I remained outside and spoke at length with the courier, who told me he was the bastard son of a clan chief. Although he held no title in his clan, he'd been educated in France. He spoke to me of many things he'd seen and instilled in me a passion for regarding our German master in London with great disdain.

I must have appeared to be lending a deaf ear, because he caught me by my coat lapel and said, "Robbie lad, beware. Many of the lowland clans are leaving our Catholic religion and becoming Protestants. That's the new faith from Germany, begun by the former priest, Martin Luther. His teachings are more in keeping with what the English parliament favors."

Taking a flask from his coat pocket, he uncorked it and handed it to me. "Have a swallow, Robbie. It's from my chief's special cask—smooth, yet potent."

Looking around to see if my father was nearby, I felt like a schoolboy about to get his first kiss.

"Are you looking for someone, Robbie?"

"Aye well, it's my father, you see. I dinna usually drink."

"Oh, I see. Well then, just hand it back. No harm done."

I quickly put the flask to my lips and let the golden elixir slide down my throat. The sensation soon turned to misery as I began to cough.

"Just wait a minute, Robbie. The fire will be out soon and you'll feel like you don't have a care in the world." He grabbed the flask, took a quick swallow, and re-corked it. "This day, to be a Catholic is suspect, as the Pope in Rome is on good terms with the French, the Portuguese, and the Spanish. We Catholics who remain obedient to him as our spiritual leader are like a thorn in the side of the English lords.

"So you see, Robbie, there are many problems brewing amongst the different factions in this year of our Lord 1745. Be on your guard at all times, lad, and speak not of which we have spoken to a living soul."

Standing at attention, feeling quite elated, I placed a hand on my rosary. "I can assure you, sir..." I hiccupped. "My lips are sealed in these matters. You have my word on it."

"Well, Robbie, I must be gone." He grabbed his chestnut mount by its mane and held it tight by the bit. In one leap, he was in the saddle. His mount neighed and reared up on its hind legs. He reined it in and eased backwards. Its iron shoes clicked on the cobblestone street. He waved his hat in the air.

"Til we meet again, Robbie Cameron. Keep your powder dry, lad."

I stood smiling at my newfound friend as he galloped down the road and out of my life forever.

* * *

Men came bringing the news. Like lightning strikes before a summer storm, they dashed between the clans who favored a Scottish King and told of the landing by the Scottish prince who had just arrived from France on a fishing boat. His ambition was to raise an army to fight the English. At first, most were skeptical as we'd been told often that the Prince would return, but this time it was different. Men spoke amongst themselves of how well he fared and how our chief was to be his confidante.

7

Cameron of Lochiel agreed to have a parlay with Prince Charlie to hear for himself what his intentions were. When we next heard from the chief, he stood in the castle grounds surrounded by the clan to read a declaration. While waiting for him to begin, I gazed at our battle pendant and the Scottish flag, the Saltire, with its white cross on a blue background fluttering in the breeze. Our patron, Saint Andrew, had been crucified for his faith on such a cross as he'd felt he was not worthy to die like our Lord and Savior on an upright one.

"I have indeed met with our Prince," shouted the chief. "It will be as he wishes." He elevated the pitch of his voice. "An uprising against the English crown!" A highland cry went up. A piper started playing a bonnie tune, "The Black Bear" Lochiel motioned for quiet. "Wheesh your tongues." A solemn hush fell over the crowd. "Ours is to be the foremost of the clans to pledge allegiance to our Prince at a place called Glen Finnan on August the 19th, 1745.

"Hear me now." As he lifted his arms to the heavens, his lace-trimmed coat sleeves slipped down and revealed a ring on his finger. Emblazoned on it was a lily on a white background—a sign of devoted allegiance to the Prince and destined to be the insignia of our cause.

He turned his upper body left and right while addressing the clan. "When men of good faith talk of this place in history, it will be referred to by all true Scots as the '45 rebellion.' Our glorious leader of this uprising is known to you all. Charles Edward Stuart, pretender to the Scottish throne, better known to all of you here as Bonnie Prince Charlie."

The crowd went wild. Pipers began to play a reel. Men tossed their bonnets in the air as crossed swords were laid down on the cold grey cobblestones and men began dancing like they'd done before battles for as long as any man there could remember. A whiskey cask appeared. The top was smashed open by the hilt of a broadsword and each man dipped in a pewter mug to drink his fill.

As I approached with mug in hand, an old shepherd knocked it away. "Away ye go, Robbie Cameron. You'll not be making this great day an excuse for breaking the pledge you gave not to touch liquor 'til you're twenty-one. Away, you scamp!"

I scurried away lest my Father see me being ridiculed and fervently hoped my wee mother would not hear of my behavior. Truth be told, I'd sooner face a regiment of mounted dragoons than a lashing from her tongue.

* * *

The Rebellion

A designated site near the Kyles of Lochalsh on the west coast of Scotland was chosen as the place for the gathering. Lochiel brought the clan to attention and all stood quiet as the Royal standard was raised.

Soon many clans swore their allegiance to Charlie and the pent-up hatred for the English was about to explode with consequences men could have only dreamed of. It was a bonnie sight, all the clans gathered, wearing their different tartans by pipers as they played in unison. My heart swelled with pride for my clan and my country. I wept unabashedly.

As a boy who'd preferred to spend his days dreaming, it was surely a dream come true. My father told me he'd travel with Lochiel as one of the chief's personal servants during the coming campaign. I was chosen to be a page for the Prince, which meant I attended to his every wish and it put me in the middle of all of the upcoming planning strategies and privy to all the latest gossip.

I was regaled in a manner becoming a page to His Highness and with my golden locks and piercing blue eyes, I became a lad to be admired by the young lassies who had come to catch sight of Prince Charlie, who was fond of the lassies. From time to time I was summoned by his aide-de-camp, Captain Lavelle, who took me into his confidence.

"Robbie, as I've explained time and time again, the Prince is a lonely man. Do you think you could find him a wench to keep him company tonight?"

"I know lots of girls who would be suitable, but I'm not so sure it's the kind of thing I should be doing."

"Now Robbie, this is not a request. I have my orders and now so do you."

I never spoke, but silently walked away in search of a lassie willing to give her all for the rebellion. I met Jane McDougal, the barmaid at the local inn and she agreed to keep the prince company. So, with lantern in hand, I led the pretty wench to the Prince's bed. Before she entered the Prince's quarters, she asked a favor of me.

"Robbie, I have a friend I'd agreed to meet tonight. Could you go the water wheel on the bend of the river...you know, near the crossroads. You'll see a lass waiting there for me. Don't tell her why, but let her know I've been delayed."

That's how I met Flora McNeil. She was a rather brassy girl with coal black hair, emerald green eyes, and a waist a man could encompass with two hands. Her firm breasts looked as if they'd burst through her flimsy blouse at moment's notice. It was plain to see, this beauty was one who knew much more about life than I and as it happened, was destined to teach me all she knew.

She was something of a gypsy, with her hair flowing over her bare shoulders and green eyes sparkling like a mountain stream, cold and dark—and bewitching.

As I approached the mill wheel, she stood up, placed her hand on her hips and began to speak.

"My name is Flora McNeil. You're Robbie Cameron, I know of you."

"Hello. Janie McDougall asked me to tell you she won't be coming to see you tonight after all. Tell me, do you live here? Surely it must be a lonely life for a girl."

"It's not by choice, I assure you. My folks have been thrown out of their croft by our English landlord who finds it more rewarding to keep sheep on the land instead of people, while thousands of good folk like me have become homeless and are roaming the countryside with their families, just trying to survive. Needless to say, we flock to the Bonnie Prince, who we all love and admire."

"I can well imagine. He's like a savior to most folks and no doubt, he has our well-being at heart. Myself, I find the man somewhat aloof, speaking in French mostly and always very particular about his dress. A 'fancy Dan' is how my grandmother would have referred to him with his silk trousers, fancy bonnet, and his emblem of a fleur de lis on a white cockade which, as you know, is the symbol of our cause.

Realizing I'd maybe said too much, I changed my tone. Looking around as if in fear I might have been overheard, I whispered. "I widna want it to get about that's how I feel about the man though. After all, he is our Prince."

"You don't have to worry about me saying anything, Robbie Cameron, page to His Highness. I'm not a blatherskite like some I could name."

* *

After a time, the cold Scottish weather had him trade in his silks for the woolen troos which were spun in his tartan, truly striking, with its red on red design. Only then did he began to resemble the people he was about to ask to lay down their lives for his cause.

* * *

As we marched into the capitol city, Edinburgh, the adjutant was riding his bay mare. I walked by his side, lest I had orders to deliver. Looking down, he leaned over to me.

"Robbie, I have great news. I've been told by one of our spies that the English General has begun to worry. It had been assumed the lowlanders would not be persuaded to join the Prince's force, but indeed the people of this city have welcomed us, especially after we defeated the army King George sent against us under the command of the English General, Sir John Cope."

After hearing the good news, I noticed that I had acquired a spike in my step and I began to wonder what would be the outcome. It was to my way of thinking akin to William Wallace, another great Scottish leader in our history, who'd beaten the English armies and could have taken London if he'd not left England after sacking the City of York.

As boys at our father's knee, like all proud Scotsmen we learned of William Wallace and his courage against that blaggard of an English King, Edward Longchamps, known as "The Hammer of the Scots" or as we highlanders called him, "Eddie long shanks." On most days if the weather was stormy, the old men of the village could be found sitting round a blazing fire in the inn drinking a dram. While reminiscing, when referring to the king, they'd say, "Aye, he was tall right enough, but William Wallace soon cut him down to size."

And so it was with Bonnie Charlie winning victory after victory—the German King prepared to flee London for the continent. That's when Charles Stuart made his greatest blunder. At Darby, against all his counselors' advice, he turned his army back to Scotland, giving the English an opportunity to reassemble their forces under the command of the King's son, the Duke of Cumberland. He met our army at Culloden and we were routed. He then proved to be a ruthless tyrant who rained terror on the Scots for more than fifteen years, killing, plundering and destroying the Scottish clan system as we knew it forever.

I well remember that fateful day of our defeat at Culloden. The highland roar went up and English soldiers could be seen running from their ranks along with a lot of lowlanders. But as the day went on, it became clear to all something had gone awry. We kept shouting for the Prince to give the command to attack, but it was slow in coming. Some said he'd spent those precious hours in the bed of a chief's wife, no less...or so I was told.

To make matters worse, the Redcoats had been trained in a new tactic when confronting the highland charge. The trooper was told to bayonet not the oncoming highlander wielding his sword, which was capable of cutting a man in half, but to aim at the man directly to his left, thrusting his bayonet at the unguarded side as he charged the English ranks with his sword arm raised to strike.

This maneuver had devastating results for the highlanders that fateful day. Because of this new tactic and the Prince's indecision to begin the battle, the Scottish army was routed. The Redcoats were told, "Take no prisoners." All of the brave men wounded by the new strategy were killed instead of being taken captive, causing the deaths of thousands that black day on the field of Culloden near the highland City of Inverness.

What followed after that day was some of the most despicable acts ever carried out by the English. In the villages near my home I saw men hanged for wearing the tartan of their clan or speaking in their native Gaelic and many more terrible things better left unsaid.

I was summoned by Lochiel. "Robert Cameron, this is a sad day indeed, laddie. We are defeated, but at all costs, we must save the Prince from the English. What Scot would want to see our leader drawn and quartered, and his head stuck on a pole for all to see? I order you to leave the battlefield with His Highness and flee across the moors to safety. He'll be dressed as a serving maid and you as her son."

As I maneuvered between the Redcoats trying to reach Charlie, a soldier not much older than I turned and saw me. He aimed his musket, but it misfired. Seeing no other ally in sight, he came running over wounded men, his bayonet aimed at my belly. Just as he took a stance, a dying Scot took his claymore and drove it between the man's legs.

He looked down, saw blood spurting profusely from his crotch, staining his blue trousers as he screamed in agony. He attempted to bayonet my savior, but then, as if in a trance, he fell over the man who had saved my life.

The Prince was hidden in what was left of a burned out tent. I saluted and doffed my hat. "My liege, I've orders to accompany you from the battle. If it pleases, Sire, don this wig and woman's skirts and let's be gone from this field of death."

* * *

Having fled the Redcoat army, we journeyed by night along hedgerows, always moving west toward the clan castle. The night we arrived, the rain was pouring down. At first we weren't recognized.

"What business have ye with this house, Ma'am?"

I stepped forward. "Duncan Bruce. Do you not recognize the Prince?"

"Robbie, is that you, lad?" Bowing down reverently, he apologized. "Sire, come in and get off them wet clothes and I'll prepare a meal—not fitting your status, I'm afraid, but we can't arouse suspicion. The Redcoats have been out on the moor most of the day searching for you. Surely a traitor or someone tortured to his limits has told his jailors of your escape route."

After a meal of cheese and bread, washed down with a glass or two of the chief's special whiskey, the Prince appeared to be less apprehensive. As he followed a servant to a room on the ground floor, he whispered in the man's ear.

The man nodded as they walked. "I will indeed, Your Highness." He opened a door to his right. "You can rest here in comfort after your long journey."

Toward midnight I was awakened in my room by a servant and told a troop of cavalry had been sighted on the road. We were asked to assemble in the great hall as soon as possible. Rubbing sleep from his eyes, the Prince seemed annoyed to be awakened from his rest, whilst a bonnie red-haired lassie tried desperately to cover her nakedness.

"You have little time, Your Grace. The news is grave indeed as a search of the house is to be made," said the man. He bowed and backed out of the room.

The great hall was in total darkness. We were taken by candlelight to the great fireplace and as a servant pushed on the great black cauldron, a secret door opened in the back of the hearth. We hastily followed a groom holding a lantern and ventured into a dark passageway that led down many steps, as if we were journeying into the bowels of the earth itself.

At the top, the walls were brick and the ceiling was arched, with iron brackets set at intervals along the walls, each with a cluster of pitch-soaked straw neatly placed, ready to be lit. Because we were in need of cover and could not risk lighting the lamps, the air was dank and cold. Every now and then, in the light of the lantern's watery beam, we saw rats scampering for safety as we hurried along the muddy floor.

The brick walls gave way to solid rock with chisel marks, evidence of the labor needed to carve the escape route all those centuries ago. As we turned a corner a niche on the right held the skeleton of some long ago clansman who could have met his death from a Norseman's bow. His remains lay where he'd fallen for all eternity. Although I was mightily worried, I must confess the escape through the fireplace filled my young heart with a sort of pride, knowing very few clansmen had ever ventured along the path now tramped by Robbie Cameron.

Pitch dark and with rain falling steadily, we soon found ourselves standing out in the open on a windswept rock, made treacherous by the green moss covering its wet surface. As the Prince faltered, I rushed to keep him upright and only then did I realize we were at the loch. A small sailboat awaited us. Waves buffeted the stern and its sail billowed in the rainy squall. The servant quickly extinguished his lamp and led us the rest of the way through the dark of night to effect our escape.

A boatman sat in the bow, while I pushed off from the shore and we headed for open water. Charlie sat huddled with his cloak pulled tight around him and nary said a word. We sailed across the loch and exited into a river heading to the open sea beyond. Soon the smell of salt air and seaweed filled our nostrils. The boatman sang a ballad depicting our predicament.

Sail bonnie boat like a bird on the wing, over the sea to Skye. Carry the lad who was born to be King, over the sea to Skye. The ballad was to become as famous as Charlie himself. After an hour at sea, we reached a shoreline. The oarsman dropped the sail and we ran aground on a pebbled beach. Stepping onto land, the gravel crunched beneath my feet. I looked up at the snow-capped mountains above us and sensed we'd cheated death. We had indeed escaped with our lives.

The Redcoats assumed Charlie would surely try to leave Scotland for France from one of the seaports, not knowing he'd only moved offshore and could have easily been taken prisoner. It was there the Prince fell in love with the Chief's daughter, Flora McDonald, who comforted him until he eventually escaped to France, never to return to Scotland. What he left behind was the worst time in Scottish history. Not only did we face the ignominy of defeat, but also the brutal treatment of the Highland clans which can only be described as barbaric.

Before he left for the continent, a strange thing happened. The Prince, who had never said more than a few words to me ever, asked me to join him in a dram. Speaking English with a French accent, he filled two crystal glasses with Drambuie, his favorite liqueur. Handing one to me, he then raised his glass.

"Robert Cameron, I owe you my life. For a boy so young, you have proven to be a man of great ingenuity and daring. I fear we may never meet again, so here's to your good health, Robert Cameron." He toasted me, drained his glass, and then smiled at me as we both smashed our glasses on the rocky shore.

As he turned toward the boat that would take him to the ship bound for France, he pulled his dirk from his stocking. Speaking nary a word, he handed it to me. It was made of the finest steel, with a fiery red ruby set in its hilt. I saluted at attention.

* * *

I remained on the island for a few weeks and then returned to my home and family. The devastation wreaked on the land and the people by the Redcoats was widespread. My Chief was forced to pay homage to the English King or our whole clan would have been wiped out.

Some of his best men were exiled to the American colonies, including my father. Had I been able to get home in time, I would have tried to accompany him. As for me, it became obvious that Robbie Cameron, the fugitive, was being sought as it was presumed I knew where the Prince was hiding. Those days after Culloden will stay with me as long as I draw breath.

Summoning up all my courage and confronting my mother, I knelt by her side. "I need to go, Mother. Staying here will only bring more misery down on the Clan Chief, and if they find out I'm your son, I fear for your life. I'll be better able to hide myself in the midst of the lowlanders.

"It's my only chance to possibly follow Father to the Carolinas, maybe as a cabin boy or junior seamen on one of the ships sailing to the new land. Who knows, perhaps I'll make my fortune, like my cousin James has done."

My mother was sitting by the window where a rain squall battered against the glass panes. I stood by the fireplace, warming my hands as she spun newly shorn wool. As she worked the shuttle, she looked from the loom to me.

18

"Robbie, lad, you're not familiar with the ways of the world. I beg you to reconsider this foolish idea. It will all sort itself out in time. If your father was here, he would strongly object to you leaving. What makes you think you'll be safer out there in the world of hangings and treachery?"

It wasn't long before I realized how true her words were. It proved nearly impossible to get through the English lines which had been drawn across the breadth of Scotland, not to mention the reward which was posted on the head of any Jacobite, as we were now called. There was a price of fifteen guineas on my head alone—a small fortune in those days of want and misery.

After leaving the relative safety of my glen, I was fair game for any no good who wanted to make some quick money. I was constantly on guard, speaking only when spoken to and making every attempt to mimic the dialect of the area in which I was traveling lest I be recognized as a hated Highlander.

The weather was difficult. One cold, rainy night, I sought refuge in a stagecoach inn where the mail coaches stopped. I inquired if I might spend the night in the stables. The landlord eyed me suspiciously, but after talking to a coach driver, he turned back in my direction, smiled and answered.

"All right then, lad, if you agree to water the coach horses and promise not to smoke in the stable, I'll agree to you spending the night. Maybe even give you some food scraps after the evening meal has been served."

With my belly full and a dry roof over my head, I drifted off to sleep, thinking that I might well make the journey with a measure of success after all.

I hadn't been asleep long when I felt a mighty jab in the ribs, which quickly brought me awake. Before a word of anger could be uttered, a small hand was placed over my mouth and a ring with the Fleur de lis was held out to me for inspection. A voice whispered in my ear, "If you want to live out this night, Robbie Cameron, be quiet and follow me. Quickly now, for we have little time."

Not knowing what was happening, I instinctively followed the stranger out to the road and onto the moor. Only when we stopped for a breath did I see that my guardian angel turned out to be none other than Flora, the gypsy girl.

Now understand the word gypsy never crossed my lips when talking to Flora as it would have been an insult. She saw herself as someone the gods had turned against and who now lived by her wits. Flora was to be my teacher in many things, not the least of which was staying alive. Looking me over as she tried to catch her breath, I couldn't help but notice her breasts heaving up and down as she leaned against a pine tree.

"Well, my young Jacobite, what troubles have you gotten yourself into? Don't you know that you can never trust an Englishman? You'd better learn here and now, my man, to trust no one and keep away from the roads. They're crawling with Redcoats who'll size you up for a Jacobite in the shake of a lamb's tail."

Before replying with some smart answer which would have only made things worse, Flora turned around and kissed me on the lips. It was totally different than how my mother kissed me goodnight. On that cold, wet night on the moor, it felt divine. We were both soaked through, so Flora decided we'd both die of pneumonia unless we could get warm.

She opened her blouse, then my shirt, and pressed me close to her to share our body heat. It was the most beautiful night I'd ever spent in my entire life as we snuggled up together with her warm body and her full, rounded breasts nestling on my chest.

Before the situation could be exploited, she scowled at me. "This is nothing more than an attempt to stay free, Robbie Cameron, and if you try to make more of it,

I have a small dagger in my skirt's pocket which will surely be at your throat."

Not knowing if I totally believed her, but being tired and cold, it was only a matter of minutes until I was sound asleep, snuggled up to the most beautiful woman I'd ever met. My dreams that night were not of America and swashbucklers, but a beautiful creature named Flora McNeil whose long legs were wrapped firmly around me. Even in my dreams I felt fortunate to have met up with this beauty once again. I dreamed we were destined to stay together now and forever.

* * *

I awoke in the early morning to find Flora gone. A panic stirred inside me until I saw her returning with two hot scones.

"So you're awake, sleepyhead? I went for a pee and found us some breakfast. I took them from an open window where they were cooling, presumably the breakfast of someone more fortunate than we. Here! Take my hat. Be careful. I used it as a pitcher for hot milk that I took from a cow in a milking house on the way back from the village."

The hot scones and warm milk were like a gift from the gods. A saying my mother would use when we were privy to a special piece of venison from the Chief's table after he'd eaten his fill. A twinge of conscience came over me as we ate the stolen food.

"Was this food stolen? I know we're hungry, but stealing food, Flora?"

Flora looked at my face. "Robbie Cameron, we're now the less fortunate. Like a parable in the Bible I read somewhere. Christ chastised the man who'd been given much and hadn't thought to care for the poor around him. We're now the poor the Holy Book referred to."

Try as I may, it was difficult to recall that sermon from my Bible teachings. Between bites of the hot bannocks, which I kept changing from hand to hand lest I burn my fingers, I asked.

"Flora, I cannot remember that parable you speak of. Where does it say, Christ knew the food had been stolen?"

"Robbie Cameron." She too was munching her food greedily as she wagged a finger in my direction. "Surely you know that the bibles we use are different. Is not mine, the new King James Bible which has much more information in it, as it was written quite recently?"

Not being fully convinced, I swallowed my mouthful and remarked. "Do you think I might read your copy, Flora?"

She scolded me. "A good Catholic boy like you read a Protestant version of the Bible? It will surely be a sin for you to read the Bible of another faith? Don't you Catholics feel you're the only ones getting into heaven? Therefore, why jeopardize your chances by reading my Protestant version?"

Not wishing to be cursed and hanging on every word Flora uttered, I gulped down a mouthful of warm milk from her hat. It proved most reassuring to have such a beautiful companion looking out for my spiritual needs, as well as my earthly ones. Not to mention the long cold nights ahead when we were forced to cling to each other to keep from freezing to death.

The first time I kissed Flora was quite by accident. She'd gone down to a fast-flowing river to bathe, warning me not to look as she undressed and swam to clean off some of the grime and dust which was our constant companion as we tramped through ditches and ploughed fields of heavy, rich, black soil.

Stealing a look through the tall rushes hugging the river bank, I marveled at her tall, slender body as she rubbed her skin with a rag in an attempt to remove any remaining clay. I was intrigued how she looked so delicate and fragile. As she moved her hands over her breasts, I felt a deep longing in my loins. Having walked for miles that day, I began to doze and fell asleep while waiting for her to return.

When she'd lain down by my side, as I was still in my dream stage, I kissed her for real and awoke to find her kissing me back, which aroused a certain feeling which proved to be very pleasing and enjoyable. We became lovers. Had it not been for Flora, I probably would have missed the whole event, not being worldly in such matters.

As usual, Flora saw to my wellbeing and guided me through my first experience.

"Robbie, I have to tell you, I was lucky to be hiding in a small cattle shed on a stormy night when a local wench and a Sergeant of Dragoons took shelter. The man kept pestering the girl to pull down her knickers and she wasn't for it. Well, that's when she ups and says, 'Okay then, but just this once, do ye hear? And I'll tell my mother to get the marriage bands posted next week—that is, if ye promise?'

"As he pulled off his tunic and his vest, he answered. 'Och fine, tell yer mother then, but come on now, dinna keep we waiting, I'm in agony, so I am.'

"That's when they made passionate love. And you know me, Robbie, ever the one to learn, I watched from a safe distance and had memorized the whole affair."

How fortunate to have such a wonderful companion, willing to pass on so much knowledge in order to help me learn about life and I so far away from my friendly glen where such opportunities would surely never have presented themselves.

* * *

One night, having made love, we lay in a haystack. Flora turned toward me, a piece of straw between her teeth. She looked thoughtfully at me for a moment and then lay back gazing at the bright, star-lit sky.

"Be careful, Robbie, who you give your favors to. It could have grave consequences."

Moving closer to her and picking a stock of straw from her hair, I quickly assured her, whispering in her ear.

"Flora, since you've taken the time and patience to further my education in these matters, rest assured being careful will be my motto. You have my word on it."

She looked hard into my eyes, brushed her lips against mine, and then put her hands on my shoulders.

"Robbie, you have certain attributes women will admire. Believe me, it won't be as easy as you imagine resisting some women who are expert at arousing a man. But just remember, a quick roll in a hay loft could bring you a minute of ecstasy and a life of misery—and a short one at that."

* * *

We moved ever south, trying to get to Edinburgh, knowing all bridges over the great river Forth were garrisoned by Redcoats and where there were papers to be shown and we had none.

As usual, Flora had an idea. "Perhaps one of us could distract the guard on duty while the other sneaked by?" She felt she was better suited to do the distracting while I sped across the bridge in the shadows.

"Flora McNeil. Why should you be the one to distract the guard?"

She looked at me as she often did, shaking her head. She leaned against me with her hand on my shoulder as she removed a pebble from her shoe. "We don't have time to wait until we find a guard that you might distract. There are a lot more of the other kind."

Not understanding what she meant, I finally agreed that Flora would take charge of the situation and Robbie would follow orders. I remembered my recent past, thinking that nothing had changed much since the discipline of the army. I was still taking orders, only now my superior was nicer and smelled much better than the others I'd known. As expected, the bridge at Kincardine was guarded by tough-looking Redcoats who spoke a kind of English not readily understood by me.

Flora explained. "They're from London and are especially cruel to anyone who speaks as you, Robbie, with that gentle lilt which all you Highlanders talk. It's more like you sing your words rather than speak them."

"It's because I think in Gaelic and speak in English, which gives a lilting effect to my voice. Does it displease them?"

"Listen Robbie, if questioned at any time from now on, just pretend to be dumb. I feel it's something you can accomplish quite easily. Just be natural, that's all, and you'll see they'll be fooled by your acting."

Not knowing quite how to react to her jibe, I decided she meant well and if it meant we'd survive, it was a small price to pay. Besides, she was right. I was dumb in the ways of the lowlanders and city life.

I'd never ventured farther than my glen, except on market days when we'd drive the Chief's cattle to Sterling for the sales. Even then I never went into town with the men. My job was always to guard the cattle against thieves like the Rob Roy Macgregor's clan and their band of outcasts, who still carried on the family tradition. They were still the finest cattle thieves in all Scotland.

Had I'd gone to town, maybe Flora wouldn't have to constantly shake her head and remind me. "Robbie Cameron, you've a lot to learn about women and life in general."

It was after midnight when Flora woke me. "It's time to go. Once you start across, don't look back or hesitate, no matter what happens with me on the bridge. Pay attention now, Robbie."

She whispered in my ear, her eyes looking from side to side as she spoke. "My mother's sister is a business woman in Edinburgh, near the Royal Mile, and that is our objective—to take shelter in her home. So keep all this in mind and do only as I say. Do you agree?"

"What kind of business has she, Flora?"

She appeared annoyed at my inquisitiveness and hurriedly explained as she smoothed out creases in her dress. At first she began by looking down, as if embarrassed, but lifted her head when she spoke.

"She's in a kind of giving favors business and those who get the favors are most generous with their appreciation." She picked off some straw from my jacket.

"My aunt's so busy with the favors, she has a lot of young girls helping her. That's what I meant when we made love on the moor and I explained about you being too affectionate with other girls could prove a little bit risky."

Not quite understanding the whole thing, I kept silent as we walked ever nearer the stone bridge with its many arches, set amongst a fast-flowing current. I remembered the favors my clan would do for others. They never amounted to more than a slap on the back or maybe a dram of whiskey was offered. How could one get rich doing such favors was indeed a puzzle to me. Clearly, the lowlanders must be more rewarding of good deeds than any highlanders I'd known.

Once on the bridge, Flora cried out saying she'd tripped and twisted her ankle. At first, the sentry was not friendly, but when he drew near, he soon became the perfect gentleman, offering to help Flora to her feet. That was my cue. When he laid down his musket and his back was to me, I scampered across the bridge like some frightened rat.

After a bit I stopped. At first, all I could hear was the sound of the current as it collided with the stone pillars supporting the arches of the bridge, but then I heard Flora talking and a man answering back.

"Have you hurt your foot, Missy? See here, let me help you up. Going to Edinburgh, are we? What's a little girl like you doing out alone on such a dark night?"

"I'm going to see my auntie. Hey, take your hand out from under my skirt."

"Come on now, lassie. Give a lonely soldier a kiss."

"Okay a kiss and nothing more. I'm a nice girl and don't want to be left with a bairn to bring up all by myself and you away in some foreign land. Now, if you're an experienced lover, I might be persuaded to go farther."

"You just come to me little girl and Tommy Atkins will show you how experienced he is."

Not wishing to hear more, I headed for the other side of the river.

I waited for Flora, who was taking her time. I wondered how she could be so accommodating to such a monster. I was annoyed at her not being in more of a hurry as the guard was surely one of those hated Londoners. All at once I heard a cry and then a splash as if someone had fallen into the river below.

Flora arrived out of breath soon after, explaining the guard had been most helpful, but had demanded a kiss for his trouble.

"It was when he began to have other ideas that I suggested he remove his trousers, which it seemed he was more than eager to do. As I began to unbutton them for him, he leaned back against the bridge rail. I gathered all my strength and while he was busily dropping his pants, I pushed him hard up against the rail. He catapulted backwards into the water below. Before the duty officer had a chance to investigate, I was across the bridge and by your side."

Standing there on the bridge, looking into the cold, dark water below, I felt no compassion for the man, trying as best we were to survive. This was to become the routine—Flora McNeil in charge and me, her camp follower, never questioning her decisions and having more love and admiration for her every day as we continued on our journey to Edinburgh.

* * *

Edinburgh, the capital, was the largest city in Scotland. It had been the home of John Knox, the Protestant leader who was no friend of the Catholic chiefs and their followers during his lifetime. Therefore, it was a most trying time for me, wishing to see the great city, but being frightened at the thought of so many Protestants and wondering, 'what would they look like?'

* * *

It took three days to reach Auld Reekie, which I cannot really explain in English, but it means "old smoky." I could understand the meaning more easily as a pall of smoke from many fireplaces hung over the city, as we approached from the north. My thoughts slipped back to the clear, cool, highland air of my childhood, which now seemed so distant. The fragrance of the sweet, burning peat fires in every cottage now seemed better and better to me. I realized for the first time that my days of daydreaming were over, so I hitched up my troos, tightened my belt, and hurried to keep up with Flora.

* * *

The day was hot and sticky as we found ourselves walking with a bunch of fellow travelers. I thought of my home, my mother and my father, wondering how he was faring in that far off land of my dreams.

Flora, who'd left to go pee behind a hedge, caught up with me. Grabbing my shoulder and pointing, she whispered. "Look up yonder, Robbie, What do you see?

I saw a church steeple and a jibbet, side by side. A corpse was swaying in the breeze, small children were playing and a mangy dog was barking at two lassies jumping rope while reciting a riddle.

"Honestly, Flora, what kind of justice is there? When a man must choose between his religion and his clan or the gallows?"

"That's English justice for you and don't you forget it, Robbie. We are as strangers in our own land, where a loose tongue or a slipped word could have you swinging up there in short order."

Partially in fear, I angrily pulled myself away from Flora, and set off down the road. Looking back over my shoulder I jibed at her. "If I had any doubts about English justice? I don't anymore." She ran to catch up with me. In her hand were two, orange-red carrots. So fresh they were still attached to their dark green stalks. Not a word was spoken, she just handed me one, and I could hear her crunching down on our new found delicacy. Knowing I'd been bloody childish by my reaction to the jibbet, I smiled. "Wherever did you find them? They're one of my favorites."

"They just jumped into my hand as I passed that tinker and his cart. Now, before you start with your Bible questions, just haud yer whisht and eat."

Craning my head to see over the crowd, "Flora, I see what looks like an arch and people are lining up. Are we in danger do you think?"

"That's the official entry into the city, but we'll skip that, and move round to our right, and wait till dark. It might be safer."

"Look, Flora, the folk are just walking through, no papers are being shown, as far as I can see."

"Right then, Robbie, get along side that family with the push cart, and when we walk thru the arch, help to push, and I'll pick up a wean, as if I'm a big sister. Be careful, don't look anyone in the eye, you might invite a question, and we have no answers."

Auld Reekie

Entrance to the city was easier from the north as it was assumed you'd passed muster with the garrisons stationed all along the route. We walked like so many others on their first visit to the capital—in a kind of daze and bewilderment. We looked all around us, gazing up at the spires of St. Giles Cathedral and across the wide street at the great law buildings.

We walked through a park and entered a busy street with its many eateries, where gorgeous smells of meat pies, treacle scones, and newly baked bread wafted from the open doors we passed. Customers sat looking out on the passing parade of those of us less fortunate as they gorged themselves on the newly baked delicacies.

I stopped at a water fountain and filled the pewter cup attached to the bowl with a chain. Crisp clear spring water flowed from the breast of a bronze cherub. The overflow then passed into a trough, where horses were being watered. As I drank I pondered on how well-dressed the people were, at least in the center of town, maybe not so much in the poor enclaves.

But for now, it was all a dream as we mixed with all kinds of well-to-do people on the street. Not to mention the fine horse drawn carriages, with their gilded crests painted on the doors of their dark lacquered coaches, establishing their rank and standing in the community.

The horses were groomed to perfection with shiny livery of black leather to match their flowing manes and tails, and their leather trappings studded with bright gleaming silver buckles. The wheels were painted mostly red or yellow and had coach lamps attached up front beside the driver. As the many coaches clattered over cobblestone streets, their eiderdown silk window screens were pulled down tight to allow sanctuary from the prying eyes of those of us less fortunate.

As they passed, I could not help but think how the horses must have felt superior to the work horses, which pulled the many commercial carts. Their coats were dull and lifeless and their trappings no more than rope halters. Their owners dressed in shoddy work clothes with string tied around their trousers at the knees to ensure no rat fleeing from a feisty terrier might seek refuge up the leg of an unsuspecting driver.

After a while, Flora suggested the time had come to visit her aunt. What surprised me most in such a large city was that nearly everyone we spoke to for directions knew exactly where we should go—especially the men.

"Good morning to you, Constable. I'm in need of directions to the home of my aunt, Jane McNeil. I know it's in this neighborhood, but my wee brother and I are having a devil of a time finding it, sir."

At the mention of her name, the man, who was of tall stature, first looked around and then putting a hand to her shoulder, pinched her bum and pointed to a large Georgian style house down the street to our left.

"Look no more, lassie, for yonder hoose doon this long street here." He pointed with his baton. "Do you see the grand looking place with the two pillars way doon at the end? That's where she calls home." He winked as he pinched her cheek.

"It's always a puzzlement to me how many nieces that bonny woman has? But no mind, she's a grand woman and I would take kindly to your giving her my best regards. Be sure to tell her, if she's ever in need of help in any way, Irvin Wilson is her man."

With that said, he tweaked his waxed mustache and then turned and walked down the street whistling the tune, Highland Laddie, and twirling his baton as he went.

When Flora mentioned the connection to her aunt, it seemed to bring on a new acceptance of us. Afterwards, any gentlemen she stopped almost begged to be reminded to the lady. I imagined she was a kindly soul.

We had long since passed the great houses and cobbled streets when we eventually arrived at her aunt's place of business. We were immediately stopped by a gentleman with an Irish brogue. He was tall with hazel eyes and red hair that hung down in locks about his face, framed by a strong jaw line. Strange as it seemed, I thought I recognized him from my past. He was all business.

"Now tell me? What is your business with my mistress? She's a busy woman, I'll have ye know. Who is this ragtail lad you have there, hiding behind your skirts?"

"My business with my aunt is no business of yours, I assure you. Be kind enough to inform my aunt that Flora McNeil wishes to see her."

He seemed to resent the way, Flora addressed him, but after her explosive response, we were ushered into a very posh entrance to the palatial house, yet the area around it looked downtrodden. There was much I needed to learn about my new surroundings and Mistress Jane McNeil.

Flora was taken upstairs while I waited with the Irishman, who commented, "See here, lad, if any gent comes by you must stay in the shadows and not be seen to be gawking."

"If you please, sir, I think we've met? I'm a Cameron of the Lochiel Camerons. I was a page in the service of Charles Stuart. As you can see, I'm on the run. Let's just say the agents of the Crown would like to have words with me."

His eyes narrowed and he answered quite harshly. "If you've a mind to be keeping that head of yours attached to your shoulders, laddie, I'd forget the past and talk to no one about where you came from. Do you understand? Do you hear me now, boy or am I going to draw a cane across your back to get you to listen to me?"

I took a step back. He loomed large as I addressed him. "I assure you sir, that from this day forth my lips are sealed and there is no-good reason for you to think otherwise."

"What's your name, boy?"

"Robert Cameron, of the Lochiel clan, sir," I answered politely.

"Well now, there's no second names here and from now on you'll answer to Robbie. As for me, I'm Rourke, Major to me friends, but as yet, Robbie, you're nothing more than an acquaintance, so it's Rourke to you. Do ya hear me, boy?"

"Yes, Rourke, Sir."

As his big hand came close to my ear, I quickly repeated. "Yes, Rourke." His hand went down and brushed across my golden locks.

"Sure I'm thinkin' you're as bright a lad as I've met around here in many a day." He looked at me wearing a big grin. "So, when we're alone and in private, so to speak, you can call me Major, right, boyo?" When a big smile crossed his face, I knew I'd made a friend for life. How long that life would be was very much up in the air.

Rourke and I were summoned upstairs by Mistress Jane into a spacious room with silk drapes and fine couches. There was Flora and a dazzling auburn-haired lady with a peaches and cream complexion. I immediately saw she looked very much like my Flora. All I could think of was how lovely Flora would look if she were dressed like her aunt. I was introduced by Rourke, who was quick to remove my hat and shove it rudely into my hand. As she spoke, I listened closely.

"Robbie, you will go with Rourke and he will teach you what you need to know to exist in this town. Is that understood?"

"Will I see Flora again?" I asked, looking back as Rourke ushered me out of the room. Once outside on the landing, Rourke put his hand on me and stuck my hat back firmly on my head.

"Of course, ye will, lad, you're not going to damnation all together when you go downstairs with me, are ye? But like yourself, Miss Flora has things to learn and when her training is over, sure you'll see her every day I'm thinkin'. Now, enough blathering, we need to get to work."

* * *

First off, I had a bath like no other I'd ever known, with scented soap and then a full set of clothes—light olive green colored britches, white hosiery, milk-colored silk shirt, and fine leather shoes with brass buckles on them. I wanted to think they were gold, so gold they were.

Rourke even took me to a shop that sold silk chapeaus—that's French for hats and I was decked out in a very jaunty one made of fine material and finished off with a feather tucked into the brim, which Rourke assured me was all the fashion on the continent.

"It won't be affected by the rain either, you wait and see, Boyo," he assured me.

Next, a haircut and then a brown tweed waistcoat with buttons made from a deer's antler. As we strolled along, it was obvious that Rourke was well known, especially when we passed an inn. He would say it was his duty to introduce me around. To be friendly like, he would have a dram in each establishment. He explained it was so the innkeepers wouldn't think he was above mixing with the lower classes. It seemed to work for everywhere we went that day Rourke was warmly accepted and me along with him. When he explained I didn't drink myself, their look of cordiality faded somewhat.

He'd say, "Sure, isn't the lad a distant relation to her ladyship?" Only then would a smile return quickly and I was once more in their good graces, even if I was a teetotaler.

Rourke would often be heard to say, "Sure the lad's a credit to his dear father, me brother." With a tear in his eye he'd take out a huge handkerchief, blow his nose, and add, "I promised him on his deathbed to look after the boy." He'd partake of a pinch of snuff and then declare, "So, he'll be taking no spirits as long as he's in my care." Then that grin would appear along with a wink, he'd touch his nose and whisper to me, "Don't bother about the facts being a bit mixed up, sure nobody will be bothering ye if yer related to meself and, of course, it kinda makes me appear like I'm in the know with herself, God bless the woman. Isn't she an angel in disguise?" He would heave a sigh and then down another whisky. By the time we returned home, the daylight was going, Rourke hurried his step, and I had to run to keep up with him.

"Oh bejasus! She'll have a fit for sure if I'm late and it's entirely your fault, wantin' to meet all me friends and associates. I'll be in trouble for sure."

As luck had it, we weren't late and Rourke quickly stood inside the entrance, with me by his side. As the evening wore on, fine gentlemen arrived in their carriages.

Rourke would open the carriage door, take the man's cloak, walking cane, and chapeau, and quickly give them to me. In turn, I gave them to old Maggie, the attendant, who brushed them and hung them on a hook. I remember wondering how this old lady could remember the names of those who came and went.

"Oh, it's easy," Maggie winked. "Robbie, my boy, when I was a girl on the stage, I had to memorize hundreds of lines, so a few names here and there isn't all that hard. Besides, I see them same old blown up red faces here most every night the good Lord sends."

On most evenings around midnight, Rourke would tell me, "Off with ye now and get a good night's sleep for there's a hard day in it for us tomorrow, don't ye know?"

When I awoke there was always a coin or two by my bed, this being part of the tips from the night before and when questioned about the small amount by Maggie, Rourke replied, "Now, I ask ye, what kind of a guardian would I be? To be givin' that poor boy all kinds of money to spend on dis and dat. Sure, doesn't he already know, if the day ever comes when he's in need of a sovereign or two, that yer man Rourke will be there for him in short order?"

I can still see Maggie, sitting on her stool, her shawl around her shoulders with her pipe in one hand and an elbow on her knee. 'If that day ever dawns, you scoundrel, I pity the boy's chances of gettin' help from the likes of you." She wagged the pipe in his direction. "I know for a fact, you've spent more money on whiskey than any other man in Edinburgh."

Rourke looked at the old woman contemptuously, but with a smile on his face. "Maggie, darlin' don't ye know? God made whiskey so Irishmen like meself wouldn't end up rulin' the world? Now, think about this, instead of them heathen English ordering all around, sure an Irishman would be doing his best to be kind to all his subjects and then what kinda of a world would it be now?"

He lowered his head 'til they were eyeball to eyeball. "You best be thinkin' about that, Miss Maggie, the next time you be givin' out with yer lectures and you yerself known by all and sundry, to be able to drink the best of them under the table...and that's no lie."

* * *

So went my life in my new surroundings in the fair city of Edinburgh. As I worked mostly in the evenings, I was inclined to sleep late, but the Major soon put that to right. In the morning, he would march into my room and I was obliged to wash and dress. I should mention, in my previous life in the highlands, washing was not a big priority on my list of things to do. Rourke instilled in me that cleanliness is next to Godliness. He'd say nonchalantly, "A Protestant idea, mores the pity, but nevertheless, a good rule to live by, lad, even if it comes from those heathen Protestants."

I soon forgot my old way of life, which for the most part I spent watching and hiding from Redcoats. Here in Edinburgh, I spent my days roaming around the city, taking in the sights and in general becoming what must be said "a more educated lad than I'd ever expected to be."

What was strange, the amount of learned men one found in the back alleys and poor districts. Men, who for the most part were those who'd lost their station in life due to drinking or womanizing to such a degree that they found themselves either bankrupt or an alcoholic. However, most of them were educated and always ready to take the time to answer any question or teach me the proper way to act. So, in a short span of time, I became more polished in not only my attire, but in thought, word, and actions.

On most days I could be found in the coffee shops where all form of business was conducted, from simple contracts to great expenditures, which usually took the form of foreign enterprises with shipping to and from all over the world. It was not unusual for me to be found carrying messages from one consortium to another and always the soul of discretion.

I was regarded as one who could be trusted to keep secret any and all messages which were sent through my employers to one another and always paid handsomely for my services. Most of my clients were also frequent visitors to my evening place of employment. I boasted casually to Rourke that I was known by all as a good lad with a head on his shoulders, who was going places.

Rourke, on the other hand, was quick to point out. "You should be careful, lest that good head on your shoulders, doesn't someday, become detached from the rest of you, lad."

He looked at me. I detected a moment of concern.

"Listen to me, Robbie, always remember the old sayin', 'If you lie down with dogs, you'll rise up with fleas.' Meaning of course, 'all those fine gentlemen are not always walking the straight and narrow path. "Someday, them fellas you hold in such high regard may find themselves on the wrong side of the law and in Scotland, as you well know, lad, they usually hang criminals of any type rather quickly."

I sometimes gave Rourke the impression of not paying heed to his words, but secretly I listened and was deter-mined to watch my back at all times. Rourke was a man of many talents and for a rough diamond was extremely alert. For some strange reason, I felt he was well-educated.

Always on my mind, was where had I seen this man before? The answer was always the same. There was no way I could have met him and forgotten. He was the kind of man others regarded as a force to be reckoned with and no one was inclined to take the chance of getting on his bad side. So, being his friend and associate, it was often made plain, most lowlifes would think twice about doing me harm, lest they had to answer to the Major. So my life and education went on, day after day, with only happy things happening to me. My days as an outlaw seemed far away and gone forever.

* * *

On entering the house by the rear door, Jennie, the cook, scolded me. "Where have ye been Robbie? The mistress wishes to see you at once, do you hear? Hurry now, lad, before you make her angry and we all suffer because of your tardy nature."

Immediately my clothes were brushed and my hair combed. Jennie lovingly wiped a washcloth across my face. She looked at me in a warm way and kissed me full on the lips. I was puzzled. I looked at her endearingly, but before I could return her kiss, she turned me around and with her hands on my shoulders she gently headed me in the direction of my Mistress' boudoir. She gently patted my backside and giggled as she left.

I knocked softly. Rourke opened the door and looked at me with steely eyes. As Jane spoke, I tried to think what I must have done to receive such a reception.

"Come, sit here by me, Robbie. I have news of your clan Chief, Lochiel. He has sent a dispatch to you personally."

"Please, Ma'am," I blurted out. "I'd be obliged if you could read the contents to me as I wouldn't wish you to think I keep secrets from you who has been so good to me."

She smiled and looked toward Rourke. "Well, I can see you've made a politician out of him, if nothing else, you rascal. Where could a young highland lad such as Robbie Cameron, learn the ways of a charmer, if not from the great charmer himself?"

Looking nervously from one to the other, I wondered if I'd said the wrong thing. My heart soon lifted when Rourke suddenly burst out laughing and slapped me on the back, nearly toppling me over.

"Robbie, my boy, you do me proud this day and that's no lie. Why, I couldn't have come across with a better answer to her ladyship, even if I'd stayed awake all night thinkin' of one."

"Enough of this blarney from the both of you." She made room on her couch and with a wave of her fan, she beckoned me to sit beside her. "Now, Robbie, for the task at hand." She turned slightly so we were practically face to face. She opened up the dispatch. "Robbie

Cameron, let me first say, I read this letter only at your insistence, less Lochiel might think I had it in my heart to pry into his affairs."

"Who would tell him, Ma'am?"

"Robbie, you must always remember, in this city the walls have ears and you won't go far wrong." She looked up at Rourke for confirmation of her words. "Is that not right, Major?"

Rourke nodded approval of her words of wisdom, adding, "It truly is, Ma'am. The boy has much to learn."

"Robert Cameron." She started to read and without thinking, I stood at attention as if in the presence of the Chief and he was addressing me.

"I'm entrusting to you a task about which I have strong feelings. I have sent with this letter, a young woman and her maid servants. My request is that you personally escort them to the port of Glasgow where they will take a ship for the Americas. There, this poor, unfortunate girl will be able to once again be united with her husband.

"This faithful soldier, who for his duty to me was shipped out of the country by his jailers as punishment for his loyalty, not only to the cause, but the young pretender, Charles Stuart. Should you undertake this charge, be aware the Redcoats will surely be on her trail, hoping to find a few of my stalwart men, whom they would dearly like to catch and embarrass me. It is my dearest wish that you fulfill my orders and see to it they get safely out of the country. For myself, I will miss her company dearly. She's been a shining light in the dreary days surroundings me after the defeat at Culloden. But for her company in those lonely days, I feel my life would have had a tragic ending. She was able to make me see our work must go on and I must put aside my personal feelings and think only of my clan and my duties."

He then went on to assure me that my mother was well and living in his care. News had reached him from

America that my father was faring better than expected. He ended by addressing me as a good soldier to the cause and someone he held in high regard.

My mistress folded the letter and asked Rourke to go and fetch the young women. She handed me the letter and then clasped my hand to be sure I was paying attention. "Robbie...this young woman's really not all that upset about her husband being in the colonies. As a matter of fact, he's what can only be described as an old man who suffers from the gout, so I'm told.

"She's in her twenties and if all the rumors are true, the Chief..." She began to wave her fan nervously as she looked to see if Rourke was in earshot. She spoke in a whisper holding the fan up to her face to muffle her words.

"It is said the wife of Lochiel was the one who thought it better she leave the castle and be sent over to her husband. I say this only to ensure that you watch out for yourself and don't get entangled in some sordid affair which might cost you your position with the Chief as it is obvious to all that he holds you in high regard."

"How can that be, Mistress? He hardly knows me!"

Running a hand through my hair, she laid her other hand on my face and looked into my eyes. I felt a strange feeling as our eyes met, akin to how I'd felt with Flora. She stood up and I followed.

"Flora told me of your nights on the moors and how for a beginner, you were a very quick learner. You're a bit of a dark horse, aren't you, Robbie? Do you think you came to me by accident? Surely you must know by now that your presence here is by design. Rourke was given the task of furthering your education in all things and I do mean all things. Knowing that rascal as I do, I'm sure he has taken great pride in doing just that. Again, she glanced in the direction of the hallway.

"You must know, Robbie, that none of us, even , is totally safe here in Scotland. We survive by our wits and good judgment." She took a step back. "The day will surely come when even I must leave my homeland lest I fall into the hands of the Crown's agents. I can assure you, my fate will be fast and lethal. As for you, young man, always be on your guard, trust few, and then only when it's necessary. She gave me a cheeky smile. "Above all, don't let that well-endowed lower portion of your anatomy do your thinking for you." She tapped my crotch with her fan and smiled with a look of feigned surprise.

"Always think through a situation, especially where young, beautiful women are concerned." I blushed. "Well, Robbie, it's plain to see that rascal hasn't taught you all the tricks he has up his sleeve. For now, that's a good thing."

* * *

When Beatrice was shown into the room, I was astounded at her beauty and her young years. Why, she's no older than myself...and so lovely. My mistress introduced us, telling Beatrice I'd been chosen by the Chief to escort her to Glasgow. She smiled, came over, and kissed me on the cheek. She looked over at Mistress Jane. She seemed to pause as if she expected me to return the kiss. At that moment, the words of my mistress came flooding back into my brain.

I took her hand and kissed it, bending slightly to indicate my respect for a married woman. As I glanced at my mistress, I could see the nod of approval and I could I could well imagine her saying, "Laddie, you passed that test well. But that won't last if I'm any judge of women and I like to think in my line of work, I have become an expert."

Rourke, however, was less frigid and missed no time in endearing himself to the young women by heeding her every wish as a command and never missing an opportunity to pay her compliments, such as holding her arm, lest she might trip or falter.

However, I was the one chosen to escort the party. Rourke was quick to inquire. "If there's a need for another sword, I would be only too happy to help Robbie in his task, Jane."

She made it abundantly clear that he was to stay in Edinburgh. "Rourke, don't think for a minute I cannot see where this is leading. You'd best watch your step. You're treading on dangerous ground here."

Wishing to take no part in that discussion, I excused myself and accompanied Beatrice and her maid servants to a private coach waiting for us and we left without further ado. On the outskirts of the city we were stopped by a troop of mounted dragoons, who emerged from a copse of silver birch trees.

I could tell by his demeanor that the officer soon fell under the spell cast by Beatrice. "Good morning to you, good Sir, are you traveling to Glasgow? I hope you weren't startled by our sudden appearance. There are a band of robbers on the King's highway bent on robbery and many other unmentionable crimes that I dare not mention in front of the ladies.

"As for myself, as I'm on my way to the city, I feel it might be prudent to escort your carriage and ensure your safe arrival. I am a Scot by birth. My name is Duncan Campbell. My father being a magistrate for the crown, I received my commission after the uprising. These men are desperate and although I do not altogether approve of the way the highlanders have been treated, the law is the law, and I swore an oath to uphold it."

What a bit of good luck. After all, who'd look for a Jacobite group traveling with the English army, albeit with a loathsome Campbell. Yes, what could be better?

"Beatrice is my sister. She's on her way to the Americas to be married and I'm escorting her party for safety sake. I'm truly relieved to have your company, Captain."

"As for me," he replied. "My work in Glasgow is not pleasant. My orders are to meet agents of the Crown who are on the trail of some Jacobites, one of whom is familiar with where the traitor Charles Stuart has gone since his ignoble defeat at Culloden."

"Rest assured, Captain, that we are loyal to the king and can only hope that your mission meets with success. Also, that you, sir, may be in line for promotion."

* * *

When we stopped for the night, he spent his time talking to Beatrice, who would occasionally flutter her fan and meet my eye, as if to say. "Don't blame me, Robbie, you're the one who accepted his offer of protection." Her ladies had been well-schooled and appeared happy to eat with the troop sergeant. As for me, I ate at the bar and found a spot in the corner where I could see everyone coming and going.

Tired and in need of sleep, I went off to bed.

I was awakened rather coarsely when my young officer friend held a candle to my face. I rubbed the sleep from my eyes. I could hear a cock crowing in the early morning light. I waved the candle away as he began to explain he'd fallen in love with my sister and desperately wanted to marry her.

"Captain Campbell, as you only spent a few hours with my sister at the dinner table, how could you have formed such an attachment over a meal?"

"Robbie, your sister and I are taken with each other." He looked away as if gathering his thoughts. "The truth of the matter is...we spent the night together and have fallen in love."

I looked at him in total shock. How could this have happened? I rose and picked up my britches. What would Rourke advise the best approach to be? Slapping him on the back as a sign of approval, I looked him in the eye.

"Please sir, allow me to dress."

He turned his back.

"I couldn't be happier for you both. Now, what will happen if you don't succeed in the duel? What will my sister do then? Not to mention your father. My God, his position will be ruined by the scandal and all for love. How touching!"

"What duel? What are we talking about?"

I thumped on the table. A beer glass fell to the floor as I feigned displeasure.

"Her betrothed, Captain, don't you see? He'll want to fight a duel for her honor when it comes out at your court martial that you and my sister slept together."

His eyes were ablaze. I could guess his mind was racing as he ran his hand through his hair. I wanted to say, "You fool," but I looked at him as if with great sympathy. I doused my face with cold water and holding a towel in both hands as I dried my face, I looked in his direction.

"Do you have sisters? If so, their lives will also be destroyed after their suitors hear of the scandal. But true love conquers all, so I'm told." I tossed the towel on the bed, sat down, and pulled on my boots.

Taking me by the arm, his head close to mine, we began to walk me across the room and back, whispering in my ear.

"Listen, Robbie, maybe I've been a bit hasty. Your sister and I've only met and can't begin to really know our own minds."

"Certainly, I agree." I stood with a finger on my lip, as if seeking an answer. I raised my hand as if I'd just thought of a solution to his problem.

His eyebrows arched in anticipation of my resolve.

"You must leave at once. That's it in a nutshell, Captain. I'll tell her you had urgent news of those damn Jacobites of whom you spoke earlier. She'll be devastated at first, but once on board the ship, she'll hopefully forget your youthful indiscretions and pick up the pieces of her life."

* * *

He assembled his troop and they rode off, just as Beatrice arrived at the front entrance looking lovelier than ever. She appeared serene and contented. I assumed she felt invigorated by her night of sexual encounter. Just as the column was leaving, she waved to her lover. He reined in his mount, doffed his hat in a wide sweep of his arm, and then charged off toward the highway.

I took her hand and helped her into the coach. As she looked at me, I tweaked my nose, as if in deep thought.

"I'm completely amazed at the tale that young man told of love and indiscretions."

She bade me sit across from her and then reached forward and took my hands in hers.

"Robbie Cameron! Sure you, of all people, could not believe such a tale? Ask yourself? How would you be able to explain all this to his lordship when he personally entrusted me to your care?"

She remained cool and reserved under fire. I envied her composure in the threat of a scandal.

"I never doubted your honor, for a moment Ma'am."

She waved her fan in front of her face, showing only her eyes. "It's just that in the future you must be careful how you act around young men like the captain. Your beauty is too much for them. They lose their head and take on flights of fancy regarding you."

"You, Robbie Cameron." She closed her fan. "How do you feel when you're around me?" Her eyes closed slightly and she looked straight at me. We were now so close I could smell her perfume. Her breasts were pressed against my chest. They were all I could see, apart from her red lips as she ran her wet tongue over them.

I cleared my throat. "Well, Ma'am, you see it's like this. I'm a soldier who's been given strict orders that must be obeyed so I don't allow myself think about a beautiful lady like you as being a woman, rather more like a package which must arrive safely at its destination. I can't begin to think of you in any other way, can I?"

"Now Robbie." She kept moving closer to me with each word. She tapped me on the shoulder with her fan. "I don't like to think of myself as a package, but packages can get dented slightly and still arrive in good enough shape to please the recipient, don't you agree?" She put her hand on my thigh and laughed.

"Oh Robbie, you're such a boy. Don't you know I'm only joking with you? I know you have a job to do. I'll not torment you anymore, I promise." She puckered up her lips, just like a bairn. "Now give me a kiss and let's make up."

I kissed her on the cheek, exited the coach, and left her laughing at my boyish ways. Thank you, Colonel Rourke! You saved me again. I wonder if you'd run from her so quickly? But we'll never know, will we?"

I climbed up beside the driver. "I'll sit up here with you for a spell. I need the air."

* * *

The ship was ready to embark, but the weather was miserable, so the Captain decided he'd stay in port for another day. "I have rooms for you at the inn. My second in command will show you the way. Until tomorrow then, Mr. Cameron." His officer was a pleasant enough man. "My able seaman will see to your needs. He'll be waiting for you at the inn."

As we entered the room, darkened by the inclement weather, shadows fell over every nook and corner. It was one of those old inns. The front was covered in ivy and a squeaky sign, possibly a hundred years old, swayed back and forth in the wind as the rain pelted against it. The only bright spot in the room came from a hearty fire in the fireplace and smells of cooking wafting from the kitchen. It took time to adjust.

Each table had a lighted candle on it. A few customers sat eating. Two men in particular eyed us for a minute and then, moving their heads close together,

47

they renewed their conversation. Some sailors sat drinking at the bar.

One crossed the room, nearly knocking me over. His breath smelled of Irish whiskey." M'name's Murphy. "Captain sent me to look after you."

"Would you and your wife like to eat a little supper after your long journey, sir? And your maid servants...I'll see to them also."

I was about to say this was my sister. Rourke looked at me and then glanced toward the table where two men sat eating. I realized they were the Crown men the Captain had spoken of. I answered loudly.

"I'd be obliged. May I introduce my wife, Beatrice? My love, this is Mr. Murphy. He was sent by the Captain to help us with whatever we require."

"Able seaman, sir, that's me title. I'm pleased to meet you, Ma'am."

"Forgive me, able seaman, my wife and I are country people and don't know much about the ways of the sea. I'm sure you'll do your best to see that we learn."

* * *

Once in our room, Rourke gave me a hug and started towards Beatrice. I put my hand on his shoulder. "What in God's name, are you doing here?"

"The jigs up, Robbie, we're all on the run, you included. Those two at the table are Crown men, and we, my son, are off to France in the morning with Beatrice and her maids. After dark I'll take the ladies aboard ship and you'll stay at the bar making it obvious to all that you and your party are spending the night. At some point, I'll come back and we'll sail on the early morning tide."

I looked around and quietly asked. "Tell me quickly. Jane...is she safe?"

"She is, Robbie, but from now on, we're on our own. I doubt if we'll be running into her for awhile. Now, Beatrice, I can call you, Beatrice, can't I?" Let me see what I can get you to eat. I'll bring it to your room as you must be feeling a little out of sorts. Those nasty men down there won't be bothering you. Have no fear, Rourke will see to that."

"Oh, Mr. Rourke." She batted her eyelashes at him. "You make me feel so much safer knowing you're looking out for me."

My poor Jane. Had she been able to escape without capture or was she already in the notorious Tollbooth? A hellish place that once in, it was impossible to get out unless, of course, you made the eight o'clock walk with the hangman. But I must not let myself dwell on such a terrible thought.

As I turned to share my thoughts, Rourke was already escorting Beatrice to her quarters and the door was closing behind them. My lord, what's to be the result of Rourke and my charge spending time alone together? It was obvious they were alike in at least one way and that one way worried me the most. My home in the glen now seemed farther away and I longed for the comfort of it.

Au Revoir Ecosse

I found myself sitting alone. Rourke was only too pleased to have Beatrice all to himself. I felt a sense of loneliness coming over me with the news of the Crown agents closing in on my mistress in Edinburgh. Maybe, at this very moment, she faced grave danger.

Reminiscing, I remembered the time I was summoned to the library and there sat Flora with her Aunt Jane.

"I want you to take Flora for a walk and maybe take tea at a nice restaurant, Bobbie." She called me "Bobbie" when she was pleased with me. If not, it was "Robert Cameron."

"Don't let anything happen to her. Here's a gold sovereign to pay for your refreshments."

Off we went, dressed like gentry—I with my brand new, sky blue silk coat and Flora dressed in yellow-silk, and twirling a parasol. We made a handsome couple. It was obvious to me that passersby admired us as we walked in the gardens just off Princess Street.

I would have thought I'd died and gone to heaven, being with Flora, but an English army band was playing a military tune. There was method to our madness. In the noisy atmosphere of the park, it was less likely we'd be overheard, if for a moment I forgot and reminisced about our adventure on the moors and our Jacobite affiliation, Flora quickly changed the subject.

There were always spies or peddlers lurking about, eager to earn a coin or two for reporting Jacobites. The Crown was in need of workers in the colonies, so anyone unlucky enough to get arrested by Crown agents would be given a quick trial and then put aboard a prison ship, what many called a "coffin ship" for a voyage across the Atlantic. Many a soul left his native land and ended up in "Davy Jones' locker" the expression used by seamen for "burials at sea.

* * *

When the subject of Rourke came up, Flora was quite bitter. She held her fan in front of her face as we passed a drunken squatter sitting on the pavement before she spoke.

"That great Irish lout. The way he speaks to my aunt and his demeanor are disgusting."

She closed her fan and slapped it against her palm for emphasis. Her eyes were ablaze with rancor.

"Lucky for him, he served the Prince—his bodyguard, I believe."

"I think you're wrong on that score. That Irish officer spoke like a laird. I remember he had red hair and an enormous beard, but he was every inch a gentleman and spoke English eloquently. I've often heard him and the Prince talking in French when they didn't want it known what they were discussing. No, this man Rourke could no more pass for the officer I remember as the Prince's bodyguard than I could."

Flora looked puzzled. "I've often heard my aunt speak of Rourke and the Prince in the same sentence when Jane and I visited with prominent members of the committee whose job it is to oversee anything connected with Prince Charlie."

The subject changed and we went on with our day together. I was wondering what lay in store for all of us and our beloved country when Flora casually dropped more bad news on me.

"Robbie, soon I'll be going to Carolina, when Aunt Jane feels it's safe for me to travel."

"What about us, Flora?" I stammered. "I mean, you know, our friendship?"

Flora looked at me as if she wanted to say more. She put her hand on mine, but then hesitated. "Time will take care of all your questions, Robbie."

51

It seemed as if she had the answers to my questions, but was not at liberty to divulge any. By the time we got back to the house, it had begun to rain heavily and when it rains like that in Scotland, it usually lasts at least a day, if not longer. Business was slow, so I quickly hung up my new jacket and joined Rourke in our usual spot at the entrance to the house. Finally, I mustered up enough courage to ask what had been on my mind all day since Flora and I talked.

"Were you ever in the Prince's party, Rourke? That's where I think I saw you before? It's been on my mind since we first met."

"Yes, indeed. He's a grand fellow, bless his heart, and a true gentleman."

"So what are you doing here? Do you know what happened to the officer who was the Prince's bodyguard?"

"Sure he's long gone, I would imagine. The Prince and he were as thick as thieves. Sometimes I think we might have all been better off if we hadn't set eyes on either of them and possibly a lot better off than we are right now with the Crown breathing down our necks night and day."

"Maybe, but at least for a time we were men again, with a cause in our heart and a love of country and its brave men. I must say, I find your remarks objectionable to say the least." I stood up and stepped back to separate us.

"Calm down, lad, nothing will be gained by you and me crossing swords this day."

He took out his tobacco pouch and began filling his pipe. He spoke in a different tone, not his usual gusto. I was taken aback. My god, there is more than one side to this man. He truly is a man of mystery.

He puffed on his pipe. "Have you heard this phrase? It's from the Latin, I believe. I'm referring to 'being incognito.' If so, that is my position at the moment 'til

I'm advised by my superiors. Just like you, Robbie, I'm told what is expected of me and I do what I'm told."

"Maybe so, Major?" I turned away from him. "But I feel we are a different breed, you and I. The Prince is my liege, come fair weather or foul. It makes no difference to me."

He sat with his hand on his knee and looked up at me. "I feel we should let the subject drop, Robbie. It's not a good thing for friends to let the sun go down on their quarrel. It's better to dwell on more pleasant matters, don't you agree? And, if you don't object to a wee bit of advice from a man who has received his share over these many years...

Never judge a book by its cover, or better still, all that glitters is not gold. There will be times when you are forced to bite into it to be sure."

I felt instinctively the words he said were meant to have a deeper meaning, but for the moment, I'd keep my thoughts to myself. I'd dozed off and awoke to Maggie nudging me. She handed me a message from Jane.

I ran my fingers through my hair as I read it. "Come at once to my quarters, Robert Cameron."

Believing it meant trouble for my remarks to Rourke, my heart missed a beat at the thought of possibly saying more than I should have. My failure at diplomacy had backfired.

* * *

Entering her study, I saw that Flora and Rourke were seated on either side of her. I advanced slowly, my head down as in shame.

"Sit down, Robert Cameron. I have things to discuss with you."

I hesitated and then Rourke spoke. "Sit down, lad, you're among friends."

Gone now was the heavy brogue and the tough manner. I sat opposite another man, who not only spoke politely, but perfect, proper English.

"Major Rourke is here on a mission for the Prince and needs to talk with you. But first, Flora is going to the Americas and plans to leave soon. If you accept your duty to the Prince, you'll be accompanying the Major, or should I say the Colonel since the Prince has seen fit to promote him for services rendered. Flora is also in the service of the Prince, who, by the way thinks of you as a personable young man with great potential.

"He sent Flora to bring you here on his orders. So you see, your chance encounter was not quite as it appeared to be. Flora is not the gypsy girl you befriended, but the daughter of a prominent clan chief, whose position would be greatly compromised should she fall into the hands of the Crowns' agents.

The conversation hit me like a thunderbolt. Her mannerism and her air of authority shook me to the core. The war was not over, certainly the cause still very much alive. It only appeared to be dormant. All that glitters is not gold. The words came flooding back to me. I quickly realized I was no longer Robbie, but Robert Cameron a soldier for the pretender to the Scottish throne, with a heritage that stretched back through the ages to one of Scotland's legendary kings, Malcolm Canmore.

Questions asked were answered faster than I could ever hope to remember:

Yes, I might meet Flora later in the Americas. No, she did not love me, but obeyed orders to induce me by any means to follow her to Edinburgh.

The Colonel was to take a large amount of gold to France and would accompany me as my man servant. It would therefore be necessary for me to learn the art of fencing and also receive lessons in firearms and, above all, I must be schooled in the art of being a spy.

I might at some time be perceived as a man of means, or perhaps a fool or a beggar scraping by under the noses of the Redcoats. Whatever the situation called for, I must be equipped to handle any and all tasks, and my teacher to be was none other than Rourke.

Needless to say, the whole operation had been approved by my chief, who seemed most anxious to prove to all concerned that I remained a man to be trusted. As pre-ordained, I swore an oath to obey all orders given to me and to work for the day when the rightful King of Scotland again sat on the Scottish throne, atop the stone of destiny.

Having taken the oath, I spent a short time with Flora, as she explained to me how she regretted having to deceive me. However, it wouldn't be prudent of me to dwell on thoughts of someday us being more than just friends.

"Who knows, Robbie, maybe someday we'll meet again." She fondled a golden earring as she spoke. "Do you remember the gypsy who wore this?" She took my hand and kissed my cheek.

"If circumstances allow, maybe someday we might even take up where we left off in the glens. It's all in the hands of fate."

I sensed she offered me hope only as a means of making it easier to accept the future. It proved to be one of those days in a man's life when he takes a step nearer to being what he will eventually become and will always remember it with a twinge of longing for things to have turned out differently.

When I went downstairs, Maggie sat in for Rourke. She pulled her skirts together and bade me sit by her. As I took up my post, she looked me over.

"Robbie lad, what's the matter? You look like you've lost a gold sovereign and found a copper penny. Why so sad?"

Not wishing to divulge my misfortune, I replied. "Och, I'm confused. Yesterday I heard a man talk about the Scottish throne and how it sat atop a huge carved stone as old as time itself. It's been on my mind ever since."

"It's not just a piece of rock, Robbie. It's the Stone of Destiny. Scottish Kings have been crowned for centuries sitting on that stone. It's magic, so I've been told, and bad luck to any and all who try to destroy it." She lit up her pipe. The sweet smell of her tobacco filled the dank night air.

"Is there magic in the stone, Maggie?"

"Robbie, being on the stage all my years in the theater, I played many parts and I heard many tales of magic and the likes. What we're talking about is the magic feeling the stone can conjure up in the minds of loyal Scots. Believing in its magic can give all of us a reason to have hope and belief in our cause."

"That reminds me of the story I read about King Robert, the Bruce. Did you know he'd lost battles against the English and hid in a cave in defeat and despair?"

Now Robbie, don't try and teach your Grannie to suck eggs. What Scotsman hasn't heard how one day he sat watching a spider as it spun its silken web and for some reason it fell. He watched as it tried to climb back up. Three times it tried and two times it fell, but the third time it succeeded."

I interrupted. "Bruce took it as a good omen and then got back into the fight? He triumphed over the English at the battle of Bannockburn in the year 1314 and chased the English out of our country. I suppose you could say that was magical right enough."

"All I know, Robbie Cameron, is that things happen that have no explanation, so what harm is a wee bit of magic now and then?" She re-lit her pipe and we sat staring at raindrops falling into puddles, each wee drop creating ripples. We sat there in silence, both of us lost in our own thoughts. Maggie puffed on her pipe. I began to see my life like a ripple, small at first, but ever-widening in knowledge and experience. I remembered those precious nights spent on the moors with Flora

and my eyes filled with tears for my love of a gypsy girl,
a young man and his misspent love.

My First Mission

Very soon after taking my oath, Rourke embarked on a tight schedule. He proved to be a dutiful tutor, teaching me not only how to fence like a gentleman, but also as a brigand, and how to load and shoot a firearm in a matter of seconds. Next, the Skean Dhu, the Scottish name for a small dagger, which I would carry in my hose, would enable me to kill an enemy if I ever found myself in close quarters with an adversary.

As Rourke colorfully suggested, "Put one in each sock lad. It's not a sin to have two. On the contrary, it might save your life someday. Above all, never under estimate your enemy. Don't be a fool and over-estimate him either. Remember, if necessary, bite into whatever appears to be gold and you'll find out what's gold and what's brass. That's one of the great secrets of being a spy. Our motto is. Stay alive and let the other man die for his country."

My training finished, I began my first mission. The Clans had in their possession a declaration of loyalty to the Scottish kings of old, which had also been signed by all those chiefs loyal to the Stuarts. Being a historical document and something more than just a piece of paper, it now became an important piece of history. Its significance showed the French and the Vatican the loyalty the Scottish clans held for The Stuarts. It documented that the signatories held Charles Stuart to be the rightful heir to the throne of Scotland and was evidence of their belief the uprising was a just and noble cause.

These men were now in great danger if this document were to fall into the wrong hands. Lochiel, who'd been given the document to hold in trust, felt it should be delivered to the Prince, who might be able to use it as a bargaining chip in any discussions he might eventually have with benefactors on the continent or the politicians in Westminster.

It had been agreed by all those concerned that the sooner it was taken out of the country the better it would be for all. We were also entrusted with a substantial purse of gold guineas, raised by supporters for the Prince in exile. I was chosen to journey to the port of Queensferry to await my man servant, Rourke. The quay was filled with four masters, all loading and unloading their cargo. I soon found the Arielle, a trim little seagoing vessel, plying between Scotland and France. When Rourke arrived, he showed me a hatbox and explained we must never let it out of our sight. "That's why I've taken on the role of manservant so I can guard it at all times. A good man servant looking after his master's property is the best way to do that, don't you think?

"Besides, laddie, what a great joy it will bring to your mother, bless her soul, to know you've risen to such great heights as to have a grand Irish peasant looking out for your every wish. Sure, the Pope himself should be that lucky."

It amazed me how much weight this man servant of mine had acquired since last we met, especially around his waist line. But it looked good on Rourke, especially with the great red beard he now sported and the earring he wore, while acting the part of a devil may care rascal.

When we boarded, I made it painfully clear to the purser that I wasn't willing to sharing my cabin with anyone.

"That great oaf of mine is to attend me day or night, whenever I feel the need of anything."

My pompous manner encouraged the other passengers to stay clear me, perceiving me as a spoiled brat, forever treating his manservant no better than a slave. I overheard one man say to a fellow passenger.

"Poor fellow, he's obviously so illiterate, he finds it impossible to find a good position, what with his uncouth manner and loud talk. It's well known the Irish are thieves and liars. If the young man did treat him with respect, he'd only take advantage as they are lazy by nature."

It looked so easy to see how well Rourke was able to pull off any type of disguise. An older gent accompanying his daughter to France actually made the statement out loud. "All that has been said is no doubt true gentlemen. However, the Irish are good for one thing, they're better than any ten men in a fight."

My ignorant man servant actually thanked the man for taking his part in the discussion. The man just smiled and shook his head, while he appeared only too pleased to befriend me, which I found strange.

When I looked, Rourke was biting into a coin. I remembered my lessons and knew immediately what he meant. Returning his kindness, I began to give the impression of being infatuated by his daughter, a blue-eyed beauty with long auburn hair and an impish smile.

The outcome of my attention resulted in her asking me to dine at their table and occasionally we'd take long promenades around the deck when she'd tell me of her enrollment in the Sorbonne, a world renowned place of learning. She also spoke of all her worldly hopes for her future. When she took her leave of me and if no one was around, she'd stand on tiptoe and plant a kiss on my lips, smile, and scurry away.

During the day, Rourke spent time polishing my livery, while I appeared on deck quite the Dandy.

Her father suggested it would be more appropriate for me to give the poor lout some time off. Perhaps share a nip with the rest of the servants and a round of cards—if he knew how to play? I immediately agreed he should have the night off when I attended the Captain's Ball and give him a chance to relax before we reached France. Rourke smelled a rat, and we agreed to let the rodent at least sniff the cheese for one night and see what happened.

"Now Robbie, go and enjoy the ball. Only God knows what life has in store for us in France? Don't worry. I'll take care of things."

* * *

The girl's man servant proved to be an unusually pleasant type. Rourke befriended him almost immediately.

"How do you stay with that spoiled brat, Irishman?"

"He's a bit of a waster right enough, but I have a wife in the auld country with three kids and a widow woman in Edinburgh with a child, so I'm obliged to put up with his nonsense. And there's me mother-in-law, fine woman that she is, always the first to see me hand over me money when I arrive home for a visit and walk me to mass on Sunday so I shouldn't be tempted to go into a public house.

"She always makes sure I buy enough drink for the two of us, saying how she doesn't like to see me drinking on me own. Ah truly, she's a grand women. Sure St. Peter himself will be seeing to her when she arrives in heaven for all the grand looking after she has done for her son-in-law in this world of temptation."

"But surely there are others you could work for?"

"Sure in the old country, getting a day's work is hard as pulling teeth so it is, and besides, I'm seeing a bit of the world at the same time. And yourself, how long have you been in your present employment? What kind of business is he in? Tell me now. Does he ever have the need for another fellah, would you say?"

"He's in trade, but seldom has the need for another man. But leave me your address in Edinburgh. I could inform you if such a time came and the need for a helper should arise."

Rourke was quick to hear the word inform, but it would not only be the master he'd be informing and if he and his so-called master ever found out what he and

Robbie were really up to, it would be a Redcoat General they'd be talking to. I can well imagine, "Robbie and I both would be his guests for a short stay in the Tollbooth 'til they found out all we knew. Then, early one morning, a walk to the gallows and we'd be left gently swinging in that breeze that comes up the river on the morning tide. If they only knew how determined I am to let them think me a stupid ignorant Irishman and what delight I take at their clumsy attempt to unmask me.

* * *

I attended the Captain's soiree, which turned out to be no grand affair. I'd seen better nights in the inn with Rourke, but at his insistence, I sat next to my newly found friends. As the night wore on the lass talked about how she looked forward to Paris. I listened intently, hoping they would make their move. Then, as her father was deep in conversation with the Captain, she complained of feeling sick and would I accompany her to her cabin?

On arrival, she fainted. I was obliged to lift her onto the bed. I then wet a hand towel from atop the water jug and placed it on her brow. She remained unconscious and I felt obliged to loosen her bodice. As the lantern in the cabin swung back and forth, I became transfixed on her milk white skin. I could only imagine she'd never worked a day in her life.

She awoke, smiled at me, and then looked down at her bodice. She finished unbuttoning, showing herself to me. She then held on to me as if she were enamored by all my attention.

"Robbie, you're a bold one right enough. I imagine you are of a mind to stay with me you rascal." She placed my hand on her breast. Ever the gentleman, I agreed, and holding her tightly I became intoxicated by her presence and the scent of her perfume, as I slowly removed her bodice. She lay on the bed now completely naked as I kissed her neck and breasts, and as I reached for her thigh, she in turn removed all her other personal garments.

As if by some premeditated plan, her father roughly opened the door and rushed into the cabin. He immediately accused me of taking liberties with his daughter. She now shunned me and held a shawl to cover up her nakedness as she quietly sobbed. He sat by her side stroking her hair.

"Sir, I am astounded at your attempt at deflowering my child. If I were a younger man or had a son, you would certainly be challenged to a duel to save my dear daughter's good name. Sir, I will admonish my daughter never to speak with you again."

As he escorted me to the door, I looked back, intent on apologizing, only to see her lower her shawl, exposing her upper body and smile with an air of endearment to me. I regained my composure and sadly walked to my cabin, dwelling on what might have been had the old fool stayed away. As I opened the door, it was plain to see the place had been ransacked. The infamous hat box was opened, the lining torn out, and the document gone.

I acted like a crazy man, turning over furniture looking for any sign of the parchment. I lay on my bunk, a sheet between my teeth, desperately trying to think what I would tell Rourke, but in spite of my troubles, tried desperately not to cry. Having lain in silent torment for hours, I succumbed to sleep.

* * *

I awoke to the drunken singing of my manservant as he ambled along the passageway down to my door, totally drunk, and in no way possible to be of any assistance in the matter. He was loudmouthed as he looked around. His speech heavily slurred and his clothes looked disheveled, as if he'd slept in them.

"What turmoil? Is there something you were looking for? You've made a dog's breakfast of the place that's for sure. If you think I'm about to clean up your mess this night, then think again, young Sir. I'm going to sit down in this chair and go to sleep." He hiccupped.

We both lay quiet for some time and I tried not to think of the trouble I had gotten us into with my stupid ignorance of women and their devious ways. Would I ever learn how to behave around them? At this moment in time, I longed to be back in my glen where life was much simpler and the wenches less corrupt.

Eventually Rourke spoke. "Well, they took the bait and found nothing. So now I can imagine we've seen the last of your fine friend and his daughter."

"What about the document? And that man servant? Where is he?"

"The gold guineas and that parchment I've carried on my person all along," he said, patting his waistband. "As for their manservant, I believe he got drunk and fell overboard. Now, do you have any further questions for me?"

"But you said the..." I looked at him realizing I'd been duped. "The bloody hat box was a ruse wasn't it?"

"Well Robbie, anyone watching us for the last few days would be conscious of it never being out of our sight and you constantly touching it as if it were a woman's thigh. So, if they were after the document it would be natural for them to think it was in the box, don't you see?" He began to set the furniture to right as he looked over at me. I got up and helped straighten up the cabin.

"When we reach Paris, Robbie, I'll be a retired business man visiting the capitol for a vacation and you'll be my man servant. I know of a place where we can get fitted out. Now you, Robbie, must learn to be the obedient servant and to make sure you're always dressed correctly at all times and be seen to wear white gloves when you're in attendance. Always be ready to complain to anyone who'll listen about how your dear old mother told you not to go into service. You'll tell of how you wouldn't listen and how you've lived to regret it."

As planned, I sent a letter of apology to the young lady regarding my bad manners and begging her forgiveness, saying how I had lost my head because of her beauty and learned a bitter lesson. I then confided in her I would be visiting the Notre Dame at vespers for the next few days and hoped to meet her there. She, in turn, sent a blank note with a rose pressed in it. I looked over at Rourke, holding it aloft as one would a trophy for all to see.

"Robbie, forget the girl, she can only bring you trouble. Just remember, there's as good fish in the sea as ever left it, laddie, and in Paris the streets are filled with many young women such as she, just looking for adventure and sexual liaisons. Have no fear."

"She had a certain thing about her, Rourke." I sounded most worldly. "I do believe she is a virgin."

"Robbie, lad, remember this...time spent breaking in a mare is time wasted if there are many more equines already used to the saddle."

"What's that got to do with a young virgin? I think she really liked me and besides, she showed a deep attraction for me after her father forbade us to meet."

"Don't you see, Robbie? It's the old story. We all want what we shouldn't have 'til we get it and then it turns out to be wanting. Now, forget her and concentrate on the Parisian ladies with their seductive natures and their willingness to please a man."

I looked at the rose, then at Rourke standing in anticipation of an answer. I took the flower, sniffed its fragrance, and then duly tossed it overboard, watching it float away on the tide. Rourke broke into a smile as he nodded his approval.

The Continent of Europe

Paris is like no other city. The grandeur of it all so stunning, not to mention the colorful people one sees in sidewalk cafes where all types mingle. There we were—I, the obedient servant and Rourke, the swank. I felt he'd planned it so as a retired gentleman he could visit all the posh places, whereas I, his man servant, had to confine my wanderings to the poorer sections of the city, if for no other reason than to learn the art of survival.

We never kept company. Each day I went out to take in the city, always on the lookout to see if we were being followed. I spent time in Notre Dame with its many brick buttresses, lending a feel of heavenly guided strength to the majestic edifice.

What a feeling of the almighty one feels, sitting in a pew listening to the choir rehearsing the many Benedictine chants and the perfumed smell of the many lighted candles permeating the air as the bright sunshine burst through the many leaded glass windows depicting such scenes as the archangel Michael locked in mortal combat with Lucifer.

On certain days I would leave early and walk along the River Seine to the Palace of Versailles with its many grandiose fountains and statues which abounded amid the beautiful gardens bursting with the vibrant hand of nature on its earthly creations.

Many mornings I walked for a bit and then waited for Rourke to see if he was being shadowed. Only once did I notice him being followed to a home in the suburbs where it turned out the man's wife waited in anticipation for Rourke's arrival.

After waiting for a time, the man entered and found the two in bed in each other's arms indulging in what could only be described as a sexual liaison.

He'd burst through the door to her boudoir and as his wife tried to cover her nakedness he wrenched the covers off the two naked bodies locked in a torrid embrace. Holding a pistol and challenged him to a duel, he persuaded Rourke to disengage and get dressed, prodding him with his pistol. A date was arranged and Rourke exited the villa.

I immediately sought an interview with the distraught husband and explained I would be acting as Rourke's second at the duel which was to take place the next day. Using his butler as an interpreter, I took the time to inform the man the danger he was in.

"Sir, this Dandy is, in fact, an ex-officer of Dragoons who is capable of shooting a man between the eyes at twenty paces."

I begged him to seek another alternative and he quickly begged me to accept a sum of money he eagerly presented if Rourke failed to show up. I further explained if he saw fit to enlarge the gift he could bring his wife along so she could see what a coward this scoundrel had turned out to be."

We became a little richer for Rourke's indiscretions, though Rourke regarded himself as the damaged party in the whole affair.

As we sat enjoying an aperitif, Rourke assured me the money would come in handy providing for our welfare until we reached our destination. When I casually suggested he had all the money we might need around his waist, he became terribly angry and his eyes became like dark pools, and his jaw was set in an impressive pose. He set his half-filled glass of merlot on the table.

"Listen to me, lad, and listen well. Where the Prince is concerned, I'm a man of honor. I would never spend a penny of that money and if necessary I would lay down my life and yours to see that his money reaches him."

Being chastised severely, I shot back. "Alright, I apologize for my stupid talk. Tell me? Where are we going? And when?"

"All in good time, Robbie." His mood had changed to one of indifference. He emptied his wine glass. "When it's safe by all concerned to do so, I would imagine." I found myself sulking. Rourke lifted my chin so I was looking straight into his face.

"This is not a game, Robbie. If anything, it's a deadly game. There are agents of the Crown who would not hesitate to kill us both if they knew we were carrying the insurrectionist document. Til now we've been able to outsmart them, but that could change at a moment's notice. The less you know the better. If caught, they would make you tell what you know and believe me it would not be a picnic. Just remember, no matter how brave a man is under torture, all men talk in the end."

Like a fool I retorted. "What about you then?" I pulled myself up straight in a gesture of defiance. With my eyes like two slits, I wagged my finger in his face. "Would you talk?"

"Yes, but before I would subject myself to the inevitable..." He twisted the ring on his right hand as he looked at me. I of course, eyed the ring. "The center is filled with poison. I would partake of the deadly brew before being put in irons."

"What about me, then? Why don't I have such a ring?"

"Because my young and true friend of this world. You are if nothing else a man of faith and it's just possible that when the time came and the decision had to be made to leave this world you might hesitate, lest you damn your immortal soul. Then all that we have worked for would be lost."

I was annoyed. Had he implied I was a coward? Then I realized he'd addressed as being a man, which I felt he now regarded me as an equal. From that day on I would only think of myself as such and my heart gladdened at the thought of his words.

* * *

"We're bound for Marseilles. When we arrive there you'll be told our final destination. For now, you must content yourself to learning some French and Italian, enough to get by in casual conversation. For example, if you were to engage a gypsy girl in some friendly barter." He smirked. "Your requests couldn't be misunderstood and you'd not find yourself in a world of trouble."

Throwing back my head in defiance, I replied. "Why should I converse with a gypsy girl? I sat one hand on my knee and the other rubbing my chin, looking off into the distance. "Believe me, I've had my fill of gypsy girls."

"Oh yes, I seem to remember that girl Flora and you, were together in the Highlands. He stroked his beard as he poked a finger at me. "I must remember to ask you about that some time. But don't let that spoil your outlook on all gypsies. If, by chance, a gypsy lass should cross your path, make sure you pay her a mind, but keep your hand on your money pouch." I just shook my head and walked away. He burst out laughing.

* * *

Our journey to the south went without incident and we arrived in Marseilles. It was hot and humid, not to mention smelly, especially the area we lived in called the Canebiere, a dangerous place frequented by renegade sailors, army deserters, whores and gypsies, all of whom would rob you in a minute or kill you just as easily.

It was a labyrinth of narrow streets and hidden passageways. Rourke figured it was a place where only fools or murderers would frequent, so we'd be relatively safe from our pursuers. It was there I found out how many languages he could speak, conversing as he did with all manner of nationalities while at the same time

69

always watching, as if he expected to be attacked at any moment.

One could say he had a very special gift. It was his voice and his eyes. I watched people. They wanted to like him. In a way he even seemed like an addiction. Once he got you in his sphere, he made sure you wouldn't want to lose his friendship.

I felt that he used my name with great affection, especially when he asked me to wait for him or manage a chore he needed doing. Being a Scot and by nature prone to being dour, I'd never met anyone quite like Rourke. He could be funny, but in an instant become very serious when it was warranted.

One day I asked, "How many friends do you have, Colonel?"

He looked at me, laying a hand on my shoulder. "Have you ever read Cicero, Robbie?"

"Yes, I've read his work. What's your point?"

He lay back in his chair "Do you know what he had to say on the subject of friendship?"

"Sure, I must have." I was looking through a periodical. "At this point in time, Rourke, what the great man said on the subject seems to elude me."

"It is said he once told a colleague, 'One can number many in his list of friends, but a true friend is rare.' I consider you such a friend, Robert Cameron."

For a moment my eyes filled up and I looked away. I took a deep breath. "He certainly knew what he was talking about, Colonel, for I too am privileged to have such a man for a friend."

Moments like that are rare in a man's life and not easily forgotten. As I've lived my life I can count on one hand all the true friends I ever had. Rourke has always remained on the top of the list.

* * *

"We're on the move, lad." He'd roused me from my slumber and stood by the window. Dawn appeared to be breaking and as I rubbed my eyes of sleep, I leaned up on my elbow.

"Have you not been sleeping then, Colonel?"

"Robbie, when a man gets up in years he doesn't require as much sleep. The faces of all those men he's killed in battle or dueling seem to come to haunt him at that time when not quite awake, but not yet drifted off to sleep. I suppose it's hard for you to understand, but I feel when a man takes his last breath in this old world, they also come back to remind him of all the mistakes he's made, along with the indiscretions he's committed."

"I never have trouble sleeping," I yawned. "I guess my memories are yet to come."

"Long may you live that way, Robbie."

Still not quite awake, he shook me again. "Wake up, Robbie, wake up!" His voice sounded harsh. He threw me a damp towel. "We must leave immediately. The Crown agents have found us and there is little time to spare. I must ask a great deal of you, lad. I need a decoy to allow me to throw them off the scent, which will give me time to get to the ship that's waiting for us in the harbor.

"It's imperative the document I carry never gets into the hands of the English. You can well imagine the effect it would have on the Prince's loyal clansmen and their families. The transport ships bound for the colonies would be filled to overflowing with the flower of Scottish aristocracy, loyal to the cause.

"There's no time to have someone do the job for us, so you must do exactly what I say. Leave the building straight away. A small fat man will approach you. Appear to be discussing with him the direction you should take. He'll eventually take you by the shoulders and point you in a direction away from the harbor. Run. Don't walk, as if you mean to warn somebody of impending danger.

"I'm sure the agents will follow you and if they split up, the one who remains to watch the house is not long for this world. Once you've drawn away the hounds, this old fox can escape to the ship. You must lose them and then return to the harbor.

"The ship must sail on the next tide, Robbie. We can't wait for you if you're late. I'll get word to you, I promise, but not in Marseilles. You must return to Paris and our old lodgings. He left my room looking back. "Good luck, God speed. Now go."

As instructed, I fled through the streets in haste, still pulling on my jacket and met the appointed decoy. After a while I felt safe and tried to get my bearings, not quite knowing which way to the harbor. I raised my head and smelled for the tang of salt air and then duly headed in its direction. But sad to say, the hound had the same idea.

Struggling to know where to go, I came upon a street fair which had all the usual stalls, acrobats and jugglers. I tried to lose myself in the crowd. Desperate, I began to wish I had a special ring like Rourke as it was plain to see my hound was circling in on me. It was only a matter of minutes before I became his prisoner.

A somewhat buxom, red-haired gypsy girl pulled me into the center of a crowd and stood with her hands on her hips in ridicule. She dared me to dance with her. My first thought was to push her away, but in my dilemma I remembered Rourke's words and I gave myself to her. She began a wild dance as she pulled me around in circles, always moving towards the edge of the crowd that had gathered to see the spectacle unfold. The music sounded loudly in my ears and I thought I might go deaf if we danced around in circles much longer. All at once she pushed me out through the crowd and we disappeared down an alley. She motioned me to be very still, motioning with a dagger she put to her lips. We spoke not a word, but her eyes said it all. Be still, very still, or you're dead.

He found me instantly. Calling out, pistol in hand, he warned me of his intent to shoot if I made a move. "I am a member of the crownnnnnn..." His word faded away as he slid to the ground, blood dripping from his mouth. It was black, so I knew she'd stabbed him in the kidneys. She picked up his pistol. In an instant we were running madly for the harbor and the ship. My gypsy friend pulled me along as we fled with her free hand holding up her skirts. I could see Rourke standing on deck motioning me to hurry. The ship was beginning to get under way as the sailors hauled in the ropes from the wooden capstans on the quayside. Time was of the essence.

As she loosened her grip, I pulled her to me and kissed her with all the admiration one could have for the person who had just saved his life. In turn, she looked at me and then toward Rourke and said in English, but with a French accent. "Go...Robbeee. Go with God and that handsome Irishman. The first kiss was ours, but now I give you one for him." She kissed me passionately. "Tell him I am missing him already. Although I know he is a rascal, I will light a candle for him tonight at the Shrine of the Fisherman and another for you, mon ami. Bon chance." She simply disappeared into an alley. I jumped on board the gunwale as the ship left the dock. Rourke held me in a firm grip. I knew, of course, I'd just been rescued from certain death and I knew as long as I lived, I would never forget her.

* * *

It felt good to breathe in the salt air and to know that all had gone well and we were safely on our way. "Where are we bound for now, my Irish Colonel?" I said in a mock French accent.

"He turned. "Rome! Robbie, we're off to Rome."

* * *

The ship was a small coaster and had only one mainsail. Rourke felt we'd be safe from any English man-o'-war as we were so small we'd appear as a little speck on a great ocean of green. Time was spent resting and brushing up on my Italian. I suggested to Rourke that before he was done with me, I'd be somewhat of a linguist like himself.

He also taught me a number of German phrases and remarked how easily I'd picked up the language. "It's true what they say, Robbie. If you learn Italian, for example, the other languages that came under Roman rule are easy to pick up as they are all somewhat related.

"English, of course, is the exception to the rule. It is simply a multitude of different languages forged together through necessity to conduct business between the different business groups and it all started in a small market town in northern England."

I listened and, of course, made a point of remembering everything he taught me. As I sat deep in thought, I glanced over at him.

"What have you got on your mind, Robbie? I know that look by now."

"Rourke..." I hesitated. He looked at me, nary saying a word.

"I wonder, would it be possible for me to see the document? Knowing the dangers we faced together these last few months, I've often wondered what it looks like."

As he picked up his constant companion, I began to fear retribution for my insolence. Looking around to make sure we were alone, he removed the grip of his sturdy walking cane by turning the ivory handle counter-clockwise and proceeded to pull out a tightly wound paper roll from inside. He meticulously unwound the yellow parchment and began patiently laying different objects on the four corners as he meticulously spread his hands very carefully across the parchment, straightening out all the creases.

Written in a language which had long ago disappeared into the mists of time, it told of blood oaths taken by the clan chiefs, loyal not to the house of Stuart, but those who'd gone before. The words were in an ancient Gaelic and had been written by a gifted hand. Almost saintly, I thought. Being a scholar of Latin myself, I found it easy for me to read the latest signatures added by men who, like their forebearers, held allegiance to Kings of Scotland over the millennium. Only now did I realize the significance of such a paper. They'd stolen the Stone of Destiny and now they hungered for this ancient testimonial that held danger within its sacred words to those foreigners who now sat on the English throne in Westminster Abbey.

* * *

On our arrival in Italy we headed for the Eternal City and most certainly the Vatican. Rourke explained the Prince had taken shelter there as the Crown agents were after him. He still remained an open wound in the side of the English government, who were determined the Scots would never again threaten their existence.

The Vatican was like a country within a city with its own laws, army, and supreme ruler. The Pope ruled this enclave, chosen by God to reign over Catholics across the world.

Here I was, a lad from the Highlands of Scotland, who a short lifetime ago seldom left his glen, walked through the great buildings I'd only read about. The pomp and ceremony became awe inspiring.

"Remember, Robbie..." Ever the skeptic, Rourke pointed to a painting of a Pope. "He puts on his trousers one leg at a time, just like the rest of us mortals. It's true that man cannot live by bread alone, but it's also true His Holiness cannot live without it. Draw the line and remember—you have only one life to live, so be a spiritual man by all means, but never forget to live life to the fullest, lest one day when you're old you might regret that you didn't."

I roamed the same streets where men like da Vinci and Michelangelo once walked and I never ceased to be amazed at the wonder of it all. Rourke had awakened my long-harbored desires to see all these wonderful things and now, because of Colonel Rourke, I was fulfilling those boyhood dreams.

"Well Robbie, now that we're in this holy place, I can assure you the Prince's document of loyalty is safely in his hands along with the gold sovereigns I carried on my person. We've fulfilled our obligation to him. So now it's time to play, and believe me lad, play we will."

Lying in the hayloft in my glen I'd read about men like Julius Caesar. Now here I was with Rourke, the bon vivant, who'd seen the best and the worst of life. Who better to see Rome with than such a man? He took me to see the Coliseum and we explored not only the upper chamber, but also the slave quarters where men had been sacrificed at the whim of demented potentates. The great fountains were magnificent and the grand galleries were proudly filled with famous paintings and sculptures. Lastly, what to Rourke was the most important thing in all of Rome—beautiful women of all shapes and sizes, eager to please a man beyond his wildest dreams. Rome had it all—the magnificent churches, but also the debauchery of which there was a plentiful amount.

When I grew tired of those activities, the Vatican offered peace and tranquility within its walls. It was a place of sanctuary for the boyish part of me. I felt its warmth and safety from the outside world; however, it wasn't enough. Often very early, just before dawn, I'd awaken and look out of my bedroom window over the eternal city as the sky turned a gentle grayish pink and the bells of all the churches called the faithful to early morning mass.

I hungered for my glen with the mists on the mountains, and the trout-filled brooks with the water running rust colored as it tumbled down from the bogs to flow into the icy cold rivers filled with melting snow cascading down from the mountain peaks. I remembered those bright moonlit nights and the sky filled with millions of stars twinkling above the glens filled with little thatch-roofed houses, hillsides strewn with grazing cattle, and red deer with their majestic antlers framed against a moon filled sky.

A special time for me was a summer evening at dusk, complete with the lowing sounds of the cattle being carried on the sweet night air and the gentle rain falling almost like a mist. I thought again of my youth. I'd seen so much and yet, God forgive me...I missed it all. I missed my glen.

The Duel

I awoke from a dream. As if by magic I could hear sheep bleating. I rushed to look into the early morning street below. A shepherd was lovingly moving his flock to new pastures. I turned back into the room.

There stood Rourke, dressed in a blood red dressing gown. In his right hand was a glass a of burgundy and cradled in his left a beautiful, scantily clad Italian signorina, with flowing hair the color of coal cascading over her breasts onto her olive skin. Like shards of crystal, her green eyes smiled at me. She then looked up at Rourke, gazing at him as if he were a Greek God atop Mt. Olympus.

"I'm going home, Colonel."

"Robbie, lad." His smile faded. "Quel dommage. Do you imagine they'll let you go back? You, who have been like a thorn in their side. Don't you realize you're the one person more than any other who has been instrumental in the Prince eluding the Crown's agents? It's utter madness, Robbie. Believe me. The Scotland you knew is gone forever and that friendly glen of yours. It's now better described as a veil of tears. Your country is one which has been conquered, tortured, and betrayed. Those dreams you have belong to a different time.

"Every day you're in Argyll, will be a day your mother is in mortal danger. How long do you think she'll last in the jail in Inveraray? The Campbells aren't known for their hospitality when it comes to a Jacobite. She'll be lucky to get something to eat and a mouthful of water to drink.

"Think long and hard on what you're about to do, laddie. Think long and hard." He'd remained silent sitting on a table with his feet dangling in midair. He leapt onto the floor. "Your chieftain...Cameron of Lochiel." He moved around. My eyes followed him. "How do you think he'll feel when for the sake of his clan he must give you up to the English? It'll break his heart for sure."

"I know, Colonel, I know, but maybe I can slip in unnoticed and stay long enough to see my mother—give her a wee bit of comfort to see her through hard times. I will at least know in my heart I've tried to make up for all the pain she's had to endure."

"And where will you go if they're on to you? There's no captain who'll risk his vessel to give you passage. The McEwens were brave enough to help the Prince, but with all they've had to endure since, I feel you'll be as John the Baptist, a voice calling in the wilderness of past friendships and associations. Just wait and see if I'm wrong."

I now stood my back, resting defiantly on the handrail of the balcony and my arms folded. "Nevertheless old friend, my mind is made up."

* * *

After much discussion and debate, Rourke spoke with the Prince and then asked me to come his quarters. His lady sat by a glowing, smoldering fire, quietly strumming a lute and singing an Italian love sonnet. Rourke sat writing by candlelight. As I entered, shadows danced around me as he rose up and leaned across the desk. He handed me the name of a bank in Switzerland.

"If you're still of a mind to go back, take these letters of credit and other papers you'll need if you're to fool the English officials."

He stood running his hand over the signorina's shoulders as he looked over. "It's all changed, Robbie." He threw his quill in the fire and began to prance around the room like a caged tiger. "No more carrying gold in your pocket. It's a sure way to confirm you're on the run." He pointed a finger at me.

"Now, it's all about letters of credit that allow you to deposit money in Switzerland. Then wherever you go, just produce them at a bank with those personal papers you now have in your hand and they will verify you as the person to whom the letters were issued and the worth of the notes in their currency.

"It seems when the clans were beaten, it was feared the English would confiscate any wealth they might haves so what gold coin they'd hidden from the Redcoats, they eventually deposited in the banks in Edinburgh. In turn it was sent to Switzerland for deposit in their many banking houses. This way they were able to keep their fortunes intact. No longer could they be waylaid on the roads by the many outlaws the English have created with their brutal treatment of our once brave comrades in arms."

I stupidly approached him in a mild rage, my arms held straight and my hands clenched tight at my sides. "But how is this any good to me, Colonel? I have no money. Maybe you forget that I'm as poor as a church mouse, living off your generosity for all this time."

"Robbie, lad." He motioned with an outstretched arm as if seeking to comfort me. I've spoken with the Prince about your dilemma. If you must do this thing, he's procured these papers for you here in Rome. Believe me. They will fool any Englishman who cares to examine them. Now, as for the money, remember what I told you in Edinburgh. If you're ever in need of money, then Rourke is the man to see. There is a fund that the chiefs have for such contingencies. Into the bargain, I have an amount given over to me by the Prince.

"But remember, whatever country you may be in at any time, you need go to the nearest bank that has dealings with the Vatican and present your papers and they will vouch for you."

I gave him a skeptical look. "I can see a Scottish bank falling over themselves to be courteous to a highlander who presents official Vatican letters of credit as you call them. Och yes, I can see that happening right enough." I sat down with my back on to my old friend and buried my head in my hands.

He swung me around, sat down, and slapped me on the shoulder. His companion brought him a glass of wine and stood by him. He sat with his arm around her, with his head on her thigh. "Remember lad, when you have money, a banker will always be your friend and will overlook your many small indiscretions. That is, if he thinks there's a chance of him getting his greedy hands on some of your fortune."

I began to calm down. "I must admit when we lived in Edinburgh, I always noticed how gracious the bankers were towards you, Rourke. I must assume they knew you had money?"

He removed his hand from her body and tweaked his mustache. "My case was a wee bit different, Robbie." He coughed, straightened up, and strode around the room, occasionally looking at me as he spoke. "You see, there's another twist to this tale." He held up the wine glass.

"If you owe them money and are, shall we say, somewhat lax about repaying them? Well, it's better to be courteous to the man who owes you money than not, as there's always the chance he might someday pay you back."

He stopped and then moved to place an arm around the signorina. She snuggled close to him, nipping his earlobe and together they walked out toward their bedroom. I stood looking out of the window. He turned back, as if having forgotten something and walked toward me.

"Now listen to me carefully. Travel by way of Switzerland and Holland. It's well known as a Protestant country and if your papers are stamped by their authorities, then there will be less chance of the English taking the time to scrutinize a wealthy banker.

"Remember! He wagged his finger at me. Rid yourself of all things Catholic on your person and never miss an opportunity to heap praise on the King, even if it sticks in your craw to do so." He hugged me and whispered in my ear. "May God protect you Robbie, lad. Have a care." He produced a large handkerchief, blew his nose, and as he lifted it to his eye, his voice faltered. "I'm missing you already, laddie."

* * *

Switzerland appeared clean and industrious. I had Vatican papers obtained for me by the prince and was perceived as a rich young man studying for the cloth. However, given my situation, I found it quite remarkable how many young women tried to seduce me. Luckily for me, Rourke's lady had taught me the technique of a woman's fan. The different movements are a secret code as to her disposition toward a prospective lover.

On the times they succeeded, which I must confess were more frequently than not, they were quick to tell me how they'd only taken the opportunity to make love to me as they were hopeful I would realize how futile it all seemed for a rich, handsome young man so well-endowed by his maker to take holy orders. I quickly chose to administer a sort of absolution for their indiscretion. A small price to pay, shall we say for easing their conscience. Yes, I'd now become a man of the world. I could imagine Rourke would be very pleased to see how his protégé had finally turned out. I imagined no one would be more surprised than he.

* * *

I reached Amsterdam and changed my identity to that of a man of the cloth. I took on the role of a young attorney traveling for the Vatican on their behalf. I checked my letters of credit, which I hoped would pass the authorities there and in Scotland. As promised by the Colonel, to put a phrase on it—they were as good as gold.

As usual, Rourke was right. The bankers were less interested in scrutinizing my personal papers than they were on getting their hands on my letters of credit. The reality that one's beliefs might have different names came second to the fact my letters all spoke the same religion—money!

* * *

The crossing was rough, but less so because the ship carried ballast. Their reason for the trip was to bring back Scottish coal. For ballast they filled the ship's hold with red Dutch clay roofing tile, which in time replaced the thatch roofs Scotland had known for centuries.

The coach trip to Edinburgh was comfortable as I was now perceived as a man of means. No more hiding in shadows for Robbie Boy. I went to all my old haunts and spoke to a few trusted friends who told me Beatrice remained in France. She'd not gone to the Carolinas as planned, but had stayed in Paris with her maid servants.

It appeared she'd had a tryst, as they put it, with my old friend and comrade, Rourke, the mad Irishman. I now realized where he'd disappeared to those many times in Paris and why he'd chosen different lifestyles for us.

What would my sovereign lord be thinking if he knew? I began to think of my circumstances and how Rourke would comment if he were with me. 'Robbie lad, have ye bitten of more than you can chew?'

* * *

By good fortune, I met a sensual young vixen named Annabelle, whose husband was a business man in the city. He had Jacobite leanings and they invited me to stay with them in their home in the fashionable part of town. She was enchanted with my stories of Paris and Rome.

I must confess, I often used Rourke's escapades as my own to bolster my prestige with not only this lady, but any who might wish to hear me relate my travels on the continent, which were far and beyond any chance they had of seeing all the places I'd described.

For the most part, they were young women married off to older wealthy men, by parents who had need of money to pay off debts. Or, they themselves felt it more prudent to be rich and have fine things rather than married to a young impoverished lad who couldn't possibly keep them in a manner befitting a fine-looking, spoiled young virgin.

I felt it advisable to remain with my hosts to see if I might be watched, but it seemed the young attorney proved to be above suspicion. Always eager to hear about the ladies in Paris and what they were wearing, together with my many stories, Annabelle became very fond of me.

One evening when her husband had gone to Glasgow on business, she asked if I should like to hear her play on the harpsichord. I assured her I would be only too happy to do so. She leaned her head to one side as she approached me.

"I keep it in my bedroom, Robbie." She took my hand and guided me to the stairway, looking back at me with an amorous smile as we climbed the stairs. "My husband is quite deaf and cannot appreciate the melody, poor soul."

I nodded an understanding as I accompanied her to the boudoir. I could see at once the furnishings said female and I assumed she slept alone. She began to play a host of classical compositions, including a new piece from a child genius named Mozart. I listened ever so intently.

She stopped, but kept her hands on the keys and began to engage me as to how I liked the city. "Do you have a lady who your heart has gone out to then, Robbie?"

I explained I had been without a companion for some time. She suggested that she knew many youthful, respectable ladies with whom I would be very well received.

"Shall we say, Annabelle, I prefer more experienced ladies who better know what a man expects of them."

She leaned over atop the harpsichord, her head tilted slightly and her bosoms crushed against the lid, emphasizing their size. "Pray, tell me, Robbie, you're not one of those..." She covered her face with her fan, with only her eyes on me. "...who's more interested in young men? I don't wish to offend sir, but I also do not wish to make your stay with us a trying one."

Reading her intentions by the movement of her fan I replied with my hand over hers. "Truth be known, most women I have befriended have been more experienced, not pretty young things who take delight in leading a man on, only to retreat when he begins to show them deep affection."

Before I could continue, she stood up facing me, slowly unbuttoned her gown, and as it fell to the floor, she hurriedly removed her undergarments, and moved to her dresser. Sitting at her mirror as she brushed her hair, she spoke not a word, but bid me take her by the hand. Together we rose up and walked over to lie down on her bed. After we'd made turbulent, passionate love, she pulled me over her once more and as she ran her fingers over my body she spoke in low, almost begging, whispered tones.

"Robbie! I cannot express the feelings I've had for you since your arrival in our home. It has been like a tonic for me just having you here and watching you go about the house with your jaunty stride, so full of self-confidence, and the compassion you show for a lonely young woman, whose husband, shall we say has lost his joie de vive."

She looked striking with her full round breasts, long shapely legs, and her milk-white Grecian-like figure, akin to those maidens one sees on the Greek urns at the museums in Paris and Rome. We'd made love several times and I began to pity her husband, as even for me she proved a handful as she never seemed to weary of our love-making.

It struck me that if this mirrored her routine, her poor husband being older wasn't long for this world. Rest assured I felt he'd probably die in the best of circumstances. A phrase I could imagine hearing Rourke comment. "It's a fact, lad. If one has to go to meet his maker unexpectedly, then it must be the best of all ways to go, by far."

Until her husband's return, I spent most of my time in her boudoir. As I lay on her bed after lovemaking she'd stroke my golden locks. "Oh Robbie, darling, you can never know how lonely my life is. You've brought a feeling of joy to me that I've never experienced before and I'm sure, will never again."

When her husband eventually returned, I made my excuses and moved into a nearby inn. I then received word that Lochiel was anxious to speak to me, so I purchased a young dappled grey, newly broken to the saddle, along with two French dueling pistols and set off for Argyll.

Truth be told, I did feel the want of the lady and her bed, even as I knew I'd done the honorable thing by taking my leave when her husband had returned. What kind of man would seduce a woman in her own house, right under the nose of her husband? Then again, it was hard to be honorable as she, the lady in question, had given me a host of very good reasons to stay.

* * *

It was good to see the purple heather-covered mountains and hear the occasional lone piper in a far off glen playing a dirge at sunset. I could almost hear the song my mother would sing to me as a boy when I'd hurt myself playing. She would have me on her knee and softly sing a song of love between a maiden and her young man. Even now, a grown man, the thought of her comforting me brought a tear to my eye. I aimlessly thought of Flora McNeil, my first true love.

* * *

The Chief met me with all the pomp and ritual of a close friend. With my lectures from Rourke ringing my ears, I was thinking, 'What does this old rascal have in mind for Robert Cameron of the glen?' I'd come home to see my mother and not to engage in any intrigue. I recalled that old Scottish saying, 'Whatever is meant for you will never pass ye by. So brace yourself and grab life with both hands.'

Taking me aside, we strolled out to look out over the castle lawns. Two brightly adorned peacocks strutted on the grass, their tails fully extended, as they showed off their ornately colored feathers of deep-greens, blues, and purples. Looking around to see if anyone stood within earshot, he then laid a hand on my shoulder.

"Will ye join me in a dram, Robert?" A simple nod brought a man servant carrying a bottle of the clan whiskey and two hefty glasses on a silver tray.

"I've had correspondence with our friend, Rourke." He sipped his drink. "He assures me you are a man to be reckoned with as far as defending yourself in sword play and the like. Tell me this, is your friend Rourke perhaps prone to exaggeration in this matter?"

"Well, Sir," I too sipped at my whiskey, holding it up to the light to admire its golden hue as I answered. "I wouldn't want to be seen blowing my own horn, so to speak; however, I've been taught by the best swordsman I've ever known and having the good luck to have him share such a thought with yourself, known far and near for your own ability with the steel." I faced him. "What kind of man would I be to disagree with my mentor? But tell me, my lord, are you in need of a swordsman at this moment in time?"

He nonchalantly drained his glass. "I surely am, Robert Cameron, and that's the God's honest truth. I recently had an occasion to meet with the Duke of Argyll to play a hand of cards and gave my opinion of his fencing master. Well, to put it plainly, he took umbrage at my remark.

"He challenged my man against his, not forgetting that he'd seen fit to put on the table a rather large sum of gold as a wager. Now the problem is..." He took a pinch of snuff, waited, and then sneezed. "My man has come down with the pox, damn him to hell, and I'm in need of a swordsman to defend the honor of the clan. What makes it worse for us, my man is familiar with this brigand and all his tricks."

"Would I know Argyll's man? Is he a Campbell then? It's possible I've seen him in action?"

"No, Robert. I should think not." He refilled our glasses and then handed the bottle to his servant who stood off to one side. "He's German, I believe."

Handing me my glass, he walked through an open window into the great hall toward the fireplace. Looking back to see if I'd followed, he stood with one hand on the mantel shelf looking into the now dying embers. He kicked at a log, which flew into sparks, and re-ignited with a renewed fury, the flames silhouetting the chief as he raised his glass as if in a toast.

"He's one of the gang who now rule from London. Not much to look at, but has a well-known reputation. Truth be told, I loathed taking up the challenge, but he goaded me into it. God forgive me, but for the whiskey and my devilish pride." He hung his head and attempted to stand ramrod straight. Rather shakily, as he steadied himself by the mantel shelf.

"If you're not up to the task, I'll take up the challenge myself, Robbie." He looked at me, then plopped down in a high backed leather chair and added as he again partook of a pinch of snuff. "However, with my rheumatism and the gout, I'm not up to prancing around in a circle as well as I might be."

He now left the conversation to me. I threw a knurled oak log onto the flames, wiped my hands together, and stood over the man. "My lord, you must surely know I would deem it a privilege to defend the honor of the clan, come what may. Rest assured I'm able and most willing to take up this challenge no matter what."

No one spoke. We drained our glasses and smashed them into the fireplace. The drops of liquor remaining in the glasses caused the flames to soar upwards, revealing a sly smile on his lordship's face. He had me cornered.

* * *

The meeting for the duel arranged, we arrived and were received with as much pomp and ceremony as what might be expected for the Wee German Georgie himself. The lords of the Isles, as they were known in Scotland are long on tradition and ceremony, it being their ties to the old ways which were fast disappearing.

I listened to long-winded speeches and toasts, which were part of this circus. As the meeting wore on, I passed the time looking at all the splendid wall coverings and paintings. I remembered a tale of Rourke's about the clan Chief who inhabited Glamis Castle which, by the way, is the line of demarcation line between the Highlands and the Lowlands of Scotland.

As Rourke told the tale, the chief had been visiting France and attended one of the grand balls held by the king. He'd engaged in conversation with his majesty's chancellor, and the renowned Dutch painter, Jacob De West. The chief persuaded him to come to his castle in Angus and paint scenes depicting the life of Christ based upon frescoes he'd seen in the Sistine Chapel.

They were to be copied on the sugar pine paneled ceiling of the great reception hall. An amount was agreed upon and the painter traveled back to Scotland with his host and proceeded with the task at hand. However, when the painter had completed his commission, there became a disagreement as to what had been promised in payment when the initial meeting in France had taken place.

Now Jacob De West, being an astute fellow, simply agreed he must have been wrong in his evaluation of the contract.

"Your Lordship, I'm sure you will forgive my misunderstanding. I wouldn't want to give the impression I'm unhappy with the figure you mention. Be assured, I will leave your beautiful home well satisfied that I've been treated fairly."

Upon reflection, the next day at lunch he explained. "Because the work I've completed has met with your approval, Sir, I feel almost compelled to paint one more painting, and if I might suggest, that panel yonder at eye level as one exits the great hall. It will be my parting gift to a most gracious host."

The painting completed, the great artist took his leave of the country and returned to France. It was quite a few years later, however, when a visiting dignitary shocked the Chief.

"I agree the work done on the ceiling is without equal, your lordship; but this painting the artist completed?" He pointed with his silver tipped walking cane. "The one, which portrays Christ on a donkey entering Jerusalem on Good Friday, is quite unique. It is, to the best of my knowledge, Sir, the only painting ever completed which shows Jesus Christ wearing a hat."

Needless to say the chief being a canny Scot, decided to leave the painting just as it appeared. "Well now, if it is indeed unique as you say? Then who knows? Someday it might become of great value."

I returned from my reminiscing by the voice of the Duke, inquiring as to what sword I would choose in the contest. I saw before me a weasel of a man, dressed in silk pantaloons and a fancy wig which wouldn't have been of much use at Culloden. 'But then,' I thought, 'had he been there, he would surely have been on the side of the Crown.' He smiled and at a clap of his hand was attended by his swordsman. The German stood about the same height as me, with a long scar on his cheek. In most cases this denoted he was of noble birth and had been chosen to train at the Deutsche Fechtschule, it being the finest military fencing school in all Germany. The scar he wore was a badge of honor held amongst the upper classes.

Rourke would have been quick to point out that such a scar could just as easily been gotten by a man trying to snatch a whore's purse as she she'd be quick to pull a dagger from her skirts and slash the culprit across the face, therefore, I did not allow myself to be intimidated by my opponent. However, his sword proved another matter as he chose to use a broadsword, much heavier and lethal, while I on the other hand preferred a lighter sword which I felt served my needs better to engage in a duel.

"No matter," Rourke would often say as he taught me the art of fencing. "Robbie lad, always remember..." He'd parry and thrust and jab at me as he spoke. "The sword is only as good as the man who wields it."

I made the decision to compensate for the differences in our weapons and asked all to indulge me while I changed from my heavy shoes to the pumps I used while dancing a reel or a jig. The old chief looked at me with contempt and I knew all present were probably thinking. Is this a duel or a dance contest we are about to witness?

I thought, Robbie Cameron, pay no attention to the old man or that weasel Argyll. It's he who wins that counts. We went to the center of the great hall with its stone paved floor and the referee threw down a white handkerchief. The duel began.

The German lunged forward like a frenzied, pent-up bull chasing a herd of heifers, but I'm no heifer. I sidestepped him and as he flew past, I administered a great whack on his arse with my sword. He was not amused. He turned again and charged. I parried, easily stepping back as he again flew into nothing but air. The crowd began to twitter and he became angrier by the minute.

I addressed Argyll. "Sir, I feel it will be impossible to continue with the contest unless you can assure me your man will not continuously have his backside to me as I can hardly be expected to engage in sword play with his German arse."

The German became furious and made a fatal mistake. He tried to cut me with a downward thrust when the distance between the two of us meant he had to stretch his whole body to do so. I waited until he fully extended his arm and then I moved to his left and brought my blade down on his outstretched hand. Immediately it produced a great deal of blood as I'd severed the vein.

He yelled in pain and dropped the heavy sword on the floor, clutching at his hand. Swiftly, I jumped forward and with my right leg behind him, threw him face downwards on the floor.

Laying there on the stone slabs, his arms outstretched, as he fell trying to save his face from harm, he reminded me of a postulate I had once seen humbling herself before God and her Mother Superior as she begged forgiveness for her shortcomings. Luckily for my German friend, he only had to ask for mine. More easily given I presumed.

"Fertic?" German for "finished." Again I asked, but this time in English. He nodded by moving his head, not all that easy when you're pinned to the floor by a man wielding a sword at his jugular. I cautioned he'd very quickly be sent to his ancestors should he decide to debate the matter. I kept the sword on the man's neck while turning to Locheill.

"Have you satisfaction in this matter, your Lordship?"

Turning to Argyll, I smiled and took the greatest pleasure from seeing him squirm, not only for losing the fight, but also a great deal of money he would now have to pay my chief. Not to mention the scorn he would have to live down that would be heaped on his name in the local inns.

The tale would be told of a great German in the pay of Argyll, being brought down by the clan swordsman wearing a pair of dancing pumps and wielding a flimsy sword. It reminded me of the well-known parable of David and Goliath. I imagined I would have to be very careful when traveling in Campbell country for now on.

My chief shook my hand. "Robert, I will use this yarn at every opportunity to the satisfaction of all the chiefs who hear it. A gallant lad from my clan, who in a mere few minutes brought down the great swordsman that Argyll had wagered, could beat any man I brought against him. Truly, this is a moment in history to be savored by all."

When the German finally rose, I quickly gave him my handkerchief to bind his wound. Obviously, no one from the Duke's side stood ready to assist him as he stood like a soul in limbo. One of the Chief's page boys brought my shoes. I placed a hand on the lad's shoulder as I removed my pumps.

I talked at length with my combatant in German, a fete which brought much admiration for me amongst my side. As the servants began mopping up the spilled blood I could hear their chatter. Robbie Cameron not only proved himself a great fighter, but a linguist to boot. This indeed is a great day for the Clan Cameron.

For Gustav, my opponent, he clearly felt no shame. "You beat me fair and square, Scotlander, and in our line of work, my friend, there is always another day."

We shook hands and he told me in his tongue, "Be careful, Robert Cameron. There are many here who hate you and would do you harm if they could. You sir, are a man of honor and I have seen little of that here today. I must tell you, my wife, Gerta, and I will always be in your debt for not rendering the death blow or a wound which would have ended my ability to ply my trade. *"Danka. Gott segne sie, mein freund."* (God bless you, my friend.) He was grateful I hadn't killed him and by not rendering a second blow, he would be able to ply his trade on the European continent for many years. As for me, I was thrilled to know I'd fought and won my first duel. I must tell Rourke all about what happened. That's when I realized that for the first time in a very long time, I felt completely on my own.

* * *

The chief held a *caliegh* as we Scots call a party—good food and wine accompanied by usage beatha (ish-ga ba-ha), the water of life as we Scots refer to Scottish whiskey in our native tongue. I looked with pride upon my mother's face as we sat next to the Chief at the dining table, being waited upon by those she'd waited on all her life.

"Mrs. Cameron." Lochiel stood. The room fell silent as he raised his wine-filled glass. "Your son has done us all proud this day. Most surely a true pity that your husband, a good and loyal man that he is could not be here to honor Robert."

My wee mother also stood and then curtseyed. "It is indeed a shame, your lordship, but we will keep him in our prayers and if it's the Lord's wish, we may still someday be together as a family in a free and prosperous Scotland, being ruled over by a true Scot."

The room erupted in praise. I sat totally surprised at my mother's answer—so clear and precise, like a woman who'd made speeches all her life. It became clear to me that my mother, like most highland women, kept her light under a bushel as the Good Book says.

The old Chief stood up again and faced her. "Amen to that, dear lady." He then raised his glass and toasted the Prince and the Clan. Last, but not least, he toasted my mother and me. The whole gathering stood and emptied their glasses. Weeping, my mother whispered in my ear, "See the tear form in the old man's eyes."

I agreed with her, but thought. Is that a tear of joy or perhaps he is remembering a certain lady Beatrice, or, at best, he'd been partaking of maybe a wee dram too many?

* * *

My mother became the overseer of the castle linens, a most privileged position of great importance, with many ladies to attend her and be at her beck and call. She took up residence in a castle apartment facing east. No more milking or gathering crops—none of those lowly jobs for her. She'd come up in the world.

* * *

"Mother, I must leave on the Chief's business and I leave you a happy woman who now has all she needs to live a happy life. I bent over and kissed her cheek. "See it doesn't go to your head," I said, grinning.

"Now listen here, Robert Cameron." She stood hands on hips. "Am I not the one who was forever telling you not to be looking up at the stars lest you might fall on your backside?"

We sat there that day over a cup of her best Indian tea and bannocks smothered in homemade butter and heather-flavored honey. I thought how this memory would stay with me for the rest of my life. My wee mother, now a woman of importance in the Lochiel household with a position worth more to her than a box of priceless black pearls plucked from the oceans depth by exotic, bare-breasted maidens of the Orient.

* * *

The next few weeks went by and I began to forget the words of my German opponent regarding my safety. After all, who would try to harm the Chief's swordsman? It could easily start a feud which could last for years— not that I thought myself all that important.

Summoned to his study, the old chief rose to greet me and inquired if I would perform a task of secrecy. He began pacing back and forth across the room as if greatly distressed.

"It would appear, Robbie, the Crown's investigators are suddenly opening up old scores long ago dealt with. It's my belief that devil's disciple, Argyll, is behind the new purges not only of myself, but into the past trials and investigations of several of my loyal clansman in the lowland areas near Edinburgh.

"It's important to get word to Jane as soon as possible, so those in question might at least move their fortunes from Scotland to the continent before they can be arrested. Information like this can only be carried in person. Nothing in writing is acceptable, lest you be detained by the Redcoats.

"So you see, Robbie, it must be someone who is trusted and known by the clan members involved in this unfortunate situation. He clapped a hand on my shoulder. "So, who better than most for this task at hand, but the clan duelist, Robbie Cameron, who we all look up to and admire?"

I rose and stood at attention. "I shall set off immediately, Sir."

"Now wait up, Robert." He bade me sit with a wave of his hand. He poured two glasses of sherry and handed one off to me. "You'll not be alone in your task, Robbie. I've sent word for Colonel Rourke to assist you in this matter. Letters from Rome tell of how you work well as a team and were responsible for the Prince's gold and that other item being safely delivered in Rome.

"Jane McNeil is not only a dear friend, but a very important link in the chain of the Prince's supporters. If she was to be arrested and the Crown's prosecutors forced her to talk, it would most surely put many loyal men in jeopardy, not the least of which I count myself."

He took a pinch of snuff and then sneezed. "They've not moved on her yet." He pulled a silk handkerchief from his coat pocket. "She's been under house arrest since you all escaped. Friends in high places who still have sentiment for our cause have let it be known to me the English believe the man responsible for Charlie's escape is himself on the way to secure her release. The Crown Generals would pay a pretty penny to get their hands on such a man, so be careful with whom you break bread. Many a greedy man has damned his soul for a purse of English gold."

He beckoned me come closer. He placed his arms around me and kissed my cheek. I could feel the wetness of his tears on my face as he spoke.

"Robert Cameron. I love you like a son. You've exceeded all my expectations. As a lad I saw your worth and when the Prince asked me to find him a page. I knew in my heart there was but one lad I could consider.

"So go now and may God protect you. We may not meet again in this world, Robbie Cameron, but rest assured, I'll be the first to greet you in the next. You have my word on it." He turned away from me and raised his handkerchief to his face.

I took a step backward, also wiping away a tear on my cuff as I donned my hat. With a hand firmly on my sword, I looked back. He stood by the fireplace peering into the flames with both hands on the mantelshelf. His head bowed as if in prayer. He seemed old. I left the room a sadder man.

The Funeral

Rourke entered my lodgings. "Where were you when I came through the door just now, Robbie? You were a million miles away. I hope you haven't taken to daydreaming?"

"Just so, Rourke, I have indeed. I've been thinking of a duel I fought for Locheill in Inveraray Castle."

It seemed Rourke felt I was restless for action. "There will be adventure enough, Robbie. We must get Jane out of Edinburgh and get her passage to France with all possible haste."

I gave thought to the problem at hand. For a moment I'd forgotten that it was our dear Jane that Rourke was talking about.

"Tell me, Colonel, how do we manage such a feat? What are we to do? We can't leave her a prisoner in her own home for much longer. Why ever did you leave her as you did? Surely it could have been possible to take her with you?"

"Robbie, lad." He took my wrist in a vise-like grip. "I would have soon as cut off my right hand than leave her, but she insisted I go to catch up with you. She felt sure you might not realize the danger that you're in. Jane felt the Chief was premature in ordering you to help, thinking she'd be able to escape on her own. Besides, she had affairs to attend to with the bankers, moving her money and the like, so she wasn't ready to go."

"I'll go and fetch her. Is she still at the house? Rourke, old friend, you must find a ship's captain leaving for America and have him make for a port on the other side of the River Forth where I'll endeavor to meet you."

Rourke had a meeting with a sea captain and learned the first mate came from a little town on the east coast of Fife named Lundin Links. He felt sure the local port official would turn a blind eye to his ship, the Pathfinder, laying over for a few days if there was a cask of rum in the arrangement. He punched my shoulder. "You have a few days Robbie, but not much more. If you have a plan, then go quickly, lest we all end up in Tollbooth, that most dreadful of all prisons!"

* * *

Reaching Edinburgh and finding Jane proved easy, but Crown agents had the house surrounded. She felt they hadn't moved in on her as they were after a bigger prize—one Colonel Rourke who'd it appeared had been informed on by one of his many enemies in the cause. My papers were in order, so I felt free to travel the length and breadth of Scotland if I had a mind to; however, Jane remained the bait intended to capture Rourke. She would not be allowed go anywhere.

As I entered the house, Jane had begun packing. I took her by the arm and we walked 'til we were out of earshot of any of the servants who might want to eavesdrop.

"How is Maggie? Is she still in your employ?"

"She's well, thank God. She'll be pleased to hear you ask after her, I'm sure, Robbie."

"I was rather hoping she was poorly. I'm in need of a funeral in the very near future. Tell me, where is she now?"

Jane finished packing her trunk, closed the lid and sat on it. She stunned me as she took an expensive walnut pipe from her pocket and lit up. With the sweet pungent tobacco smell swirling about us, she moved waved the smoke away.

"Please forgive my unladylike behavior, Robbie, but when I'm nervous, it helps to enjoy a pipe." She packed down the tobacco in the bowl as she continued. "After the Crown agents came snooping around, the place became deserted. Our clientele went elsewhere, not wishing to be associated with an establishment being spied on by the authorities. Maggie, poor soul, decided to move into the area around St. Giles Cathedral. You know, where all the poor of the city live. She's living with some man I gather."

The room felt warm and stuffy. I took off my jacket and sat down next to her on the trunk. As I looked into her eyes, I felt the need to make love to her. I quickly glanced around the room, then stood up and opened a window to avoid eye contact lest she guess my feelings. I fidgeted nervously, as I continued talking.

"Because in her younger days Maggie chose the role of actress, I have need of her services, Jane. Can we have her come to the house? Tell her she has a very important part to play and only she can fill the role."

I made my excuses, picked up my jacket, and headed for the door. As I looked back, she sat looking at me with a winsome smile on her face. She'd read my innermost thoughts. To Jane McNeil, Robbie Cameron, the lad from the glens, remained an open book.

* * *

Maggie arrived, pleased and excited at the acting part she'd been promised. When she saw me, she fell into my arms with a joyous grin on her face.

"Robbie, lad! It's now many a year since last I stood on stage, but it's like having sex. Once you have experienced it, you never lose the taste for it. As for Rourke, that lovable rascal would say if he were here, 'Sure, doesn't practice make perfect?'"

"Maggie, this role will be the most important part you ever played." I moved her to arm's length. She smiled at me with grandmotherly pride. "It requires you to...die!"

No one spoke. Maggie looked mightily worried. I laughed. "Not really die, Maggie, Just play dead long enough for me to take you back to your home town of Lundin Links to be buried."

She raised her hand to interrupt. "Now I know you're not from there, but that's of no great value. You'll see when we put you in your coffin."

Maggie turned white as a sheet and began crossing herself and praying in a low murmur, her rosary clenched in her gnarled, arthritic hands.

Jane interrupted by pulling me around by my sleeve. "Robbie Cameron, have you gone mad? What's this all about?"

"Jane, it's really simple." I placed a hand on Maggie's shoulder and hugged her to me. "Maggie plays dead and you and she are carried out to a hearse in a special built coffin which will hold you both. Maggie, on top, I'm afraid." Maggie's tormented face now showed a weak smile of appreciation.

"There will be air holes so you can breath and when we're far enough from the house, we will let you out from time to time to stretch your legs. Then, when we reach the port of Lundin Links, like Lazarus, you will both miraculously rise from the dead. You'll both be put onboard the good ship Pathfinder bound for the Americas by way of France, so we can pick up Beatrice."

Maggie cheered up when she knew her mistress would also be playing dead. The only difference was that she would have to look and play the part.

A doctor friend, an old customer of Jane's, came to the rescue. He prescribed a drug he'd dabbled with in India.

"Maggie will be out like a light and will surely fool the undertaker himself."

Next we needed a cabinet maker to furnish the box. Jane immediately thought of a fellow who, although not a customer, always got the job if one of her unfortunate clients passed from this world while indulging themselves of what her premises had to offer.

Maggie exclaimed the work was elegant, as she touched the ornate oak coffin. She sighed softly.

"I only hope when my time comes, I'll have as nice a piece of furniture to carry me out." We laughed with gallows humor and then the two soon-to-be occupants tried out their means of transport to America.

* * *

Maggie "died" and the undertaker was summoned. He was a rather shriveled up old man sporting a large tin horn that he inserted into his ear when anyone addressed him. I assured him that although he would not be furnishing the coffin, he would still be paid his normal fee, not forgetting there would be two coaches traveling to Fife, which itself would prove costly because of the distance they had to go.

When all of the arrangements were made, the carriages began to move off. The cortege was stopped by the special constable who had been keeping watch on the house. He was tall and sported a waxed mustache. After a small sum of money changed hands, he laid his hand on my shoulder.

"I could swear we've met somewhere, Sir."

"My face is one that has that effect on some. Maybe I'd asked for directions of you at some time?" I thought of the day Flora and I had asked him for directions to her aunt's home. I recalled he pinched her bum. It seemed like a hundred years ago. He jiggled the money pouch I'd given him, tweaked his mustache, looked me up and down, and then shook his head as he strode off to supper, not wanting to be there when the funeral procession began its long journey.

* * *

Needless to say, when we were free of the immediate area, I decided our plan had worked so well that the two ladies were allowed to give up their charade. Some heavy boulders, along with a dead dog, were interred in the coffin which continued on its way to Fife.

"But why still send the coffin, Robbie?"

"Well, Jane, if they find us gone, the first thing they'll do is chase after the undertaker, who firmly believes he is burying Maggie. If stopped, I hardly think the Crown agents will want to open the coffin after that dog, begins to smell and they read the note signed by the doctor alluding to cholera.

"Remember, if Rourke was in charge of this operation, he would surely say. 'Never leave anything to chance whenever the Crown is involved. So what if it cost few shillings more, we got the job done right."

Jane agreed and we began to discuss our plans for sailing to France. Realizing we were now out of danger, Maggie tugged on my coat sleeve. I excused myself to Jane, and looked down at Maggie, took her by the shoulders and heaped praise on her for an outstanding performance.

"I feel proud of my performance, Master Robbie." She took a pinch of snuff. "But I feel I'm a tad too old to go traveling half way around the world. Not only that, I recently took up with an ex-preacher. He and I make a reasonable living preaching the Bible to any who'll listen and are amazed at the coins we collect. My suitor is convinced it's my oratory, you see, which endears the converts to us. So I'd surely settle for a small gratuity, which I could put away to help Simon and me in our old age."

I handed over a small leather pouch full of gold sovereigns and left our old friend by the roadside, sitting on her valise, happily counting her newfound wealth. As we sped off in the direction of Fife and freedom, my last sight of Maggie was her busily laying a pinch of snuff out on her hand. I felt a tear form and quickly wiped my face.

As the coach rumbled over the Forth bridge crossing, my mind went back to the night Flora and I crept stealthily across in our quest to escape from the highlands, where she toppled the trooper in to the river as we journeyed to meet up with Jane in Edinburgh.

I looked out on the scene. Who would have believed it? We once again caught up with my old friend, the officer of dragoons, who'd so graciously placed Beatrice and myself under his protection on the way to Glasgow and had a dalliance with her.

He explained he'd been transferred across the Forth and now saw to the needs of travelers going north to St. Andrews. He added that he'd be pleased to escort us as far as Lundin Links.

"Your sister, Beatrice. Does the lady enjoy good health in the Carolinas? And her husband, sir, does he fare well also?"

I ignored his remark and introduced him to Jane. "This is my other sister, Jane. She has recently had a death in the family and is making the trip to visit distant relatives near the town." As we talked, a dragoon sergeant came to inform him of a robbery of a mail coach and how they must leave our company at once.

Kissing Jane's hand, he remarked how he hoped we would soon meet again in the near future.

Jane whispered to me as he galloped away. "I hope not, Robbie. The man looks as if he's the kind that would take advantage of a woman, given half a chance."

Thinking back to his dalliance with Beatrice, I smiled and said, "Who knows, Jane, maybe he's been taken advantage of himself a time or two."

* * *

We eventually reached our destination. The small fishing village of Lundin Links, known to be the home of Alexander Selkirk, the sailor who'd spent four years on a deserted island. We took rooms for the night and spoke with several fishermen who'd heard from Selkirk's own lips his tale of adventure on an uninhabited island in the Indian Ocean.

* * *

In the morning I looked out to sea and saw our ship, Pathfinder, at anchor in a small cove. I met with the Harbor Master, who seemed nervous at my interest in the three-master just off shore. He explained she'd be going to sea on the next tide having made much needed repairs. I felt sure he thought I was an agent for the Crown who might investigate this affair, but I quickly assured him my only interest lay in ships in general. For my part, I was visiting with the relatives of my sister-by-marriage near the town and had come to spend some time exploring, maybe partake of some ale. "Would you be interested in joining me?"

Needless to say, he took the opportunity to have me leave the harbor area and we adjourned to the local inn for a respite. Upon entering the establishment, I could see the seating area had several windows, which offered a view of the harbor and the sea wall beyond. Each window had a small, square, leaded-glass sash. Pathfinder lay at anchor with her sheets tied at the spars and the tide tugging at her anchor chain.

We were met by some members of the crew who'd finished their watch and had come ashore for the last time. Try as he may, the Harbor Master couldn't pass them by and they, in turn, offered to buy us a drink. One able seaman came from Ireland. Soon he and I were chatting away as I explained to him how I'd arrived with my sister, Jane, and would be visiting for a few days.

"Now, there's a pity." He rendered a healthy slap on my back. "If we ourselves were not planning to leave on the next tide, sure you and your sister could come on board and see what a ship that sails the seven seas looks and feels like."

"I would surely like to take advantage of your offer," I replied.

He raised his hand and pulled on his beard for a moment. "Come to think on it, we're going back to the ship and will return one more time for the last of the supplies before we leave. Mind you now, you'll have to look smartly, as time is off the essence."

Pointing out toward Pathfinder, he said, "You can see she's a tad restless to be gone, as she rides out the incoming swell, dragging on her anchor. So make haste."

"Oh my." I sounded quite feminine. "I'll get my sister and be down shortly. I know she'll be so pleased to have the opportunity to look around your vessel. We'll be safe enough amongst all those strong swarthy men, won't we?" The Harbor Master looked over at the crew and gave them a sly wink.

Jane came down and we set off with the able-bodied seaman on our tour of the ship. Soon we were aboard and Rourke showed us to the Captain's cabin and ushered us in. Once he had the door closed, he picked up Jane and began to do a jig of sorts, singing, "Janie is my darling, my darling, my darling, Janie is my darling and I'm a buccaneer."

"Let me down, Rourke! You're crushing my dress. God man, you don't know your own strength."

Rourke stopped, looking all apologetic.

"No matter," she said. Looking up, she smoothed out her dress. "Your heart's in the right place and I'm so glad to see you here. I no longer have to fear the Crown agents when Rourke is looking out for me.

"As for Robbie Cameron..." she said, giving me a hearty clap on my back. "Never again, as long as I live, will I ever make light of your teaching abilities, Rourke. You've done a masterful job of teaching him all he needs to know and then some. I tell you, Rourke, he's without a doubt, he's a chip off the old block as far as being able to come up with remedies that normally only you could imagine."

She then proceeded to tell the tale of Maggie's funeral. We were joined by the Captain, who informed us we were now out to sea, heading for the French coast and the lady Beatrice.

"But I thought she sailed for America long ago, Rourke? What happened?"

Jane interrupted by turning me in her direction. "I've been told, Robbie, that she met up with some fellow and decided not to make the journey as planned. She took the money given to her by Locheill and stayed in France, co-habiting with the scoundrel."

In my best country gentleman English accent I replied, "Some fellow, you say? He wouldn't be a tall, handsome, red-haired Irishman, would he? Would that be the rascal you speak of, dear lady?" I said, smiling at Rourke.

Rourke looked daggers at me. "Now, Jane." He stood looking like a rainy Friday. "Have pity on me. Sure you know me well enough? I'm what might be better explained as a man who has a great liking for the ladies and when that worldly girl wiggled her you know what at me..." He paused and sighed. "I was done for sure."

Jane raised her skirts slightly and mockingly. "From what I've been told, maybe the two of you were doing a bit of wiggling together, as I have knowledge the girl is with child. She tapped him with her fan. "Rourke, my friend, I'd say your wandering, wiggling days are over, wouldn't you?"

Rourke just stood there with a confused look on his face, thinking he was in trouble when Jane burst out laughing.

"Well, Rourke, for the first time since I've met you, I never saw you at a loss for words 'til now. Truly it must be love."

Turning to me, she poked her finger at my chest and looked at me with smoldering, questioning eyes.

"Robbie, see you don't get to learn that wiggle your friend has become such an expert at or who knows...maybe your wiggling days could be over too!"

The Captain came back and looked in at the three passengers who'd taken over his cabin, not to mention the racket we were making. There sat three old friends, lounging in his chairs, united once more, and damn glad to be.

* * *

By the second morning, we had sight of the coast of France. The Captain assured us Beatrice would be coming alongside in a small fishing vessel quite soon. There was no intention to make port, we would simply pick up our passengers and be headed on our way. When the crew hoisted Beatrice aboard in a boson's chair, the Captain ordered full sail and with a stiff breeze blowing, we were soon well out to sea as the sun slinked out of sight in the western sky.

When you're at sea there's nothing much to do. For their part, the crew has their work cut out for them, but for the passengers, we spent our time reading and playing cards, eating and making conversation. It soon became apparent, Rourke and Beatrice sat with their heads together as if they had much to discuss. So that left Jane and me to spend our time together.

We sat across from each other in her cabin. The ship rolled slightly and the ceiling lamp swayed back and forth. I'd emptied my sherry glass and motioned with my eye to inquire if it would be possible to have a refill. Jane rose and stood behind me. As she leaned over my shoulder to fill my glass, she kissed me on the cheek. She then pulled back, handing me a full measure of Spanish sherry.

"I'm sorry, Robbie, I couldn't help myself. Ever since I heard of your romantic tryst with Flora and how she used her charms to lead you to us, I've felt a strange mix of pity and admiration for you.

"Sometimes, I think we should have left you in your glen, amongst friends and family. Truth be told, Robbie." She leaned over me and her hair brushed against my brow.

"I've become taken with you and feel guilty that we chose to take you from that simple life and involve you in all this intrigue and mayhem."

108

I reached back to catch her arm and looked up into her face. "Jane, I for one don't attach blame on anyone. Surely it's my destiny. Who knows where I'd be after Culloden if the dreaded Redcoats of German Georgie had caught me? Probably, they would have sentenced me to banishment and left me to rot body and soul on some plantation in the Indies, with no chance of escape from my bondage."

We stood up. She laid a hand on my shoulder, as she set down the sherry decanter. I took her in my arms. She felt soft to my touch and I felt overcome with a need to have her. No words were spoken, as hand in hand, she walked us across the cabin and locked the door. We moved to the bed and I waited like a little boy full of anxiety. This would be my first time making love to a worldly woman. Jane carefully guided me through the encounter.

"Robbie, Robbie, slow down. It's not a horse race, lad. If nothing else, let me teach you how patience has its own reward." No longer a sprint, our lovemaking soon became a marathon and I the long distance champion. I longed for the times we would find ourselves alone. She'd take my hand and I'd begin to slowly unbutton her dress as she smiled encouragement.

I'd press my lips to her neck and then with her hand on my head, she'd push me to her full breasts. Thus would begin anew the amorous relationship that we shared throughout the voyage to New York.

In between our bouts of lovemaking, we discussed our future and how different it was going to be for all of us in the new land, not to mention the joy of not being constantly on guard from the authorities. From time to time, the captain joined us and we discussed the problems we faced as we sailed nearer to the Indies. There were always pirate ships abroad and one could never know when the silhouette of billowing sails and the skull on crossbones pennant flying from the highest spar might suddenly appear on the horizon.

I suggested that he should have a word with Rourke. "He's a man with considerable experience in these matters, Captain. I'm sure if he took the crew in hand, in a very short time he could turn them into disciplined soldiers, more able to fight these brigands with their foul tactics of no quarter given."

Rourke agreed with the Captain's decision and those men not on watch reported to the Colonel every day to be taught the art of hand-to-hand fighting.

* * *

One evening we were gathered on deck to watch the sunset when the lookout called down from the crow's nest.

"Ship aft, Captain, Sir! Gaining fast she is."

The crew went on full alert and quickly raised every sheet they could lay hands on in an attempt to outrun whoever it was pursuing us. Just as it seemed they might be gaining on us, the sun dipped under the horizon, daylight faded, and we were able to escape under cover of darkness.

The Captain called muster of all passengers and crew not on watch. Standing under a ship's lantern shielded under a seaman's coat, he bade all doff their hats. He read a parable from the good book, how Jesus saved the disciples from a storm on the Sea of Galilee and then added, "Let all on board bow their heads and pray for a moonless night so we might lose whoever is following us."

I shot a glance at Rourke as we all replied, "Amen to that."

Rourke took me aside. Turning his back to hide his intentions, he pushed a small double-barreled primed pistol into my hand. He looked over at the women and nodded in their direction. "They must not be taken alive. You realize that, don't you, Robbie?"

Battle Stations

Jane and I had spent the night in total abandon, thinking it might well be our last. When dawn broke, we learned all on board had spent a sleepless night. We scanned the horizon for billowing sails, but none were to be seen. Then a voice from the crow's nest in obvious distress rang out. "Sails off port bow."

All those of us on deck eagerly rushed to see if the Union jack was flying from the yard arm. Alas, to the disgust of all, she flew the skull and crossbones.

We now began to appreciate that prior to this event, Rourke had the ship's carpenter cut out an extra port on each side of the existing cannon mounts. This allowed us to bring two cannons together to give bigger fire power from the ship. If it could be determined from which side we were to be attacked by the brigands, hopefully we'd do more damage with each volley.

Rourke explained to us our small vessel sat much lower in the water than any pirate ship, so our chances of damaging their masts and superstructure was virtually impossible; whereas they could easily destroy our masts. Our only chance would be to hole them at the water line and maybe cause them to turn about if they began to flood.

"All this is hypothetical," he explained, but needs to be said. The last thing we wanted was to have the crew believe all was lost, as they would be more likely to give up and become the slaves of the pirates.

The Captain again packed on more canvas, but they were gaining on us fast. It looked hopeless. Rourke then suggested that the Captain give way and let them think we were surrendering. As they approached us, at the last minute, we'd fire off some volleys in an attempt to cripple them if we got lucky.

We knew our lives were to be short-lived if they boarded us. Though they'd be much abused, the crew and the ladies might survive for a while. On the other hand, Rourke and I would soon be disposed of.

As she gained on us, she turned broadside so better to board us and fire a volley, if necessary. However, that would be their last resort as they would want to salvage the Pathfinder, if possible.

As they grew nearer, the Captain ordered the helmsman, "Make to starboard" and the ship turned left as they were turning right. Rourke fired the two cannons, but the shots simply bounced off the hull as they hit at an obtuse angle. They were caught by surprise and their shots also fell wide of our topsails. Again, Rourke fired a volley, this time one bounced off but the other holed their vessel at the water line. A huge flash shook their ship violently.

Rourke shouted, "We must have hit one of their powder rooms!"

Immediately they began to give way. We all cheered, but our Captain looked confused. "If they were badly damaged, they'd take us down with them. What's going on here?"

As the smoke began to clear, the lookout shouted out, "English man-of-war, off the port bow, Captain, Sir. Coming up fast she is."

Then began a running battle with the pirates and a man-of-war sailing under a Union Jack and heavily armed. We kept on course, not wishing to be around if by some stroke of luck, the pirates proved their fighting skills outdid those of the English. As we looked back, the sun began to set on the horizon, we could see the ignited illumination of cannon's firing in a conflict of equals, each determined to expunge the other from the engagement.

We took advantage of a friendly breeze and once again packed on more sail, eventually anchoring in the main British port of the Indies. However, before we could drop anchor and pass muster with the port authority to gain access and tie up alongside, the British man-o'-war, tattered and torn, dropped anchor.

A great cheer went up from the sailors on board. "Hip, hip, hooray!" they shouted again and again.

The harbor began to take up the chant and as I turned to Rourke, I caught sight of him jump overboard and swim for the harbor underpinnings so as to become invisible to all.

A delegation soon arrived from the Governor inviting us to his residence. The Captain, the ladies and I, along with the junior officers, would dine at the Governor's table. Not wanting to steal the gunners' thunder, Rourke had graciously bowed out and would allow them to take full credit for the bravery and determination shown in their defense of their ship by its crew.

I hoped there would now be some sort of reward or testimonial which would ensure their being able to get a seaman's place on any ship sailing from the British Isles flying the Union Jack. Discretion won out, the crew proved more than willing to go along and take the credit for the planning and execution of their deeds of heroism.

When the Governor pressed the Captain for the name of a gentleman whom he felt must have something to do with the execution of such daring, the Captain reluctantly replied, "The man to your immediate right, Governor, is the man in question. Mr. Robert Cameron, late of the King's army, who fought as a loyal Scotsman in all the battles of the insurrection began by that upstart Charles Stuart. Damn the man to hell!"

A cry of "Here, here!" went up from the table and when the Governor questioned me at length, it wasn't difficult to relate all that had happened. I merely crossed my fingers under the table and put myself in the ranks of the Redcoats, telling the story as it would have been seen from their prospective, even alluding to the Prince's obvious lack of good judgment and his amateurish attempt as a leader. Lastly, I mentioned the dire consequences that befell the traitorous Scots who had struck a back-stabbing blow at the Crown.

Delighted to hear my story, Sir Harry stood to make a toast. "To His Majesty and to Robert Cameron, a truly loyal subject of King George...a man destined for great glory and much wealth in the service of his King."

He then decreed the gunners be given a barrel of his best rum and free board for a week in any inn on the island, together with a prepared scroll commending them for their bravery. He ordered his adjutant to deliver the message personally in his name, while simultaneously calling for another bottle of his best port.

As for the ladies, they were treated like royalty by the young officers of the garrison. They attended all the functions that were given in the Captain's honor. Jane remained somewhat aloof, not wishing to give the impression she and I were more than friends.

Beatrice disappeared for a day and a night. Most wondered where she'd gone. I suspected a red-bearded Irishman to be at the bottom of it all. The days were spent re-fitting the ship and repairing damage done in the fight. We also took on cargo for New York and Albany, all of which seemed to be connected to the Governor and his brother-in-law, who was the chief port officer for the Crown in New York Harbor.

The Governor assured me we'd have an escort to the port of Charleston on coast of the South Carolina and eventually to New York. It had been decided to embellish the story of our gallant fight against the pirates, to bolster the belief that even a small craft could be successful when it stood up to these brigands.

The mention of the English man-of-war might just cloud the issue of our bravery, so that part of the story wasn't included in dispatches. On our last night in port, Sir Harry gave a ball in our honor and during the taking of coffee, the subject of Beatrice's marriage and what only could be referred to as the wife of a sympathizer to Prince Charles Edward Stuart.

Beatrice was at her best ever. She first sat with her head bowed and her shoulders shaking. Wiping a tear from her eye, she began.

"Like so many others, Gentleman, I have paid dearly for our affiliation with the pretender to the Scottish throne, Charles Stuart. Because of what he'd been told was his duty, my husband lost everything he owned and for a time, his loving wife's attention.

"Cameron of , gallant gentleman that he is, took up my cause to be with my loving husband. He wrote a decree telling all how his clan had been duped by that upstart. He then felt honor justified I should be allowed passage to Virginia where I would be able to make whatever time my dearest has left on this earth as bearable as possible."

When she finished, there wasn't a dry eye at the table. One got the impression that the older gentlemen, like Sir Harry, were perhaps slightly envious of the man's luck to have a bright young thing for his bed— one who obviously remained as virtuous as a nun and who surely doted on the old scoundrel.

As we left the party, I saw Beatrice leave by coach, no doubt going to the bedside of some poor soul in need of comfort and attention until our ship sailed for the Carolinas.

* * *

After we were at sea, my Irish friend appeared on the well deck and began long discussions with the Captain about his cargo. Not wishing to appear rude, I made some excuse and went about my business; however, not before I made note of the fact that one of the crew had disappeared and his place taken by a stranger, who at all times could be seen lurking around the hatches. I wondered which master he served.

Soon after arriving in the Carolinas, accompanied only by a few hired hands, Beatrice left for the new territories which lay to the southwest where she knew her husband to be. After a day or two, one of the bodyguards arrived back to say they'd been attacked by hostiles and that the lady Beatrice had been taken prisoner and the rest scalped. He alone escaped. But for the grace of God, no one would have survived to tell the story as it happened.

My instincts told me that somehow Rourke was at the bottom of this situation. When the proclamation was posted, it suggested that in good taste only announce the lady known as Beatrice, late of the Pathfinder, had been ambushed and killed by a renegade band of Indians in the forest west of the township. May God have mercy on her soul.

For our part, we began to make haste to sail on the next tide. The crew and passengers were the same as before minus the lady Beatrice. As the ship was about to sail, a bonded woman bound for Albany arrived by a wagon pulled by oxen. She would be handed over to her new owner as soon as the ship arrived in port. The Captain decided to put her in a small cabin next to his own. That way, she would be away from the paying passengers and the eyes of the crew.

She would receive all her meals in her quarters and Rourke took on the difficult task of looking to her wellbeing, which included walking the woman on the well deck at night, away from the prying eyes of the crew. She exercised under the supervision of Master Rourke himself. It appeared he deemed the chore a most unpleasant task and could be heard to murmur so under his breath for all to hear.

I later learned that Jane had bought an Inn on the road between Albany and New York, where all the coaches had to stop on their journey north. She announced she was having plans drawn up to enlarge the inn and dining areas. It was to be a place fit for passengers of high pedigree, who were used to the better things in life, but it would not be cheap.

Just in case the odd skinflint might happen by, there would be several of the original rooms left to accommodate anyone who was not prepared to pay the new rates; however, they were welcome to share their beds with ordinary people and the traveling companions they normally carried with them.

To my knowledge, no skinflint ever refused to pay the going rate when confronted with the other accommodations offered at bargain rates to one and all. Jane was an extraordinary woman and I was very fond of her, but my vision of Flora was always foremost in my mind and I remained blind to all other women.

* * *

When we landed in New York, a surprise beyond my wildest dreams awaited me. My father was standing on the dock. He looked fit and well, maybe more fit than he had been in years. He'd been subjected to hard honest work by his master, but had been well-treated in the bargain.

His owner's son had accompanied my father to New York and intended to leave for upstate in the hope of buying some land and starting his own estate. His name was Andy Ferry and his family came originally from Ireland.

I explained I had a good friend from Ireland he should meet. He explained he had some errands to run for his father, but would return to our lodgings in a few days prior to our leaving by boat up the Hudson to Kingston.

During that layover, when the ship was being unloaded, it appeared some of the boxes of Sir Harry's we'd carried in the hold were missing and soon after an investigation began by the port authorities. The stranger who'd shipped on in the Indies went missing and the

117

police deduced he'd stolen the boxes and whatever they contained. Eventually, Sir Harry's brother-in-law arrived and proclaimed a bounty of 100 gold coins for the capture of those responsible for the theft.

Rourke took a keen interest in the chance of a reward and forever brought tidbits to the attention of the authorities who soon tired of his blarney and blathers, suggesting he had better leave the investigation to those more capable than himself.

My father and I spent the next few days getting to know each other again. We sat enjoying each other's company and drinking a goodly amount of ale. With a tear in his eye he commented, "When we last met, you were no more than a boy, Robbie, and now here you are a grown man taking care of me." He slapped his knee. "Our roles have indeed reversed, laddie."

Trying to hold back tears, I replied. "Mother's in a highly envied position now, Father, running part of his lordship's household and is very well regarded by all who know her."

"Is that a fact, Robbie? Needless to say, I'm happy. Who can tell, maybe one day, God willing, we'll be able to return to our native land and live peacefully again." I sensed his answer was more of an impossible dream than reality.

* * *

The country upstate appeared mountainous and covered in forests. The Indian tribes were friendly, for the most part and the hunting and fishing was like no other place I'd seen.

Andy arrived back and as far as I could tell his business dealings had gone well. He was eager to accompany us to my cousin's estate up the Hudson valley on the way to Albany. Jane was to go with us.

She took me aside and held both my hands in hers. She squeezed them ever so tight. "Now Robbie, listen to me. Flora is coming with us, but you should be prepared for some changes that have taken place. She spent all the time away at a finishing school for daughters of English upper classes, and has changed beyond belief.

"You see, she never was the gypsy girl she impersonated. Rather, she'd received a formal education and when the rebellion failed, like so many she fled and what better way to disguise one's identity than to take on the role of a gypsy, the lowest of God's creatures according to English standards. I ask you, who would look for the daughter of a clan chief in a gypsy camp?"

I felt stunned, but nevertheless I prepared for Flora's arrival several days later. No doubt about it, she was a lady. She acted and spoke like one. Gone was the familiarity we'd shared and in its place a certain reserve which bordered on arrogance. Disillusioned, I soon found ways to avoid her.

On the other hand, Andy was fascinated with her and lost no time engaging her in the political talk of the day, as well as books they'd read and plays they'd both seen and enjoyed at one time or another.

She remained polite to me, but any thought I had of us being as before was gone forever. She didn't seem to know she'd broken my heart. Simply put, she'd been my first love, and I'd made too much of our relationship. We'd survived a journey together and that was all it had meant to her.

For my part, I immediately decided to forget the past and dwell on the future. I took the opportunity to make my feelings known to Jane.

"I really tried to save you this, Robbie, but life has a way of getting in the way of the best of intentions." She pulled me to her and we wept together: I for the loss of my first true love and Jane for her love and infatuation with me.

* * *

The journey took several days. We stopped at various inns and Jane was quick to assess the quality of the rooms and cuisine, much of which was poor. It made her all the more determined to get her place finished as soon as possible. "Who knows, Robbie? Maybe I can have several inns along the route to the capital and one day a grand hotel right in the heart of Albany."

Not being as business-oriented as Jane, I listened and, for the most part, believed she would accomplish her dreams, knowing if anyone could, she could. For myself, I longed to find out more about the land where a white man had never stood, where there was abundance of game and fish, and a man could have as much land as he desired.

* * *

The Indians laid claim to the land as that of their ancestors, but they didn't farm or cultivate it. They were constantly moving around from one spot to the next. Not having real shelters, they lived in giant tents. When they moved, they simply took their homes with them. In the summer, they hunted and trapped in the high country and in winter they came down to the lower elevations to survive.

Their culture appeared to be in some danger of being lost if we whites were to expand our hold on the land. Every day more and more people were coming from the Carolinas in search of a new start. The older white trappers, who'd been there even before the army, were fearful of an uprising amongst the tribes and what it would mean to all those farmers.

The Redcoat commander, a true loyalist, General Webb, had told the farmers that if trouble came, they would bring their families into the newly built forts along the trail to Albany where they'd be safe from attack if, in turn, the men would form a militia to help put down any rebellion that might start.

The old trappers began to talk about the Huron and their signing a treaty with the French in Montreal to drive out the English and restore the land to the tribes.

Most of the Redcoat officers scoffed at the thought of the French marching from Montreal to attack British troops.

As one pompous ass put it to me, "What gentlemen would think of doing such a thing as to make a treaty with the red man against another white man? Surely this would bring chaos to the land and things could never be the same between the European Rulers. For one thing, there would be no honor left.

"Having studied strategy, young man, it would also mean a conflict that would be the beginning of what could become global. Next you'll be telling me those Frenchies will allow enemy officers to become targets for their men...then where will we be?"

I'd seen enough things in the '45 rebellion to know that all these words were only talk. If the English could do to the Scots the things they'd done, then I could easily see the French with their Indian allies commit to a war with England and its loyal tribes. What of the farmers and merchants that lay in the paths of destruction? Who'd care about them and their families?

What these times needed was a soldier—one who had no allegiance, either to the French or the English, who could organize and train the militia? If the day ever came when the Redcoat generals in Albany abandoned the farmers to the mercy of the French and the Hurons, the militia would be able to survive on their own terms and the generals be damned.

My words were not readily accepted by the farmers as they had good relations with the army up 'til then. They could never see the things I discussed coming to be. Nevertheless, having a good soldier to train and unite them in a common approach to the defense of their properties made sense to quite a few.

"Just how much would you charge for your services, Robert?" The committee had taken a vote to enlist my services.

"I'm not qualified to take on such a challenge, but I know someone who is. If you're sure this is what you want, I can try to find him for you. There will be fee and from what I've been told, he has a new wife and possibly a child on the way, so yes, gentlemen, a fee will be required."

One suggested we could give him some land as payment. I smiled. "The man I have in mind, gentlemen, would no more fit behind a plough than you would on a cavalry horse charging into battle."

After our meeting it was agreed we should send for the man and I decided we should next meet at the home of my cousin, James Cameron, where we could map out a strategy.

Someone asked, "Should the meeting be kept from the army?"

"No, we must be able to have a good liaison with the Redcoats. Remember, united we can succeed. If we don't have the support of the military, we lose and so will they. Therefore, it's all for one and one for all."

I was called to the local commander's office. He wanted to know more about this officer who would be training the militia. I told him I thought he was Irish, a mercenary of sorts with allegiance to no one and he'd fought with Prussian army for pay.

The English army was respectful of the Prussians as a fighting force, so that part went well. If Rourke could convince him of his past history, I felt he could well be allowed to command the militia. Who would suspect such a mercenary to hold allegiance to Charles Stuart? If and when I was to contact Rourke, I would have to school him well in the explanation I'd invented for him.

As it happened, Jane knew where to find him. She assured me that she would contact him immediately and have him arrive with his family as soon as possible.

As for Andy, he was going on with Jane and Flora to supervise the building of her inn. She'd asked my father to come along, reminding him he would be sorely needed to help run things when the inn was complete. She explained there would be good pay and free board.

He looked the happiest I'd seen him since I'd met him in Virginia. I felt it was because he was needed again. I thanked Jane for her kindness to my father and assured her that Andy would do a good job for her.

"Tell me, Jane, whatever induced Andy to agree?"

Jane explained that she'd suggested a partnership, if all went well, but there was the other reason. Flora would be there and he would be in her company every day. I wished them all God speed.

Rourke soon arrived with a very pregnant wife who he obviously adored. It wasn't hard to see why. With child, Beatrice looked even more beautiful than ever. I'm told some women are blessed with that effect when they're going to be a mother and Beatrice was surely blessed in that way. I drilled into Rourke what was to be his story and we presented ourselves at the Garrison commanders' office so he could approve of the choice the militia had made.

The Hudson Valley

Rourke strode in with the air of a general and greeted the commandant with a sort of salute and sat down. The officer was clearly ill-at-ease in Rourke's presence and I was beginning to think my idea may have been too hasty.

"Good day, Captain. How are you this fine day?" The accent was Irish, but perfect and polished.

The Captain replied that he was well and pleased to meet the officer who he believed wanted to command the militia. Rourke insisted on first names and I was at last to know his name.

"My name is James and yours, Sir? What is yours?"

"Peter Richards."

The meeting began.

"James, I believe you served with the Prussians. Do you speak German?"

"*Ja Wohl. Spraken Sie Deutch?*"

Peter smiled. "German is not one of my languages."

James continued. "*Parlay vous, Francais, mon ami?*"

Blushing slightly, Peter replied. "Sorry, I'm afraid no French either."

"*Entonces habla español, mi amigo?*"

Peter fidgeted with the collar of his uniform and said rather quietly. "I'm almost afraid to admit, sir, I speak only English."

James responded. "I assumed German is mandatory now in the English army, so one could converse with the king. I believe he can only speak German. Is that true?"

"I'm afraid I don't mix in such high circles, James. I'm just a simple soldier."

Rourke continued with a commanding manner. "Discipline, that's the secret of the Prussian army," he mused. "But Peter, if you've never been on the continent, there's no way for you to know their ways, is there? So, let's get down to brass tacks.

"What do you wish to know about my career, other than I held a rank in the Emperor's cavalry in a heavy dragoon regiment? I've fought in many battles and was wounded twice. As I've said, feel free to ask...anything at all, old boy."

Peter cleared his throat as he began. "I'm well satisfied with your excellent record, James. It speaks for itself as far as I'm concerned. As we speak, I'm busily penning a document to send up to headquarters. It will contain notice of my approval to whatever rank the civilians feel would be appropriate for your duration as their commander."

We stood to leave. Peter looked up from his desk and asked. "I say, James. Why didn't you join the British army?"

For a moment, I felt weak at the knees at what might be coming. Rourke turned back and placed his boot onto a chair and looked down at Peter.

"Well, you see, it was like this, Peter. When I was a young man in Ireland, there was this general's daughter. I applied for a commission in her father's regiment. It turned out he wasn't all that keen on me, sad to say." He winked. "I had to beat a fast retreat from the old country." He stood up ramrod straight and touching his nose, leaned over the desk. With his sword handle dangling in Peter's face, he said, "I'm sure you understand. Surely you've been in such dire straits yourself at one time or another. You wouldn't be a true soldier if you hadn't, would you?"

Peter stretched his cravat, stood, and held out a hand.

"James, I must say, by Jove, you do like to live dangerously, don't you, old boy?"

James smiled and heartily shook Peter's hand.

"Ah, those days are all gone now, Peter. I'm a married man with a pregnant wife. No, I'm afraid I leave all that kind of thing to you young lads. Don't have the stamina for all those shenanigans any more. A wise man knows when to quit, I always say." He turned and left Peter standing, favoring his right hand and looking at me.

I shook my head and smiled. Once outside, I sat down on a log, removed my hat, and wiped my forehead with my hanky. "Well, Rourke, old boy, that was the finest performance I've ever seen. It surely beats any play actor I've had the pleasure to watch."

James also sat down, removed his hat, and said some words I'll never forget.

"Robbie, if you're going to tell a lie, then make it the biggest and best you can. Remember, you're just as well to be hanged for a sheep as a lamb."

We burst out laughing and went for a drink at the ale house.

* * *

Once there, in a pensive mood, Rourke stared into his ale, musing.

"Robbie, I must watch myself from now on, lad. No more taking chances, no womanizing, and no more cursing out the English."

We met Jane and discussed Rourke's new command. "Now listen, if you're in need of some money to a purchase house..."

"Don't bother about me, Jane. I've come into a bit of money recently."

"As recently as the Indies," Jane remarked. "I seem to remember some boxes belonging to Sir Harry went missing, along with his spy onboard ship. Tell me now, just what was in those boxes?"

"Now, Jane, remember the old saying, 'A man must do what a man must do. I have to do what is best for me, Beatrice, and the baby, not forgetting my militia.

Heavens yes, I have a lot to accomplish and what's more, if what I hear is true, I don't have a lot of time to do it in."

Peter and I went back to my cousin's farm and discussed the possibility of war with the Indians and the French. "When it comes, Robbie, it will be in the fall. They must find winter quarters for their women and kids and old folk. That will give us time to get the crops in the storehouse and prepare our defenses.

"The army has suggested that at the first sign of trouble, the families must move into the fort and stay there 'til the war is ended."

I looked at Peter. "Captain, do you think this war will spread up and down the state?"

He took a moment before responding. "Yes, I'm afraid that's what headquarters is thinking, Robert." He spread his hands out over a map. "What's more, if things go well for the French, they might even make a bid from Canada." He was pointing at Quebec with his long clay pipe as he spoke. "We are rather thinly stretched out, you know. So yes, it could well become a bigger war than most think."

It was strange for me to be mixing with what had been my sworn enemies and when I mentioned that to Rourke, as always, he readily answered with a quip.

"Now Robbie, don't you know war makes strange bedfellows? Look at me! If not for the war of '45, I wouldn't have given a second look at you and your clansmen, dressed in skirts and playing those awful bagpipes. I don't know which I can't stand the most—the damn Redcoats or that screeching noise you fellows make with the bagpipes, which you call music!"

"Well, Rourke," I smiled, clapping him on the back. "You'd better get used to it as your militia has some of the best bagpipe players in the Hudson Valley and they love to practice."

* * *

Training the men began in earnest. Many had fought the English and were easily disciplined. The young ones were shown the ropes by the old soldiers which made James' job much easier. The biggest problem arose when James decided to make himself a Brigadier.

"Don't you like the sound of it, Robbie?"

"No, James, I don't! You'll only make yourself too conspicuous with that title. Colonel will suffice nicely."

"But Robbie, that means you can only aspire to the rank of Major. Are you sure it's grand enough for you, lad?"

"What are you talking about? What are you hinting at?"

"Laddie, when you saddled me with this job, I assumed that you would put your shoulder to the wheel with the rest of us. Besides, what's good for the goose is good for the gander. You got me into this war and by Harry, that means you're in it too. Anyway, I couldn't handle this without you, old man. You have great sense of what needs doing and you tend to have a calming effect on me at those times when we're under pressure. I depend on you totally."

"There's no race on this earth that has the gift of the gab like you Irish, is there? You think you can charm the birds out of the trees, I'm sure. But just to let you know, I accept the job, but through true friendship, not any of that blarney you've been spreading around like horse dung."

We both laughed and as usual, Rourke suggested we retire to the inn and spend some of that hard-earned money we had acquired for our services. The locals had already got to calling James "Colonel" and true to his colors, James had not seen fit to chastise them for it.

Upon entering the inn, a kind of hush went over the men. A buxom blonde waitress approached us and asked if we needed a private room. Rourke laid a hand on her shoulder.

"Now, lass, that would be a huge mistake for at this very moment the drinks are on my new adjutant, Major Cameron."

A swarm of troopers descended on the bar. A few Redcoats, who were also there, took advantage of a free drink. As they toasted my appointment, I couldn't help thinking what Cameron of Lochiel would have thought of me buying drinks for the damn Redcoats.

Rourke took command of the training. It was harsh. Teaching the recruits to load a musket and fire in so many seconds and then reload again and fire. Next bayonet drill, which happened to be that used by the Redcoats at Culloden.

Peter remarked, "This looks a lot like the bayonet drill given to the British infantry in the Scottish campaign."

Rourke replied. "It was so successful against the insurrection in '45 that it became famous all over Europe. If it was good enough to defeat the Jacobites, then it's good enough for the French and their allies, the Hurons."

When we were alone with the militia, Rourke explained that he knew a lot of the men under his command were Jacobites and had fought for Charlie.

"Listen up now, men. This is a different war in a different time. To lose means disaster for you and your families. So, above all, we must win against the enemy and this bayonet drill could save lives and win battles."

After a few weeks the men really began to come together. Rourke admitted to me he was surprised at their ability to react to his commands so quickly. As he took a pinch of snuff, he remarked, "When I see how our men react to commands, Robbie, I understand better how we lost at Culloden. The men were great fighters, but Charlie was the problem. I knew that day we wasted too much time and yet he wouldn't listen. Had he paid attention to his officers and with such men as these lads, we could have won.

"Now it's different. We won't allow anyone to put us in the wrong position ever again. This time, we'll choose the time and the place."

* * *

He gathered the men around him and began to enlighten them as to our strategy.

"First, we won't fight like the Redcoats. We'll fight our own war, which will be on our terms. It will upset the English, but no matter. We fight when it suits us, not the enemy. Our plan will be to hit them with lightning attack, then retreat and then hit them again when they least expect it. Never pitched battles for us—hit and run, hit and run. That will be our tactic."

We suspected when the raids came they would attack the farms nearest to the frontier. Mohicans hated the Huron, so sent their scouts to watch for any sign of their presence. When the militia was told what farms would be first, the women and children were to be passed down the line to the fort.

The men would stay on. At the first sign of attack they would fire their homes and barns. Needless to say, the livestock would also go with the families to the fort. When attacked, they would retreat in an orderly fashion in a direction Rourke would choose for them.

"The plan is to lead the Huron until they are in a place I deem favorable, then spring my trap. One thing, no Huron or Frenchie must be allowed to escape. The order of the day is we take no prisoners. I know the English generals will never agree, but what they don't know won't harm them, boys. We know, if even one man escapes, the next attack will be much harder as they will know how we tricked them."

"The French officers will not be up front, sir. How do we keep them from escaping?" a lieutenant asked.

"Our Indian scouts will get behind them. They will take care of our French brethren. Don't worry about that part of the plan."

Family

There was a lull in the training and the men went home to finish bringing in the harvest. I took time to visit my cousin James and his family. Their home was beautiful, with white painted wood clapboard, fine brick fireplaces and pitch, pine-plank floors polished so you could see your face in them. Heavy cut-cedar shingle roofs adorned the building and a grand staircase led to the second floor.

There were four dormer windows in the roof that housed four more grand bedrooms. All in all, it was a home to be proud of. Likewise, the stables and granary matched the house in design, so their place looked like something out of a painting—a place for everything and everything in its place.

When I arrived, I couldn't help but think of the house James would have if he had stayed in Scotland and the land he now owned would have been home to hundreds of crofters, not just one family. It pleased me to see that one of the Cameron lads had become a man of substance. I smiled as he approached.

"Robert." He hugged me. "Good to see you, lad. Come in and have a dram, then we'll talk a bit and sit down to a meal."

This was the way of the Scots. A drink for their guest, then a meal fit for a king so the visitor knew he was welcome. James' wife, Lananwachee, which meant "singing waters" in her native tongue, welcomed me in true Scot fashion with a warm hug and a kiss.

"Welcome to our humble home, Robert Cameron. You must think of it always as your home. Come whenever you like and stay as long as you like, my brother."

James had explained there were four boys, all born a year apart. "James is the eldest at eighteen, Paul is next in line, Ian, third and lastly Bobbie, whose just gone fourteen. They all will be coming in from the harvest soon and we'll sit down to the evening meal."

When they arrived from the fields, we went into the large room with a large friendly fire burning in the fireplace. Again, James handed me a dram. We sat and talked about Scotland and all that had happened there. Lanawachhee played her harpsichord. We sat around her, drinking in the sweet sound.

"Sing, Bobbie lad," said James, lifting his glass in encouragement. "Sing a ballad for your cousin all the way from Scotland to see us."

He seemed a bit reluctant, but Cousin James suggested it was good manners to entertain our guest. "What's better than a Scottish song to make our guest feel at home?"

Accompanied by his mother on the harpsichord, Bobbie began to sing. I marveled at his voice. It was like an angel singing and the song, well known in Scotland, albeit the songwriter anonymous, went like this.

> Now there is a lass in Lourie glen,
> and she's the finest lass I ken,
> how I wish I was home again,
> with the Bonnie lass of Lourie.
>
> Her hair is fair, her eyes are blue,
> her lips are like the honeydew,
> and I've a secret I'll tell you,
> about the bonnie lass of Lourie.
>
> There's not another lassie fine,
> I have her heart and she has mine,
> and I'll always worship at the shrine,
> of the bonnie lass of Lourie.

"He sang all the verses. It was plain to see tears fill up in the eyes of James and myself. The young man's song brought back like a flood all the best memories we kept in our heart for our beloved homeland. When he finished, James played a few reels on his violin and we danced the night away.

After all the family had gone to bed, James and I found a chair on either side of the fireplace. With a dram of whiskey in our hand, we watched the flames dance high in the hearth after James threw a large pine log onto the grate. We stretched our feet toward the flames and inevitably took up the subject we'd tried so long to avoid.

"Do you really think there will be war, Robbie? Surely the French will not be so stupid as to break the treaties with England and join with the Huron, the most hated tribe in the Hudson valley. My God, man, they must realize the rest of the tribes will side with the English. God only knows where it will all end."

I told him of my involvement and Rourke commanding the militia.

"You know the English generals will use your troops with little regard for them. They're smart enough to know that if your men prove to be up to the task, they could someday be a threat to the Crown, especially if they try taxation and the like. They will say that's not in the cards, but win this war with the Huron and the French, pacify all of New York state and things could well change in that regard."

"You're right, of course, James, but for now we have little choice. Fight or be massacred. But we do have a trump card in Rourke. He has little time for the Redcoat generals as you know. I cannot see him lie down and march to their tune. If there's the slightest chance of his men being put in harm's way by the English, I know he won't let that happen."

"You're right, Robbie. I've heard of the man's Irish temper. If they try any of their tricks, it won't be pretty."

We started many times to go to bed, but another memory would induce us to fill up our glasses and stoke up the fire as we shared our memories, laughed and cried together. I told of my journey from our glen and the many trials over the past few years. Try as I may, I couldn't talk of Flora and my ill-begotten admiration for her. I felt I'd spend my life remembering my love for her and I felt sad. Little did I know, at that very minute, fate had already taken a hand in my future and what lay before me would surely wipe away my boyish fetish for a woman who had seduced not only my body, but my very being.

Tom McHugh

Next morning I set off to visit Jane and see how her inn was progressing. Andy was really doing a great job of managing the building. Jane kept busy buying bits and pieces to fill each room. I stayed about a week and had almost forgotten about the French and their allies when my cousin arrived with a friend I hadn't seen in a while.

His name was Tom Mc Hugh, a farmer. He and his wife, Anne, had come to the valley from New York, but were originally from Co Mayo, from a village called Doouagh, which was Gaelic for something I never did find out. Tom had finished bringing in his harvest and along with his old Indian farm hand, Two Shoes, he'd decided to go hunting and relax a bit after all their hard work.

They were in the forest for about four days when they saw tracks that they recognized as horses with iron shoes, something the Indian ponies never had. It tweaked Tom's interest, so they tracked the riders for a day and a bit, finally coming upon an Indian camp with many lodges. As there were no visible signs of squaws or children, they took it to be a war party.

Tom realized at once the danger they were in and at the suggestion of Two Shoes, it was decided that Tom would back track for a few miles to a waterfall they had passed earlier and wait for him to return. His laborer would enter the Huron camp and act as if he wasn't altogether in charge of his wits. Indians felt those kind of people were somehow protected by the gods.

The Huron could easily pick up their trail. Running was out of the question. Tom stayed long enough to see the young braves torment the old man, scoffing at his antics. Soon one of the medicine men came across the situation and immediately forbade them to bother him anymore.

For his part, Tom very carefully backtracked using a leafy branch to wipe out all footprints as best he could and hoping for a rainy day to wash out what he might have missed. Two Shoes had been gone three days and Tom was beginning to worry. As for himself, he couldn't light a fire or hunt game or fish, so he picked wild berries to sustain himself. The cold at night was almost unbearable.

He heard a rustle of leaves. Before he could call out, his man covered his mouth and signed for to be very quiet. His ploy had worked and the Huron let him move around the camp without an escort. He'd been able to listen to what the braves were discussing. He told of French Army officers and the war chiefs meeting for hours, hammering out a treaty, giving the Huron guns and iron tomahawks, ammunition and salt, a rare commodity in the forest. They were going to attack the settlers nearest to them and then spread out in an ever-increasing arc, killing all in their path.

The French had signed a paper which gave the Huron control of all lands taken in the wars. In turn, the Huron gave the French the right for their trappers to hunt for beaver, muskrat, and all other kind of game. It seemed everybody was to get a piece of the pie. The English soldiers were to be massacred along with the settlers, thus ending British rule in the state and then, if possible, the rest of the English army in Canada. It was a very bold plan indeed, not altogether impossible if they had the element of surprise over the English.

It was a very bold plan indeed, not altogether impossible if they had the element of surprise over the English. Tom hadn't taken the information to the local garrison. They would have immediately have dispatched their own scouts and then everyone, including the French, would have known the English were aware of their plan. Tom felt he should come to me and let me talk to Rourke and try to find the best way to handle the situation.

Tom McHugh stood over six feet, with a high forehead and a terrific sense of humor. His wife Anne also shared his good qualities and together they'd decided to journey to Kingston where their two children, Mary and John, attended school with the local priests and nuns, thus ensuring them a good Catholic education. As Tom put it, "There are enough dumb Irishmen in the colony, so maybe a few educated ones would even the scales."

Rourke received my message carried by young James, who was now a scout for the militia. It was a job Rourke had decided on to calm Lananwachee's fears for her son. Rourke had Paul with him when he listened to the news. Paul acknowledged that the generals in Albany would want to send out more scouts.

Rourke took him aside. "Better you go back to your troops, Paul, and wait for my signal that the French have attacked. Then make all possible haste to come to our aid, while sending news to headquarters. This keeps you out of any arguments later and ensures you don't face a court martial."

For our part, we alerted the farmers in the area and suggested that they should casually start pulling their families into the fort with their livestock, leaving only the men to first defend their farms and then quickly retreat in a direction Rourke selected. This would give him the best chance in the event of an ambush.

He also decided men should get behind the raiders and thus cut off the retreat of any French officers who would undoubtedly be present at the rear of the attack to observe. It was important that no one be left alive to tell the tribe the strategy Rourke was using, thus we could use it again and again.

Not having the English army involved meant we could fight this battle on the same terms as the Huron. No mercy for the enemy. As another trick, Rourke had several of the men dress up as women to lull the Huron frontal scouts into sending back reports that the farmers had no idea what was about to happen.

Rourke chose a valley with an almost flat terrain to spring his trap and then waited. All was quiet and soon the forest filled with the sound of birds and animals. Occasionally a large boom might be heard as a tree limb would break off and fall from a tree, disturbing the eerie calm, but otherwise it was deadly silent as the men waited at the salient.

War Drums

Tom had arrived, having left his good lady with their children in Kingston. He'd volunteered to go with the men who'd attack the French in the rear. Rourke promoted him to Captain. He was surprised at his promotion. Rourke assured him he considered him the best man for the job.

"Tom McHugh, you're a man's man and that's important when you ask men to die because of your orders."

"Colonel, when the plan succeeds, will we then attack the Huron camp?"

"I have a different view of how we can succeed, Tom. Better to let them try again, not knowing what we were up to will avoid having to maybe fight them on their chosen ground."

It wasn't long before we were informed that the attack had begun. Unfortunately, some of the lads had been killed, but, it only incensed the rest of us and also gave the enemy a false sense that victory would be theirs. When they descended into the valley, they were like crazed animals seeking vengeance on the few men they saw left to fight and they came running to skirmish attack our decoys.

We could hear them screaming and chanting as they came onto the valley floor. Rourke sprung the trap and the result was a wall of gunfire from three sides, cutting down the enemy mercilessly. On they came, almost up to our lines with their tomahawks wet with fresh blood before they were cut down by our musket fire.

* * *

It took about two hours before they broke, but by then we'd gotten behind them and they were doomed. No Huron was allowed to leave the field that day. Tom's men killed all the Frenchies and their Huron guards. It was a complete victory. Rourke then sent word to Paul, telling him of the battle and their success and explained he wanted to show the generals of their ability to defeat the enemy using their own tactics. He then turned to me.

"When those fellas engage the enemy in the future and maybe lose because of their tactics, it will only strengthen our position that we must be allowed to fight this war our way and not in some line of bright red coats in a green forest, marching to a drum, which will only make them an easy target for the Hurons to annihilate them en masse."

* * *

The generals in Albany were furious at this militia rabble taking matters into their own hands.

"No sir," the General shouted at Paul. "No, this will not stand. We are the army of His Majesty and as such we make the rules and others follow. The militia must be disbanded and sequestered into the army."

Rourke was delighted. He told Paul that he and his men were only too keen to get back to their farms. Rourke immediately advised the farmers of the decision of the generals in Albany and ordered all the women and children to evacuate to a line south of the English forts. As previously agreed, they'd be taken in by the farmers in that area who'd look after them until such time as it proved safe to return to their homes.

For their part, the militia under his command melted into the forest and waited. It was not long before the Huron moved toward the nearest fort, this time with French regulars. Rourke sent runners advising them of the imminent attack, but it was to no avail. They sat in the fort and waited as the French moved their cannon closer.

Before long, the fort was in range of their mortars. They opened fire and immediately the English cannon opened fire on the French, and so it went on for days, all the while the English were using up their ammunition and not dislodging the French guns one inch. It soon became clear that the fort was in trouble. Rourke explained that to attack the guns was futile. The Hurons would be the final factor, not the French artillery.

By messenger, Rourke informed the English Colonel that his position was deteriorating and he, in turn, requested Rourke send word to Fort Pitt. The answer was not favorable. They were under attack, surrounded by Huron. Any attempt at moving troops to their aid was unthinkable, as they would surely be cut down before they went a mile in the forest.

Of course, this is what Rourke had foretold. The army would eventually be overrun by the Huron. His decision was to keep his powder dry and wait until the Huron were in a sense of frenzy and ready for the final assault on the fort.

He suggested that a raiding party would descend on the French artillery, dislodging them and rendering their mortars useless. He would then commit his men in a flanking maneuver and with the help of the men in the fort, catch the enemy like beaver in a trap. He knew that many would escape, but if he could avert disaster at the fort, then maybe those idiots in Albany would realize the potential of his militia. If not, he would fight a war of attrition against the Huron and the French, independent from the English.

How would all this be accepted by the Crown? None knew, but those who ventured a guess thought most likely the generals would try everything to disperse the militia into small ineffective bands that could easily be out-maneuvered and controlled. All, of course, would be possible if not for one man—Rourke, who was in no mood to be dictated to by the very men who had massacred his Prince's army without regard for their families and their livelihood.

Would history try to repeat itself? His men would win the battle at the fort and then he would confront the generals in Albany, giving them the option to accept his militia as equals or have them fight the French on their own terms. The battle was fought as Rourke had planned it. He knew it would be successful. The Huron and the French withdrew.

As we sat staring into a dying campfire, the embers cascaded one into another, sending sparks shooting skyward, Rourke turned to me. "Winning is not always the case, Robbie. Remember the battles we won against the Redcoats and yet the war was lost because our leaders lacked vision. We must learn from their mistakes and be sure we're always ready."

Westward

Rourke objected vehemently, as did Robbie, but the general in charge shot back with an implied threat that any opposition to the army's plans could lead to the disbanding of the militia.

After much discussion, word was sent to the commanding general that we'd decided to go along with their wishes, knowing full well his informants had already given him the information. When we were alone, Rourke admitted that his being found out to be a Jacobite was a distinct possibility.

"They would have moved heaven and hell to examine my past had I stayed. Who knows? They may have been aware of my past all along and were waiting to expose me as a traitor to the king."

"But what will you do now, Rourke? If they're aware of your affiliations, it's only a matter of time until they spring a trap to get you."

He took off his sword and together with his pistols, removed his Colonel's coat. He turned toward me. "That's if they can find me. I'm going west, Robbie, across the Appalachian Mountains. There are many Scots and Irish emigrants clearing the land and beginning to farm."

I'd started for the door. I turned and pointed at him.

"You, of all people, a farmer? I'll believe that when I see it."

He sounded more like he was trying to convince himself as he spoke. "Now listen, Robbie, there are many different things I can get into there. For instance, a store—I can become a merchant. I have the head for organization, why not business? Besides, they'll be in need of protection from thieves and the like. These men are farmers for the most part and know nothing of fighting. They'll eventually be in need of law and order."

"Maybe there's a place for me, Rourke? What do you think?"

He put his hand on my shoulder. "All I know, Robbie, is Beatrice will remain with Jane until I can provide for her properly. If you decide to come, so much the better for me. Tom and Anne have decided to leave. After their farm was ruined, Tom sold out and is free to go."

"What of his young ones?"

"They're not so young anymore. Mary is quite the young lady. Her pigtails are gone and she has passed all her exams from school."

"She's that old? I can't believe she's that old!"

"Listen, lad, have I taught you nothing of women? Her father and mother are of the old school. Mary was with the nuns, so she dressed as they instructed her to do, but even nuns can't hold back the hands of time, lad. So be prepared for a woman when next you see Mary McHugh."

I wasn't convinced, but it was of little or no interest to me anyway. I set off to see Jane and my father.

* * *

Jane acted differently. "Robbie, as much as I love you, lad, I must look to the future. In a few years the wrinkles will begin and the waistline will expand and then I'd be an embarrassment to you, laddie. No, I must find and marry a man of means."

"But Jane, where would you look for such a man?"

"Well, for a start." She twirled around like a young girl and placed a finger to her lower lip. "Maybe a widower or an officer retiring from the army who wants companionship in his later years. Someone will turn up, Robbie, you'll see."

"You with some Redcoat officer, Jane? Really? What are you thinking?

"Now Robbie, think about it. Who would go looking for an aging Jacobite in a Redcoat officer's bed?"

It made some sense. I was moving on and Jane had to think of the future. I wished her well. She'd been a good friend to me and an endearing lover. Above all, she was a true defender of the cause. Feeling really down, I decided to have a meal at the inn and go to bed.

When I entered the bar, Rourke was holding court, embellishing on the many battles we'd fought and, of course, had no need to buy a drink as men were only to keen to buy the great man a dram.

"Come Robbie, meet my friends. This gentleman is my adjutant. A brave man indeed, if I may say so myself. Saved my life on countless occasions, don't you know." The crowd cheered and whiskey flowed like water. Everyone was having a good time. I was feeling miserable.

"What's wrong with you, laddie?"

I told him my troubles.

"Listen, lad, you know what they say. It's always darkest before the dawn. So cheer up, tomorrow's another day."

Just then Tom appeared. "Have a drink, Tom?"

"No thanks, Robbie. I have my family with me and we're about to eat dinner. Come join us and bring along that rascal you call your friend."

We went into dinner. I was prepared to be miserable, although I knew I must not show my feelings because that would be bad manners.

"Look Anne. I brought two rascals to join us for dinner. Say hello, John! Mary, make room for Robbie beside you. Mother, you squeeze Rourke in beside you and we'll eat."

As I turned in the direction where he'd pointed, I was standing next to the most beautiful woman I'd ever seen in my life. I was speechless. As I looked into her green eyes, I felt that I was looking into her soul. Whatever was happening to me was terrifying. I wanted to run as fast as I could, but I knew my running days were over. At first sight I'd fallen in love with this wondrous creature. My life was never to be the same again.

Through the haze, I was sure I saw Rourke look at Tom and wink as if to say, He's hooked all right, but I couldn't feel bad about his humor tonight. Nothing could make me feel anything other than blessed to be sitting next to an angel and she was smiling at me.

"Well Robbie, what do you think of Mary?" Anne asked. "She's all grown, would you say?"

"She certainly has," I stammered. "She has certainly grown up is right, Anne."

Mary laughed. "My God, Mother, you'd think Robbie had never seen me before by the way you're talking. Robbie, don't let them goad you. Tell them I'm no more than you expected." She nudged me. "Robbie, tell them."

"Well Mary, it's true, I did expect to see you, but you've changed. I can't say how exactly, but you've changed."

"Maybe it's my dress. I had to have a new one. I've recently grown out of all my dresses. God, I hope I'm not going to end up being tall?"

"I don't see that happening, Mary. Not at all...you've just filled out a bit is all."

She railed at me. "Filled out a bit? Do you think I'm fat, then?"

"No, no...not at all, I mean... Oh, I don't know what I mean. I'm confused. It's the whiskey Rourke was feeding me." Mary looked puzzled, but started her meal as did the others.

"You're not eating, then, Robbie? Are you not hungry?"

I looked over at Rourke and screwed up my lips and turned slightly in Mary's direction, trying to get him to shut up. She caught me and sort of turned her head to one side as if to say, 'What is the problem with you, Robbie?' I only smiled and looked stupid. Luckily, Tom turned the conversation to the militia, asking if I was going back or what."

"No, I'm thinking of going with Mary. I mean...with Rourke to the new territories over the mountains from Virginia."

Anne spoke. "Well, that's great news indeed. You'll be company for Mary on the journey, having someone to talk to and all." There was a pause, Mary pushed her plate away.

"I won't have pudding. I don't want to get fat, do I, Robbie?"

I could only smile and hoped I could live this night down in the very near future.

"Come on then, let's go for a walk. You can tell me all about the battles with the French so I can compare your stories with that of the greatest liar that ever came out of Dublin, James Rourke himself. It won't do me any harm to walk off a pound or two, will it Rourke, you rascal!"

* * *

"Mary, I feel so foolish talking like I did in there. It's just...well it was a shock to see you again and you so changed."

She took my hand. 'Listen, Robbie Cameron. Rourke and my father were being really nasty springing me on you that way. No doubt you expected to see the Mary I used to be and I've grown up some. You were...confused, right? I understand, really I do. You meant me no harm, did you? I asked you to walk to give you a chance to slip away and see whoever you're seeing these days. So be off with you and don't keep the poor girl waiting."

"I don't have anyone to see, Mary...really I don't. I would love to walk with you, if you don't mind? To be truthful, I can't think of anyone I would rather walk with."

"Robbie Cameron." She sat down on a fallen log, took my arm and pulled me down beside her. She clasped her hands together on her knees and looked at me. "Are you playing with my affections?"

I looked away as if seeing someone coming. "Why do you say that?"

She gentle turned my face until I was look directly at her.

"Well, let's face it Robbie, you've known me..."

I clasped her hands in mine. "Wait, let me explain, Mary. I don't quite know what's happened to me, but I think I've fallen in love with you and that's the truth. Tell me, what should I do?"

"Well, for a start, you can kiss me. Not one of those 'nice to see you again Miss Mary type of kisses either. I want one of the ones you save for your other girlfriends."

She closed her eyes and waited. Before I knew it, I had her in my arms, frantically kissing her and she responded in kind.

As I kissed her neck, she seemed to cry out ever so softly. I whispered in her ear. "Tonight I realize how much I love you, Mary McHugh."

"Robbie Cameron," she whispered softly in my ear. "I've been in love with you since the first time I set eyes on you. I never imagined this night would ever come to pass. You were always so worldly and I was a skinny, lanky kid. I told the girls in school all about you and they decided I was crazy to think you would ever even know I existed, so I'd go to my room and cry myself to sleep.

"Yet tonight when you looked at me, I felt a warm glow all over and it seemed you saw only me at the table and no one else. I was sure we had found each other at last and no one would ever come between us as long as we lived."

We walked along the river bank. The moon shone on the water like it was a silver highway. Mary clung to me and I to her. We would stop and kiss for the longest time and then walk a bit farther.

"Mary, Should I tell you about my trysts?"

She smiled. "Robbie, I only want to know about from tonight on. The past is the past. Starting tonight, we have no secrets and whatever went before is gone. I only want to know you love me and I you. Nothing...nothing in the past means anything, no matter what it was. We are starting our lives tonight and that's all that matters."

When we arrived back at the Inn the place was quiet. I walked her to her door. Just then it opened and her mother appeared. "I thought you two had gotten lost. It's late, Robbie, see you tomorrow."

Just as she went to close the door, Mary brushed past her and kissed me. "Mother, meet Robbie Cameron, the man I'm going to marry."

"All that money spent on making you a lady and here you are acting like a scullery maid."

"Well, Mother, I'm in love, so lady or scullery maid, what does it matter? I'm in love with Robbie Cameron, late of Locheill, Scotland." She laughed, winked at me, and closed the door.

I slept very little that night. Had I been in my mother's house, she would have scolded me. "'Robbie Cameron, that lassie has put a spell on you, sure enough. My only hope is she hasna had a witch to do it. Better say your prayers like a good boy. If you're lucky, the Virgin Mary will break the spell that binds ye two together and all will be well in the morning.'"

As I walked back along the river, a water hen took flight. I looked upwards at the night sky filled with a million stars. "Well, Mother, if it's a spell, it's the nicest spell I could ever hope to have put on me, that's for sure."

* * *

The plan was to buy good horses, some pack mules, and provisions for living in the wild. We bought ammunition and trinkets so we could barter with any Indians we might encounter on the way. Mary arrived for lunch dressed in buckskin with a pheasant feather in her hat. Her mother was taken aback.

"Mary, whatever is wrong with you? Have ye no shame dressing like a trapper?"

"Mother, this trip is going to be long and difficult. I want to be as comfortable as possible. If you're smart, you'll do the same. What think you, Robbie?"

"I think you look wonderful, Mary. Honest I do."

"Well now, Mother, what's good enough for my intended is good enough for me. I should tell you, Rourke, that Robbie and I are to be engaged soon. Are you surprised?"

"Not really, Miss Mary. It seemed to me we all knew, with the exception of Robbie Cameron, of course. The poor lad didn't know what hit him. But a man of the world such as I could see right away he was a goner soon as he saw you. Yes, Ma'am, as soon as you looked at him, he was a goner."

They both laughed. "Rourke, if you're a gentleman, maybe...just maybe I'll let you be the best man."

"Well now, if you're a lady, maybe I'll let you be my child's godmother. Then you can practice doing all the things mothers have to do before and after they have a baby. That is, if you think you're up to the task?"

"Is this how it's going to be all the way to the frontier?" Tom asked. "Because if it is, I'll definitely require another bottle of whiskey to keep me from going mad, listening to your constant banter."

Appalachia

We set out on our long journey. The weather was mild, but we knew winter wasn't far away. We needed to make good time or we wouldn't be able to get over the mountains before the snows arrived or we'd be spending the winter in Virginia.

I had a pleasant surprise. My father decided to come with us. It made my heart soar to have my one true love and my father with me on the journey. Could life be any better? If my mother could have been with us, then truly I would have felt more blessed, but someday, who knew? Maybe it would be possible.

We made good time, always staying to whatever trail was available. The journey proved pleasant as we were in a country that was inhabited by folk just like us, seeking out a new life. We knew the time was to come when we would be setting our own trail, as the number of people who had crossed the mountain range was only a few thousand at most. This was indeed a new land for everyone, with the exception of men who were trappers. They'd preceded everyone else across the mountains.

They were the first to tell of virgin forests and lakes with beaver and trout in abundance, not to mention the green meadows and many herds of different species of deer. For the most part, the settlers were Scots and Irish. Discontented with the land that had been made available to them, they simply moved on because the English gentry were given the best acreage and always bigger portions than the ordinary people.

The trek across the mountains was not for the faint of heart. Apart from the elements, there were Indian tribes who had no love for white men, because they'd stolen so much from them in the past. The Scots and the Irish seemed to get along better with the tribes. Maybe it's natural for those people who've been treated badly in their own country to feel some kind of bond with their neighbors who got the same treatment that they'd experienced in their own lands.

Needless to say, we were apprehensive about the journey, until we met up with Dougal McLeod and all that changed. Dougal was an old soldier who'd fled from the English after Culloden. He was one of the first Scots who'd trekked over the mountains to escape retribution from German Georgie as he still referred to the king.

Dougal admitted he was not shy about borrowing a cow or a plough or any such thing he might need to survive, but never from a poor soul. He only borrowed from the ones who did no work themselves, but were more than willing to have others do it for them. He was certainly a man who marched to a different drummer. When he heard who Rourke and I were, he at once acknowledged that our stand against the Crown in Albany was well known and admired by most, with the exception of a few loyalists. If the army had decided to investigate Rourke, then meeting up with him ensured our party a safe crossing over the mountains into comparative safety.

"I've decided the good Lord must have sent me in your way to ensure the Crown agents would have no success in your capture. You are, if I say it myself, in safe hands with the McLeods."

He felt it was a pleasure to help us. It wasn't a stretch to imagine his deed was tantamount to sedition against the Crown. I could see Rourke was getting more enthusiastic with every word he heard.

He inquired of Dougal, "I know there are Irish and Scots settlers over there and knowing my countrymen as I do, I suspect you Scots are treated decently by your betters. Would you agree with me now?"

Tom stood between them lest blows were coming and told Dougal. "Don't pay any attention to the man.

His brain has melted from all the Irish whiskey he's consumed in his worthless life. Sure, don't we all say in the old country, that the Scots are by far the smartest of our Gaelic folk and that's a fact?"

Dougal smiled and looked at Rourke. "You know, Colonel, in a way you might be right, as you'll find out sooner or later. The Scots are a generous lot and virtuous to a fault, so it's not a stretch to figure we have helped the poor Irish as best we could to manage, even maybe to our own detriment. But now that we have such a man as you amongst us, sure we'll be letting the Irish do for themselves and that's a fact."

Tom added. "Rourke, I think we've found your match at last. Now for God's sake, will the two of you stop your jabbering and get us up and over the mountains before we freeze our arses off in Virginia?"

* * *

Mary and I never lost an opportunity to be by ourselves and were oblivious to Rourke and Dougal who were forever bantering with each other in good humor. Mary and Anne did the cooking. We men hunted and carried firewood for the camp and always cleaned up after we finished our stay, leaving the forest the way we found it.

It became unwritten rule amongst the pioneers. You take care of the land and it will take care of you. This was also the way of life of the Indians, perhaps to an even greater extent because they regarded the land and animals as sacred. When they killed a deer or such, they would always thank their brother for sacrificing his life so they would be sustained in this great land they both shared.

As Dougal knew the landscape better than we, it was decided he would be point man. Anne, Tom, John, and my father would be responsible for the pack horses, while Mary and I would bring up the rear, always keeping a safe distance from the others. If an attack from behind came, we would then have time to warn the others to prepare.

In that event, we would have to race to catch the others as we had only ourselves and our horses to worry about. As for Rourke, he was always way out in front looking for any troublesome signs or laying back to take care we weren't being followed as that was the tactic most used to attack a group traveling in the forest in these vulnerable areas.

I was a fairly good shot. To my surprise, Mary was a great shot. Her father deserved the praise, as he made both children learn to fire a musket and pistol, as well as be able to use a knife if need be.

Mary explained. "My father's theory is simple. If attacked at close quarters, always use your knife. It's faster and less chance of a ricochet hitting off a button or belt at such close proximity. If possible, always drive the knife between the shoulder and the breast of the attacker nearest to the person's heart. It means instant death."

I sat sharpening my knife on a stone. "Could you use a knife like that, Mary?"

"I used to wonder if I could, Robbie, but now that I have you, if the thought of losing you depended on killing a person and saving you, believe me, I wouldn't hesitate."

Just knowing how she felt about me greatly affected my outlook on life. She was prepared to kill if my life was in danger. That was a strange feeling and strengthened the already tight bond between us. Needless to say, I would do the same.

At night, we all took turns on guard, with the exception of Anne as she was always up early to make breakfast. So our everyday tasks were organized. I always took the watch after Mary, so we could have some time together. Our rule was to kiss and then sit back to back so no one could approach us if we became engrossed in conversation of what our future plans were, if we would ever see Scotland and Ireland again, and all the other silly things lovers talk about when they are totally alone.

There was the color of our eyes and eyelashes. "Your eyelashes are quite long for a man," she said. We felt our hands fit together well, and how it would be to snuggle up together in a bed in our own home. Silly things that young lovers talk about that always brought warm feelings.

There were the exceptions, like when she asked if I had ever cuddled up in bed with a girl and felt wonderful. I stupidly went on to describe the cold, wet moors in Scotland and how Flora and I had kept each other from freezing. When I finished re-living the adventure, she replied. "I've never been in a situation like that myself."

I quickly realized how dumb I'd been. "Of course, I was only a young boy, you understand, and as for Flora, she said that in many ways it reminded her of cuddling up with her collie at the fireside, while her mother read her bedtime tales."

Mary got over her obvious annoyance and laughed in my face. "Robbie Cameron, if you learned anything at all from that scoundrel, Rourke, it was diplomacy or blarney, I can't quite figure out which, but I'll want a running commentary from you when and if I ever agree to marry you and we're in bed some cold night and have to snuggle up together. When I do, it better be as good as the one you just told."

She'd been peeling an apple and handed it to me. "I'll insist and believe me, for your sake, it better hold as much passion in the tale as the one you reminisced about this night."

As I sat there crunching on the apple, I was tempted to ask if she had any like experiences, but was afraid she'd tell me and then I felt my jealousy would not have been so easily abated as hers.

As Rourke would say, "Robbie, just remember, lad, never give a lass the chance to make you jealous for it seems from the day they're born they have that ability. It's a gift, lad, a gift from the Almighty."

I was ill-at-ease for being such a fool, telling her of Flora. I felt for my dagger with a ruby in its hilt. "Mary, take this and keep it on you at all times. It was a parting gift from Prince Charlie to his page boy, these many years ago."

"Robbie, I couldn't. It was his gift to you."

"Truly, it was that, but now I wish you to have it. If nothing else, it's been lucky for me, so wear it and feel safer knowing you have it with you always." She kissed me. I could see a wee tear slip onto her eyelid.

* * *

When the fall arrives in the mountains, it gets really cool in the evenings, the sun sets earlier, and the leaves change to reds, greens, gold, purple, and a lot of colors in between. The moon seems to be larger and its bright golden light gives everything the look of gossamer. It's enchanting, even mystical, and one can understand why it is that the Indians worship nature in all its grandeur.

Occasionally, if you're really lucky, you can experience what we call an "Indian summer." Unexpectedly, the temperature warms up and the birds sing more, and there seems to be more animals to see. It confuses the hell out of the bears that are getting ready to hibernate.

It was a night such as this when we all sat around the fire, reluctant to seek sleep for tomorrow it could all be gone and we would be subject to the first signs of winter, with its short days and cold nights, just waiting for snow to cover the forest floor with a carpet of silence for months. As we sat around talking, Tom asked, "What's it like on the other side of the mountains? Is it the same as this side or what? Tell us Dougal."

Knowing he was holding the fort, so to speak, Dougal first poured another cup of coffee and lit his pipe. He blew some smoke and then with pipe in hand and hand resting on his knee, he turned to Tom. He looked up at him and began to give them a picture of what we would expect.

"First off, there are no Redcoats or English law. The only law there is the Bible—an eye for an eye, a tooth for a tooth, and all abide by its good word. For the most part, people have experienced a hard life, having been a bonded man or woman. They know what it is to have little or no rights or equal justice and believe me when I say, they don't want that kind of justice ever again." A kind of hush settled over us.

No one spoke. We sat, each in their own thoughts, looking at the flames and listening to the crackle of the logs amid the surrounding silence of the forest, broken only by the sound of swishing, as the wind rustled through the tops of giant pine trees. Occasionally, a log would tumble down through the embers and hosts of yellow sparks would fill the air, as a lonely owl sat nearby, hooting into the silent, starry night.

Dougal broke the silence as he reached to re-fill his coffee mug. "Everybody is helpful and no stranger is without aid. The farms are large and prosperous. The merchants are fair and their businesses profitable. We're mostly Scots and Irish, and there are very few preachers, so there's little religious intolerance. There are a few bandits, but they mainly ply their trade on the river where all goods must be carried. When caught, they're executed quickly and then we go about our business."

He sat cleaning his pipe and in a somber mode, he continued. "I feel having lived in your company, sir," pointing his pipe at Rourke, "there is without a doubt, a position as chief law man waiting for you to take over if you so choose. The farmers and merchants take turns being lawmen, but truth be known, they're not happy doing so. It really needs a man with military experience such as you, to introduce law and order on a permanent basis."

It was a rare moment indeed, as both men stopped their baiting each other and spoke as friends. Rourke fidgeted a bit and scratching the earth with a branch he'd picked up, he looked up as if he were speaking to himself.

"Dougal, I'm not as young as I once was. I have a wife and child to look after. I need to build a house and settle down, hoping to make a fresh start and a new life for my family. Lawmen don't usually end up rich and few live to old age."

Still leaning on one knee, Dougal moved his other arm holding his pipe in a wide arc as he looked around the fire for support.

"Man, I'm not talking about some hands on lawman. I'm talking about a man capable of building a force to meet the growing needs of the community, someone to make the place a man can bring his family and not fear for their lives, not to mention the few Indians who get drunk and cause trouble.

"They need a professional like you. Hell, one day you could be the governor of the area or if not to your liking, how about a magistrate? You can have your pick, lad. I only wish I was a few years younger and had your skills. I sure as hell would be looking to have that job myself."

That being said, he resumed puffing on his pipe while staring into the burning red glowing embers as all around him sat silent in deep reflection on what had been said.

Tom spoke. "Rourke, he's right. If it's like he says, then they need a man like yourself, skilled in warfare, yet able to be fair and above all, reputable. It seems to me the job is made for you. I can see Beatrice, fine woman that she is, leading lady in the community, doing all kinds of charitable works while you keep the peace."

I quickly quipped, "Aye, and maybe in time you'll be able to find out what happened to all that gold Sir Harry lost on the ship we arrived on from the Indies?"

Not knowing the whole story, Dougal was quick to say, "Well, if you ask me, I'm sure, Sir what's his name never came by that gold honestly, and good luck to the man who relieved him of it."

* * *

As predicted, the next few days were beautiful. Mary and I were always together, talking of all the plans we would make come true and the grand estate we would have.

Dougal suggested that John stay in town with the merchants. "With all that schooling, you'll be a much sought after young man and have the pick of what you want to do and who you want to it for. There are a lot of young daughters of merchants you might be courting. Believe me John, you won't want for company. No sir."

John blushed and I could see Tom and Anne deep in conversation after Dougal had spoken. The next day Tom stayed back and joined us.

"What do you think you'll want to do, Robbie? Be a second in command to Rourke?"

"No, Tom, I want to go out to the edge of civilization, find land and build a house, marry Mary, and become a farmer."

"How much do you know about farming, Robbie? Out here in the wilderness it's not just about growing crops, it's about clearing land and knowing the seasons, and above all, picking the right crops."

"I know I have much to learn, Tom. Are you suggesting I may not make it work fast enough and go broke?"

He leaned on his saddle, staring at me. His horse moved slightly as a nerve in its leg jerked. He pulled up on the reins. "No lad, not at all. I was just thinking, how would you like a partner? Someone to share all that work and learning. Anne and I were talking and Dougal is right. John is not cut out to be a farmer, more likely a lawyer, and we don't want to start a farm only to see it sold when we pass on. Now anything you and I create, will be for you and yours when were gone and that means a lot to us. We won't interfere with you two, and there's also your father. He could be with us too, which would allow us to take a bigger piece of land when there are three sets of hands to work the place. What say you, Robbie? Do we have a deal?"

After supper we talked it over and Father agreed, so we shook hands on the proposed partnership.

Mary then loudly inquired of her mother, "Do we have a choice in this matter, Mother?"

Anne, who was busy boiling a ham hock, replied, "Mary, knowing you, dear, I'm thinking you'll have a lot to say and do with what's going to take place. So I for one am not worried in the least."

Attack

All went well 'til we arrived at the river. Dougal explained we must now follow it until we reach the settlement and that we were in some danger of being attacked by robbers. Rourke suggested we stay together and be alert for any trouble that might erupt on the trail.

* * *

They appeared from nowhere. There were three robbers on horseback wearing cloth around their mouths. Rourke charged, two pistols firing. Two fell, but as he charged through, the third man came toward Mary, pulling her down and putting a strangle hold on her throat.

Pointing a pistol at her head, he shouted. "If you follow, she's dead."

He then fell back into the forest away from the trail, leaving us standing there with very little that we could do. As he backed up, Mary feigned a fainting spell. He dragged her by her waist into the deep underbrush and disappeared saying, "If you make a noise, you're dead."

All concerned stood still and each listened for the approach of the other, but no one moved. Rourke motioned for us all to listen in which direction they might be moving. A deadly silence followed, with the exception of the horses occasionally beating the ground with their hoofs and their tails swishing away flies as they munched on the lush grass growing alongside the dirt trail.

As Mary later told us, her dead weight began to take its toll. He pulled her up and around, then re-positioned his arm around her waist. He turned slightly to his left, looking for any dead logs or branches which would

161

impede his retreat. As he turned slightly, his right arm with his pistol also moved with his body. Mary, who'd taken her dirk from her boot as she fell limp in his arms, now drove it into his breast up to the hilt. For a brief moment, he looked at her with anger! She wondered if she'd failed in her attempt to kill him and be free. Panicking slightly, she struggled to unwrap his arm, but to no avail. Blood began to trickle from his mouth onto her bodice and she called out. "Robbie!"

Rourke was the first to arrive. 'He's dead, Mary, trust me!" He tore the dead man's arm from around her waist and he slumped onto the forest floor. By then Robbie had her in his arms and carried her back to the trail. Rourke pulled the dagger from the man's chest and cleaned it on his greasy trousers.

Momentarily, as he gazed at it, he wondered how she came to have Charlie's dagger, with its red ruby crusted handle.

What seemed like disaster had become a victory, thanks to Rourke and Mary, who was now hyperventilating, having begun to realize what had happened and what she'd done.

Anne comforted her saying. 'Mary, it was his life or yours. Pull yourself together. You're safe and sound and that's what matters most—not the death of some lowlife who I have no doubt needed killing."

In all the excitement, no one had noticed poor Dougal, who'd been wounded in the shoulder and now lay cradled in Tom's arms. Rourke laid him flat on the ground and ripped open his shirt to reveal the wound.

"Light a fire, Tom. Boil some river water and lay his dirk on an ember till its white hot. He looked earnestly at Dougal, who smiled weakly at the Irishman with whom he bantered time and again. Rourke ran his handkerchief over Dougal's brow. "You're a brave man, Dougal McLeod. Don't fret yourself over this, all will be well when we remove the lead bullet and clean the wound."

Dougal lay quiet and Tom produced his extra bottle of whiskey to cleanse the wound. "I hope yer no gonna waste that elixir in my shoulder, Tom? I'm sure taking it internally would be just as good and besides, I could do with a slug anyhow."

Rourke had him take a few slugs before he started to remove the lead and by then Dougal was feeling no pain. He sang Scotland the Brave over and over, stopping only to wince when Rourke began to operate. Anne dressed the wound with whiskey to help kill infection and then Dougal had another swig and fell asleep.

"Let him rest a while and then we'll proceed, Anne. By the way, Mary, if you're feeling bad about the killing, just remember, the fine dagger that saved your life also saved Dougal's. It's possible you're the bravest women I ever known, bar none. Robbie Cameron is damn lucky to have you for his future wife and partner."

Mary just smiled, laid down on a blanket next to Dougal, and fell asleep. The rest just sat quietly, pondering on what else lay in store for them.

* * *

On the way to the settlement, they came across a young couple and their baby who freely admitted it could just have easily been they who were attacked. The husband put it to Mary. "I would've been dead along with my baby and my wife a slave to that pack of cutthroats back in the swamp where they live."

Rourke sat listening intently and then asked. "Why hasn't something been done about them before now?"

"It's been tried, but where they live in the swamp, it's very dangerous to infiltrate, what with poisonous snakes and insects, not to mention the alligators. Oh, many have tried alright, but only some came back to tell the tale," he replied wistfully. "You would think they used some magic, but I for one don't believe it. They're like all kind of lowlifes I've seen time and again. They exist because of other people's fear.

When they reached the settlement, the word soon went out about the encounter and its results. People flocked to get a look at the strangers who'd beaten off an attack by the swamp dwellers. For his part, Dougal told everyone that the town elders and the merchants should have a meeting and persuade the man they called Rourke to be the new permanent law and order man for the whole area.

* * *

The next day, a meeting was called between Rourke and the townspeople, who made a formal proposal to him. They would build him a house, give him a grand salary, and a bonus when he retired. He'd have complete control over law and order, and he was to be given the title of Chief Constable and as many deputies as he felt necessary. All was to be written down in a form of a contract, binding on both sides.

Rourke was overwhelmed, but kept his composure. "I'll want my house finished by spring, furnished as well, mind you, and the payments to be in coin every month. I'm to have total control over the law and order, and I won't be interfered with in my duties by the council."

It was agreed and drawn up by the town's newly arrived businessman, John McHugh, who got busy while Rourke worked with a Scot named Arthur Wood to plan and build his home on a site chosen by Rourke, which proved to be one the finest.

Knowing that his house was underway, Rourke began recruiting his deputies. He called on me and inquired when we were moving out to stake out their land? I explained we'd move out in the spring. Meantime, we'd stay at the inn.

As for Tom and my father, their time was spent fishing and hunting, and visiting the families that might be their neighbors when the land was legally theirs. Then they'd start to clear the land and mill the great trees that grew in abundance. It was decided to build a smaller place and then some time later on, they'd build Mary's home. Anne and Tom would stay in the original house.

"So you see, Rourke, we're making progress." I sensed my friend had another purpose for his visit and knowing him so well, I asked what ailed him.

He was sat whittling on a piece of pine. "Well, Robbie, I just feel in my gut that there needs to be an end to those swamp rats and their robbing and killing. I want to go into the swamp and nose around. I wonder if you'd back me up, so to speak, as I don't want to make it known what I have in mind. I fear these lowlifes have a spy or two in the settlement."

I pulled my musket from the saddle. "Of course, old friend, when do we go?"

"Now listen, Robbie, it's not that simple. Men have gone in there before and never came out, so I want you to think about this before you agree."

"Rourke, I know as well as you, nobody will have peace of mind 'til they have been wiped out once and for all."

As he checked out his flints and powder, Rourke had a glint in his eye. "I thought we'd go fishing and just kind of meander into the swamp casually, not attracting anyone's attention while we take look around, that's all."

The Swampers

We set off the next day at first light in a small boat. We soon realized the size of the place and by noon we were lost and sitting on a sand bank wondering where to go. When we saw a canoe approaching, we tried to hide, but the man called out to us, and we drifted into the bank.

"What are you two doing here, Colonel?"

At the mention of Rourke's rank, we turned and looked at each other in surprise. "We're trying our hand at fishing, but I'm afraid we've gotten lost, is what we've done, Sir. Can you guide us back to civilization? We could pay you for your help."

"I won't want any payment, Colonel, but some tobacco would be appreciated." Rourke passed his pouch over to him.

"I've heard about your run-in with the swampers. Killed a few of them, I hear? They won't be too happy with you, I'm thinking."

"You have us at a disadvantage, Sir."

"My name is Rodger, John Rodger, but folks around the settlement call Preacher, on account of I used to be a man of the cloth 'til my wife and kids died of the fever. My life went all downhill from then on, I'm afraid." He pulled his canoe up on the sandy bank.

"I eventually dried out and found it easier if I didn't have to live with the good folks that I had ministered to. I guess the shame of my going to hell altogether has turned me into a kind of hermit. So I live in the swamp and rarely feel the need to come out."

"That's interesting. So you know these swamps pretty well, would you say?"

He looked at Rourke and for a while said nothing. In turn, we waited, not knowing where we stood and certainly not wishing to enrage the man, lest we never find our way back to dry land.

We just sat, no one spoke. All around could be heard animal sounds and birds sending out distress signals. Occasionally, a gator could be heard, slashing and turning in the greenish algae-covered water as it drowned its victim and took it down to the depths and hid it from sight. Buzzing mosquitoes would land on me, on and off. As I swatted them away, I felt a shiver run up my spine as in the distance, I could see the form of a gator slithering by on the hunt for prey, almost invisible in the green sludge, but for its eyes. John stood up and stretched.

"If I were a betting man, who I'm inclined to think you are, Colonel, I'd hazard a guess that right about now you're thinking, 'This old coot could probably lead us right to those murdering bastards, but I don't want to scare him off. How in the hell do I get to asking him? How's that for mind reading?'"

"Well, John, you could be right, but then I'd ask, 'How come he never took the other people there instead of them getting lost and dying all those other times?'"

"Now you, sir, as my Mamie used to say, are a different kettle of fish. I think you'll have a plan of attack if you ever go up against them and what's more, I think you're a lot smarter than old Henry Bell. Cunning as he may be, he's gotten a mite arrogant these last few years. I bet right now, at this moment in time, he's surely underestimating Colonel Rourke, late of Charlie Stuart's bunch of brigands and that, Sir, could be his downfall for sure."

"John Rodger, aren't you a man of mystery. I'm thinking it would be foolish of me, to underestimate you, and that's the truth. Tell me, who is this Henry Bell and where is he from? Do you know?"

"He's an old dragoon like yourself, but a bit before your time. Had a spell with the pirates in the Indies, got to cheating them, and had to get out of there quick. He came to Virginia and killed a traveler for his purse. He made the stupid mistake of killing a Crown magistrate, who went from district to district hearing cases for the Crown.

"Well then he hightailed it over a trail cut through the wilderness and for a while was a mite respectable. That didn't last too long and he ended up in the swamp with a band of butchers as evil as they come. Since then, they've killed, robbed and raped, stolen women and the like, and that's the story up 'til now.

"Then his men met what they thought was easy pickings on the river road, all hell broke loose, and they ended up dead. No, Sir, Old Henry won't be happy about you coming on his patch at all. As I see it, he won't have much say in the matter, will he, Colonel?"

"If you decided to show us how to get into his camp and out again, there would be a bit of change in it for you, John. Maybe even enough for you to make a fresh start, get acquainted with your neighbors again, and take up where you left off all those years ago."

John sat down on an old log, took out his knife, and began to scrape out the bowl of his pipe. He put the stem to his lips and blew into it a couple of time. He tapped the bowl on his boot, then looked up at Rourke, pointing in his direction with the knife blade.

"You paint a rosy picture, Colonel. Yes, you do. That tongue of yours would put Da Vinci's brush to shame. You paint a pretty picture ever so well."

"Well, John, I think that's maybe what you had in mind all this time you've been chatting with us. In fact, I think that's what you've had on your mind since the day you heard about our little fracas on the river road. Now, could I be right?"

"Colonel, I think you and I are birds of a feather. I feel we'll end up being good friends because if there's one thing I admire in this world, it's a man such as you who has mastered the art of getting folks to do dangerous things for him, all the time them thinking it was their idea. Yes, Sir, you were certainly born with a gift of gab and spinning of the blarney." At that we began to laugh so loud that John motioned with both arms to quiet down.

"Our voices can be heard for miles in the swamps, there's always the chance some of Henry's men are out and about in a boat and if you're gonna win this fight, Colonel, you'll need the element of surprise."

It was decided to make another trip in about a week to see him at the dark of the moon's phase. John was confident we could slip into Henry's camp without them knowing, so we could make our plans to ambush them and destroy the camp. As for the spies, we would have to find out who they were before we did anything. A trap to catch them was devised, just before we struck.

It was John who came up with the idea. "Why not ask for volunteers to go into the swamp just before the fight begins to supposedly keep an eye on their movements. Only a fool or a person confident he'd be safe if captured would volunteer for such a mission."

We had a meeting and Rourke asked for volunteers for a dangerous, life-threatening mission to spy on Henry's camp. Two men volunteered immediately. They were told because they could be captured and tortured, we would not include them in the planning. Rourke assured them we would send them out two days before the attack was to occur, knowing they would report this to Henry Bell and his bunch. The hope was that they would think themselves safe 'til the night in question and they would then prepare their defenses accordingly.

Revenge

Rourke knew most of the men were scared. He pointed out that's what the pirates were counting on. Hadn't Mary McHugh killed one of the cruelest of them and lived to tell about it? Mary stood up and looked around the gathering as she talked about how frightened she was. She spoke in low tones at first, but as she went on about the confrontation, she became more animated and confident.

"I remembered all that Rourke had taught me on the trail and even though I was a scared girl, I got the better of that worthless trash."

All heads were nodding in approval. Rourke spoke again. "Listen men, I know a lot of you have served with Charles Stuart in the '45 rebellion. So did I and I remember how scared we all were facing those lines and lines of Redcoats, not forgetting the pounding of the drums and the noise of their tin flutes.

"If you've forgotten, let me recall for you how when Locheill had his pipers play and the Highland cry went up, I swear to you that many a Redcoat relieved himself in his troos right on the spot.

"I can well imagine in this band I have the honor to lead there are a few pipers who can still blow a tune, so you who fought side by side in the uprising will go in with the pipes sounding strong. We'll be whooping our cry and let me assure you, even the Irish amongst you will take courage from the sound."

"Now, who among you has the tune we should pipe? The Black Bear, said one. Pushing his way through the crowd another shouted Bonaparte's Retreat. A youngish lad with the face of an angel threw his hat in the air and cried out, "What about Scotland the Brave?" Robbie looked at John Rodger, who was smiling from ear to ear, as he leaned over and above all the cheering and whistling said, "How that Charles Stuart ever lost when he had a rabble rouser like Rourke on his side will mystify me 'til the day I die."

The crowd was stirred up now. A few of the Irish lads lifted Rourke onto their shoulders and carried him around the hall. Next it was Mary's turn to join him in the air. Soon there was the sounds of pipes. A hornpipe, thought Robbie. No, a jig, he decided on second thought.

As the men lowered the two heroes of the river episode to the floor, Rourke leaned down to Robbie said, "This is going better than I could have imagined, so if you'll permit me the liberty of dancing with your betrothed, I feel we'll have gotten our little army in the mood for a fight."

The whole place cheered as Mary and Rourke took the floor and before long there were women squeezing through the crowd to dance with their husbands. I felt a tap on my shoulder. Anne stood there smiling.

"Robbie, now is the time to find out if you'll be able to keep from standing on my toes when we have to lead off the dancing at your wedding when you become my new son-in-law. Besides, that great oaf of a man of mine can no more dance a jig than he can fly in the air."

Someone brought a barrel of homemade whiskey and before long and everybody was having a grand time.

* * *

Clearly out of breath, Rourke tugged on my coat sleeve. "Come outside with me for a breath of air, lad."

Seated on a stoop fashioned from a redwood log, Rourke began.

"Robbie, for the first time in many a day I feel I'm at home here in the wilderness. Who could have imagined it so? I only hope Beatrice will be as happy as I am right now. It's a grand feeling to be amongst friends and not

171

watching your back all the time. I can finally relax. Do you feel confident we'll beat them, Robbie? It won't be a problem if my plan is successful. We must totally surround the camp before we begin to fight. John Rodger tells me the slaves—the locals captured by the gang—will be in a kind of a compound where they're locked up for the night, so at all costs, we must keep any of the brigands from hiding in that compound once the battle starts."

"But there might surely be some brigands in the compound, don't you agree?"

"I do," Rourke smiled. "So when it's over, we'll hang them last."

"Hang all of them?" I sounded surprised.

Rourke's eyes met mine. "Yes, we must make an example of them, but we'll allow one to escape, to go amongst his kind and tell the tale so never again will brigands think they can enter into our land and live to tell about it...most of all the English. We must let them see we are a free people here and want no problem with the Crown. If trouble comes, then they too must be prepared to suffer the same fate as these cowards who would rob us of our freedom."

I knew the folks believed they had found a leader and above all, James Rourke had found a cause! The plans were simple, but deadly. We would descend on their camp area and kill the entire band. No one was to be left alive, with one exception. A hard decision, but in this land where there were no prisons, to let these cowards go free was to invite some poor soul somewhere to be slaughtered for maybe only a few pence in their pockets.

"I don't necessarily want their deaths on my conscience," Rourke told the men assembled and I doubt you do either. If they're allowed to go free, next time it may be you or your wife and children who die at their hand. We have one problem, we think the men I sent in to watch the camp are members of the gang, so although I gave them the wrong day, they may still be waiting for us."

John Rodger stood up. "Colonel, Sir, I don't think those two will be doing much talking. Their boat somehow capsized and the gators got them, God rest their immortal souls."

"How did it happen, John?"

"Well, Sir, they seemed in an awful big hurry to get to the camp so I decided to swim a little bit and help the boat to overturn so to speak."

"But what if they were innocent, John?" another asked.

John was silent for only a moment. "Well now, that will be something I'd have to live with. I realized I could live with it, but not the death of half our comrades because the spies told of our plan. Besides, I told myself, 'John Rodger, if these men are innocent then it's you the good Lord will be sending the gators after, not them. Well, as you can see, I'm still alive and kicking."

Rourke laughed with the rest, but cautioned. "John, my man, if I were you I wouldn't be tempting the Lord. He may get the idea that you've come back into his service, in which case, we'll all have to be watching our language and our bawdy talk lest we get a lecture from His preacher.

"However, as you seem to be in pretty good with him so far, would you be taking the time to give us his blessing and the work we're about to undertake this night?"

All the men knelt and John raised his hand and gave the blessing, not for victory but for justice for all those folk who had died and those made slaves by the gang, and asked to help this gathering be successful in their task.

* * *

They arrived in darkness and surrounded the camp. At Rourke's signal, a lone piper began to play. Immediately the camp arose in panic and then the highland cry went up. Other pipers joined in and the men charged, as they would in battle formation when fighting against the Crown for their beloved homeland. They cut down all in their path and when the cowards tried to get into the slaves compound, the people inside led by a giant of a black man held the gates closed against them. They turned into the approaching men led by Rourke and they were mercilessly slaughtered, just as the others had been minutes before.

Henry Bell and some of his men locked themselves in the food store which was built on stilts to keep the vermin from entering the storeroom. The cowards threw out their weapons and begged for mercy. Rourke gave them an ultimatum. "Come out or be roasted alive, your choice. We don't much care how you die, so make up your minds."

They came out and were immediately tied up and sat down on the ground. Rourke then picked twelve of his men to be a jury and allowed Henry Bell, the gang leader, to be their defense counsel. The trial lasted about an hour and with the exception of a young lad, all were sentenced to be hanged, but one.

Rourke then had all the slaves come out of the compound and challenged any one of them to speak on the gang's behalf, but his words fell on deaf ears. Rourke could see women, old and young, some from the immediate area and others from the coast. He gathered them together and explained their plight was not their fault, so there was no reason to feel shame for what they had endured.

However, if the decision was made by a slave not to return to their original area, they were free to go with him and his men to the settlement, where they could stay or come spring, if they wanted to move on, they were free to go and seek a new life.

Many decided to do just that, not wishing to bring shame on their families. Some said their previous home life hadn't been much better than that of a slave. One black man and his wife approached Rourke. He'd been taken from the coast and made to do all the building work. Did they have need of his skill?

It was decided they'd go with Robbie and Mary's family in the spring, but in the meantime, work would be found for him and his wife in the settlement.

"My name is Joshua. This is my wife is Mirabelle. We had two little ones, but they died with the fever and so we're all that's left of our family."

Rourke put his arm around his shoulder. "Well, Joshua, we need scaffolds built and we need someone to supervise the work, so get to work supervising."

Joshua looked surprised. "Don't you think a white man should be the supervisor?"

"No, Joshua, I don't. Most of the men here have been in bondage to others and have no wish to see any man have title over another. All men here are free men and that includes you. You have a talent which we as a group are in need of and you are qualified more than some to accomplish the task at hand. You will be the supervisor and let there be no more said on this subject again. You're among friends now. Besides, your action at the compound gates tonight saved a lot of lives and we are grateful for your quick thinking."

The scaffolds were finished and when the gang was made to stand on the platform under their ropes, Rourke asked if they had any last words. Henry Bell spoke eloquently. Robbie imagined in another life he well could have been a preacher. He stood out from the others in line awaiting their fate. He removed his hat and used it to point out his comrades who stood silent with their heads bowed.

"Brethren. We are men like the bible says who have fallen by the wayside. I know to a man that if given another chance at life, they'd be a God-fearing Christian from this day forward."

Before any amongst his band might begin to have second thoughts, Rourke interrupted. "While a change

of heart is admirable, we are also men who have read
the Good Book and what comes to mind is the chapter
where God demands an eye for an eye, and a tooth for a
tooth, and by hanging you we are obeying the word of
the Lord."

Upon hearing that Henry Bell began a tirade,
cursing all to hell and wishing all their seed perish for
the act they were committing this night. Rourke saw the
men flinch in the face of such words and as Henry
finished, Rourke stepped up on a fallen log and
addressed the crowd.

"I have no feeling of guilt at hanging these men.
They are a curse on the land and if there is to be blame,
then let it be mine."

Soon four men stood forward and said, "No, let it be
me." Then the entire crowd answered, "No, let it be me."
Rourke said, "Let's draw straws and it will be seen that
no one seeks revenge, only justice for the souls whose
lives were taken by these cowards."

When it was over and the dead were buried, all that
was left to be decided was the fate of the young boy who
had been caught with them and the one offender who
Rourke allowed to leave immediately, never to return.
Tom asked if he could have the boy and take him with
us in the spring.

"Do you feel malice toward this boy, Joshua? If so
speak up now."

"No, Tom, I feel only pity for him. When he learns
the ways of good people, he will have to come to grips
with his past life. I think that will be punishment
enough."

Having accomplished what they set out to do, they
burned the place to the ground, loaded everyone in the
boats and headed home.

* * *

The town merchants announced that there would
be grand party to celebrate their victory. Rourke was
formally decreed to be the head of their defense force,

with powers to do all that was necessary to keep law and order.

With Joshua's help, Rourke had his house finished by the time Beatrice and his family arrived the following Spring. He seemed to be the happiest he'd ever been.

Winter was over and the snow was melting fast. Mary and I, Tom and Anne, Joshua and Mirabelle decided it was time to head into the wilderness and start our new life. We had one last night with Rourke and after a lot of whiskey and a lot of songs, there was sadness and tears.

In the morning light, we all agreed it had been a truly momentous night and surely we would all meet again soon. What great liars we were. It was obvious that no one felt sure that would ever be possible. After all, the new land held many dangers. We were setting out on a great adventure, so we put ourselves in God's hands. We prayed He would look kindly on us and bring us to our promised land.

D. N. Curran

Homesteading

When the wagons were loaded and the mules were harnessed, we went to say goodbye to Rourke and Beatrice. How much he'd changed these past months. No longer was he the hard man he used to be. It was difficult for everyone to say goodbye. We'd shared so much together, especially me, who had been in the Prince's entourage with Rourke one way or another from the beginning.

* * *

Mary and I had decided to wait until we could find a priest to marry us. It was rumored there were a few priests and ministers who had become disillusioned with the colony of Virginia, so they'd packed up and crossed the mountains to try to start a new life, leaving behind the bigotry that existed in the English-ruled Americas.

Tom had a theory about that. "The English can only be successful if they keep all the poor people divided against themselves. This way, religion is a tool they've learned to use very successfully."

For his part, Rourke was really amazed how he'd been able to settle down, and become respectable. It was going to be strange to plan his future, knowing he was not going to roam any more.

'Truly, Robbie, in a way I envy you your adventure, but I now have a new life to lead which I feel will be a happy one. My thoughts will be with you always, my friend."

* * *

We set out along the river trail, passing through small towns bustling with river trade, which was all part of the goods and crops being sent up river from the farms and trading posts farther into the wilderness.

It was strange, but most people we met had never ventured farther than where they'd decided to stop their trek, so nobody really knew too much about the next bend in the river, let alone the distant outposts where we were heading, and then some.

There was a sort of an unwritten law that you kept your knowledge of the wilderness to yourself and if anyone wanted to try to move up, then it would be on their head. As always, Tom had a theory, including one about the kind of people who made up the new land.

"It's obvious that only the strong had survived the journey from the old world, therefore, they're part of the strongest and the best of all who left. That's the Lord's way of making it possible for this land to be successfully inhabited."

The journey was pleasant enough and we had plenty game to feed us and there was always a river for fishing. When we stopped at an outpost trading station we replenished our tea, cooking oil, flour, and oats for our porridge—a breakfast eaten by Scots on a regular basis.

At first Joshua thought we were mad to eat the gooey mess and when we put salt on it to flavor it, he was convinced he was right about these crazy Scottish folk, who ate what they ate and played their noisy pipes.

"There's black magic in that pipe music. You become very quiet. It's like you're in a trance whenever this loud noise starts. I see tears in your eyes. There's magic air in the bag and you squeeze to make the magic come out."

We laughed and Dougal repeated his usual answer. "Pity the man who hears the pipes and doesna come from Scotland."

Mary and I would steal away and spend time holding each other, kissing, and talking about our new life and how great it would be, all the time hoping that just around the next bend in the river we would come upon a priest who would take pity on us and agree to marry us immediately.

As the weeks went by, we met more and more folks, but never a priest. Everyone would say they'd heard tell of one up at the next settlement.

At last we found a place where the latest group of settlers had put down their roots. We were careful to choose land higher than the river and close to the high country which we reckoned to be where millions of years of floods had deposited good topsoil and where the runoff had deposited rich black earth from the higher ground.

Time and again my father would say, "If we don't find a priest, I'll marry you two myself." He'd wink his eye, as if to say he had something up his sleeve.

After we'd mapped out our boundaries, we fixed on an area with good drainage and tree felling began.

It was agreed Joshua would be in charge of the building and the rest of us would begin clearing the valley for crops. This would entail having to drag the roots out using the horses and mules or burning the trees if they were too deeply rooted in the ground.

When needed, we'd rip the tree trunks required for planking for the roofs, doors, windows frames, floors, and so forth. This was accomplished by digging a long pit in the ground, then one man would lay on his back in the pit and another atop the trunk to saw the logs into planks by hand. It was back-breaking work, but the rewards of having a nice home made it worthwhile.

Mary would go out hunting deer or birds to keep the larder filled, allowing the rest of us to work on the land and help the builder. Maribelle would assist Anne with the cooking and at times was a helper for Joshua. The young lad, Ian, was now an apprentice to Joshua and proved to be a quick learner.

It took several months, but eventually things began to take shape and we all were feeling excited about our future. One evening as we sat at our evening meal, my father stood up and suggested that we should plan on taking a day of rest apart from the usual Sunday. It was decided we'd take off the next Saturday. He also suggested we all dress up a bit and be in a festive mood. We were all a bit surprised at his persistence, so he explained.

"Remember when we were leaving the last settlement, I promised you I'd have a surprise for you? Well, I think it's about time I keep my promise."

When Saturday arrived, we all dressed in our best clothes. It seemed we were looking forward to the day, no matter what the surprise was to be.

My father led us into the forest carrying lots of food and such. We all followed after him, hoping for the best. Pretty soon, I noticed Mary and Anne were missing and when I inquired, me said they had something they had to do and would catch up. Strange, I thought. I only hope they manage to find us wherever he's taking us.

Eventually we arrived at our destination. The first thing I noticed was a large tree stump had a beautiful tablecloth draped over it and on it was a crucifix and two candles. My father bade us all stand around in a half circle, and bow our heads.

Mary appeared in her wedding gown and stood by the altar. My father then asked me to accompany him and stand with Mary. Before I could question him, he began.

"Friends, we're gathered here to have a wedding, not the usual kind, but one in the old tradition of Scotland. Many years ago in Scotland if there wasn't a priest available, the couple would come together among friends and take their vows before God. It was customary for the couple to repeat their vows as written on this paper."

Handing the paper to me, he said, "Who gives this woman in matrimony to this man?"

Tom answered. "I do."

"Then, before God and this gathering let them say the words which by old Scottish law will bind them in holy matrimony and may God be their witness."

I spoke first. As told by my forefathers before me, I repeated the following. "Mary McHugh, I love you, I will cherish you, and want you for my bride above all others."

Mary replied. "Robert Cameron, I love you, I cherish you, and I want you for my husband above all others."

My father then asked all present to bow their heads and ask God's blessing on this union.

"These two wonderful young people are so much in love. May the Lord grant them many years of happiness and good fortune which they so richly deserve."

All present answered, "Amen."

My father then announced, "By the ancient laws of our homeland which have endured for centuries, I now pronounce you man and wife."

As he spoke, a ray of sunlight broke through the forest canopy and flooded the altar where Mary and I were standing in a brilliant glow of warm sunlight.

Tom said, "Well now, it seems the Almighty agrees with all here that truly Mary and Robbie are now man and wife."

Mary looked into my eyes and I into hers. Words were not necessary, for we knew that our love had found a way for us to be together as man and wife forever.

Our New Home

Leaving Rourke in the settlement, we decided to move along the river where there was unsettled land for the taking. All that was required to claim it was to clear the trees and break up the virgin soil. Work had progressed satisfactorily and I helped Joshua so things would progress faster.

Work on the house had begun and I helped Joshua so things would progress faster. We chose the home site, cleared the forest floor and work began. We could see the beginnings of our house, which was big and airy, which meant the doors and windows would need a substitute for glass. It was decided fine cotton would keep out the bugs and let in sunlight. During the colder months storm windows on the outside would help keep us warm inside.

We gathered rocks from the riverbed to build the fireplace and soon began to think about the day we would move into our new home. Mostly chimneys were made of wood, but they constantly let smoke drift back into the house, which sometimes became engulfed in flames. Although I knew it would take longer to build, I felt a stone fireplace would be best and when it was finished, it would give the house a look of grandeur.

Naturally, Mary was impatient to see it finished. Both she and Mirabelle were busy making drapes for the windows from material from a river salesman, who supplied the fine linen weave they required in exchange for meat.

All in all, it was going just as we hoped. We were getting to know all the neighbors. They were Irish, so Mary felt closer to them. Their son had taken a beautiful Indian girl for his wife and they had two children.

She was Algonquin. They were known as "river Indians." As new settlers arrived, they traded with those already there, as well as the local Indians. They gave us meat and furs but also helped us with clearing the land and were assured a share of the crops which we intended to grow in exchange for their labor, which meant they would have flour and vegetables to eat in the winter.

Before the white man came, Indians had no concept of farming. They lived off the land really well when food was plentiful, but could go hungry in the winter when the snow fell. It became clear to the chiefs that our approach to living was better than theirs and so they began to adapt to our ways a little at a time.

One thing was clear from the start, you could only expect them to do what they wanted to, but you could never hurry them along. Secondly, we soon found out that whiskey was a problem for them, which later proved to be a major problem for all of us.

Mary had a way with the squaws. Although at first she could only gesture and sign, it seemed they were able to understand her. She listened to them talk and soon began to speak to them in their language, which proved useful when negotiating their labor or goods, as it prevented a lot of misunderstanding between us. She became our translator.

Anne was a big help when the children took sick. She had knowledge about how to treat some medical problems and, in turn, the Indian women taught her many natural cures using plants that grew in the forest.

By the end of our first year we had accomplished much and were very pleased with our efforts. It was decided some of us would make a trip down the river to the settlement to buy seed for the coming year. Mary was with child so I felt it would be safer for Tom to remain with the women and I decided to ask Dougal to accompany me.

He agreed to come along. We set off, aiming to be back before spring plowing began.

First, we built a raft and floated downriver until we reached the nearest settlement and then trekked the rest of the way on foot.

Rourke was pleased to see us all again. He decided we would stay with him and no discussion to the contrary would be acceptable. He was now in his new home. Beatrice was with child again. Their twins were growing like crazy. I thought about how this would be me in a very short time. He was pleased to hear that I was soon to be a father and jibed me constantly. Rourke was as content as I had ever seen him.

As for problems, Rourke explained there were some river pirates, but in general, he had everything under control. The Redcoats had made some sorties into the area and their navy was getting closer to reaching their harbor, but the merchants felt it could be a good thing as it meant the trading business could expand. Rourke was not convinced, of course, telling them that once the Crown gets a foothold, things could change and maybe not for the best. A meeting was held and over Rourke's objection, the majority were convinced it was worth the gamble.

"Robbie, they have no idea what they're letting themselves in for. Mark my words, we know firsthand what the Crown is like. It's them first and everyone else second, but I couldn't convince the merchants to be cautious."

* * *

I spent some time visiting old friends. The news from Kingston was good. Flora had married James and Anne was engaged to be married to a magistrate whose wife had passed. At long last, Jane had found her place in society.

After a few more days had passed I became restless to be with Mary and I decided to make my way back home. I bought some supplies and a couple of mules to carry the goods home, with the understanding they would also be used for plowing and gathering the crops. All in all, things were looking good. I also hired a laborer who was willing to work for his board and a share of the profits from crops sold at the season's end.

It was decided the others would leave first and I would spend a few days more with Rourke—a decision I would live to regret.

I visited with John Rodger, now the settlement's acting attorney. John was anxious to hear about our family and delighted to hear that Mary was expecting. He was still single, enjoying his freedom and all that went with it.

Kidnapped

Because of the snow run off, the river rose, allowing a British merchant ship to venture into the area for the first time. It lay anchored out in mid-channel and was bound for Scotland with its hold full of tobacco and rum brought from the Indies. Here it took on beaver and muskrat pelts for the furriers in Edinburgh. I'd decided to spend the night at the inn and leave early next day, hoping to pick up some news of the old country and how things were for the Highlanders after all this time.

The Captain seemed intrigued with my history and experience with the pirates off the Indies. He had never had a run in with them, but as he put it... "there's always a first time." We dined together, sharing some of his ship's wine. After a while, I wasn't feeling well and decided to go to my room. I bade him farewell and safe passage back to Scotland.

When I awoke, the first thing I realized was the room was swaying back and forth. Then it hit me, the room was not a room, but a ship's anchor hold and the vessel was at sea. I immediately tried to jump to my feet, but I was shackled to the floor.

What in heaven's name is going on?

I cried out loud. "Who has done this to me?"

The silence was deafening and stayed that way for most of the day. That evening an old salt brought me some gruel and a mug of water, then turned and left without responding to my demands to speak to the captain.

Next morning the first mate came into the room and removed the shackle around my ankle. He had a loaded pistol at the ready, so I was not about to start anything, lest the man panic and kill me. All I could think about was Mary and my unborn child as I politely asked what was happening to me. He remained silent as he ushered me out at gunpoint.

As he guided me through the bowels of the ship, I could hear rats scurrying. We arrived on deck and I breathed in as much sea air as I could while being pushed along. I was shoved into the Captain's cabin and he motioned me to sit.

Gone was the friendly nature of the captain I'd dined with last night. He stood, looking down at me with a scowl on his face.

"Before you say anything, let me tell you I have a warrant from the Crown to press men into service, if I have a need of able-bodied hands. You, sir, fit that bill."

I looked at him and thought for a moment, then smiled at him. "Captain, Sir, I'm not without means. I will reward you handsomely if you put me off at the next port of call for your vessel."

He sat down at his desk, silent for a moment before he replied. "That sir, will be Leith docks in Scotland, as we are now in open waters and will not sight land 'til we drop anchor there."

I took a step toward him and the First Mate struck me from behind, knocking me to the floor. I tried to rise, but his boot was pressed firmly against my neck. I turned my head as best I could with my cheek flat against the floor boards.

"This is an injustice to me, sir. I will seek redress from your company when we land."

As the First Mate pushed down hard on my neck with his boot, he poked me with what can only be described as a long wooden baton. "If you make it that far," he snarled.

The Captain sat with his arm on his knee, bending down to have eye contact with me. He motioned for the First Mate to ease up on me. I rested on my elbows as he spoke.

"Do you not see the position you're in, man? Would it not be better to accept a position on board, say, as a seaman?" He said with a contemptuous smile. "Come on now, shape up and make the best of your life until we reach Scotland. Then, God willing, you will return on another company ship to your port of embarkation and be able to take up your life where you left off."

I lay there trying desperately to think about my situation. I decided to say or do nothing to endanger my life. As I slowly rose to my feet, I wondered if at any minute I'd be attacked from behind again.

"I'll serve on your vessel, not because I condone what you've done, but because I have no choice. I realize it's the Crown that's to blame for my misfortune, with its barbarous practices of pressing men into service. Therefore, I hold no grudge against you in this matter...Sir."

I got the feeling he was immensely relieved, knowing that he had made a terrible mistake. He was eager to endear himself to me, lest he pay dearly for his blunder if the ship's owner found that he was foolishly creating mistrust between the shipping line and the newly acquired merchants along the river as customers.

"That's better," he replied, helping me to my feet and rubbing at some stains on my jacket. You'll share a cabin with the First Mate here. Had I known your standing in the community, this would not have happened. I'll see to it you receive special privileges not normally given and you'll sleep well and eat with my other paying guests. However, I must have your word that you will not speak of this unfortunate situation."

I intended to make this individual pay dearly for the trouble he had wrought on me and my family, but as Rourke would have said, "every dog gets his day" and I intended to get my day and then some.

There were four passengers on the ship, one a Redcoat colonel, retired from the regular army and on his way home to England to sell off his estate. He planned to use the money to purchase some land in the new territories that were opening up across the Appalachians. He was most interested to talking with me. In a drunken stupor, the First Mate had told of my being pressed into the ship's service after meeting the Captain at the inn.

I explained I'd been on my way back to my estate in the new territories, west of the settlement. I assured him that land was abundant if one was willing to first clear the forest of the trees and undergrowth and then break up the soil for the first time. "It's not an easy task by any stretch of the imagination."

I could tell he could afford to hire an agent, if he was lucky enough to be able to purchase good land. I explained it was virgin land, there for the taking if one could establish a friendship with the local tribes.

Unaware that I already knew, he explained to me about the trouble in upstate New York where the tribes had risen up and killed many settlers and how it took the English army to bring peace to the region. I was careful not to mention my part in all of the battles and simply chose to agree with his version.

"I've been told the French had a great deal to do with the unrest and subsequently that war, Colonel. Now, in the new territories, there are no armies as yet, French or otherwise, so I don't see a man such as you having a problem with the local tribes, unless they were to feel cheated in some way."

He agreed. "We may someday pay dearly for our administration of these new lands where the people are a different breed from the average Englishman. Are not many the same stock as the English in London? Therefore, more than able to administer their own country with little or no need from the Crown. Try telling that to the king and his cronies."

I nodded and shook my head in agreement, then excused myself and went about my duties as best I could under the circumstances.

When the storm hit on my watch, it was almost as if the sea was rearing up on its hind legs. The constant hammering of huge waves as they pounded the deck gave me cause to think that any minute now they'd eventually swallow the ship.

I must give praise where it's due. The Captain was a true seaman and without his guidance we surely would have perished. With all the knowledge and skill learned over many years at sea and his determination in the face of certain disaster, he brought us through the storm. We were thoroughly battered, but still able to make way, even though the shrouds were nearly torn to shreds.

We were blown off course with little or no way of knowing just where we were, other than we were far south of the shipping lanes. We were at the mercy of the elements in uncharted waters, but eventually we rounded a tip of land and headed east, hoping to bring us to our known port of departure. We stopped only to take on any fresh fruit and water there might be available, but never venturing inland from the shoreline.

After many days, we found ourselves to be in a bay with land on three sides and no visible signs of our known territory. It was decided to land and try to get our bearings.

I reckoned that if I were to journey north, it was possible we were west of the new territories and that heading east by land would bring us to Virginia, or if lucky, maybe nearer to my home.

Needless to say, I wasn't about to give any indication to the rest of the crew what my feelings were, but I was determined to escape from the ship's company as soon as humanly possible. I made sure I was amongst the crew chosen to man the longboat. We rowed ashore in hopes of finding fresh water and, if possible, contact someone to find out where we'd landed.

The tribe was not unlike the Algonquin I knew, but I kept my own counsel and listened while the First Mate tried to parlay with the chief. It was obvious to me the chief had at least seen a white man or had them described to him by someone as he was not all that surprised at our appearance, and that struck me as being strange.

When time came to go back onboard I explained to the First Mate my sea legs were not as good as his and I would spend the night on the beach where I could rid myself of the obvious motion sickness, I'd acquired during the storm.

He was only too happy to have me stay. I imagined upon his return to ship he would joyfully inform the captain that I was a hellish sailor and he was weary of my constant complaining, so he'd bid me stay ashore for the duration of their stay.

I watched the crew clamber aboard ship for the night, as I settled down and prepared to sleep amongst sea weed on the beach, just above the high tide mark. The sky was filled with a million stars. I laid there gazing at the heavens, in awe of the Almighty, praying that I'd find my way back home to my Mary.

A few tribesmen came by. Each one had two or three mullets on their spears. Using sign language, they bade me go with them to their camp, and spend the night. I was obviously an oddity to most of them, but I intended to use all opportunities given to me to find out more about their tribe and where if they could help me figure out where I was and how to get home.

By signs and some words Mary had taught me, I was able to find out from them that their tribal name was Montagnais and when I mentioned the Algonquin, they pointed to the east and showed little interest.

I signed. Had they been to their lodges in the east? They motioned no, but then surprisingly, in sign they told me that one white man like me had come from there many moons before and if I wanted to travel east for one moon I could meet him.

The chief then showed me a trophy from the man, alluding to the fact that I had yet to given him one. I immediately cut off two of my seaman's brass buttons from my coat and offered them to him. He tried to place them on his necklace next to the other trophy he'd been given. As I admired his handiwork, I saw a crucifix.

My heart leaped in my chest. I knew that the white man might be a priest, or at least a Christian. I tried not to be overly interested in the information I'd been given, but I hardly slept that night, thinking about it; however I made up my mind that be parting company with my seafaring friends.

* * *

The next day, the First Mate tried to barter with the tribe for the jewelry they wore. Iron hatchets and cooking pots were exchanged for trinkets as the ship's crew went about the business of replenishing the stores lost in the storm.

For my part, I began taking certain items I would need if I dared to trek east toward home. First, a water flask, pistols, and a hatchet. Every time the longboat went from ship to shore, I added to my stash of provisions.

The ship waited all day to get the tide and by early evening it was running, as we prepared to get underway to the south as far as the tip of land, then north as far as we could. The Captain explained that we would then pick up the shipping lancs for the trip to Scotland. As we tacked on sail, the ship heaved and then began to move. I jumped ship, not from the deck as one might if swimming, but by climbing down the gunwale where I gently slipped into the surf.

Within a few moments the ship was gone and no cry of "Man overboard!" was heard. I guessed it would be at the change of watch that I would be missed. I felt positive there wouldn't be a hue and cry from the captain to go back to look for me. Better I drown in the sea and prevent any future problems for him.

The Odyssey

I felt free. Ahead lay the task of setting a course on land. First, I had to get to know my Indian brothers a bit better. Maybe a guide would be given to me for at least part of my journey back to my beloved wife and child, be it a boy or a girl. Just the thought of them would sustain me throughout my journey.

The chief was surprised when I appeared next morning, but I motioned that I intended to go overland to the land of the Algonquin. He appeared to understand and I managed to swap my seaman's uniform for buckskins, which I figured would make it easier for traveling through the forests.

No one came near me, but when meals were being served I would share whatever they were eating. The Indians were friendly, but cautious. I respected their approach to me. When the chief was ready, he came to see me and together we spoke of my journey to the Algonquin tribe. It was difficult, but strangely enough, when two people don't speak the same language, they communicate by signs and gestures. I understood that danger would be my constant companion for most of the journey.

When I left, wearing my buckskins, the chief stood waving goodbye, sporting a naval uniform complete with cap. Not having a compass, I traveled into the rising sun. I made my observations at sunrise, plotting my route by sighting on a mountain or some such landmark and then heading in the direction of the marker.

For some reason I felt I was being followed, but dismissed my feelings as my mind playing tricks on me.

It could well be my imagination at work. After two days I arose to see someone standing near me.

With the morning sun in my eyes, I was temporarily blinded. As I adjusted to the sunlight, to my astonishment I saw not a brave, but a young girl. She stood very still and then spoke to me in English, saying she'd been taught by the missionary when he'd lived in their midst for a year.

She told how most of her friends could not master the white man's language, but for some reason she was able to do it. She described how he'd told her of a great father who lived in the sky and if she believed, she would find great happiness in her life. Unbeknownst to the chief, she had become a Christian.

Before he left, the priest told her to teach others about her newfound God, but she was afraid and when she heard of my journey, she decided to follow me to the land of the Christians.

She had stayed a distance away from me all this time as she feared the chief might send warriors to seek her out, and if she'd been with me, I might have been killed. However after some time had passed and no braves came, she imagined the chief thought she'd been killed in the forest by a bear or a big cat.

I was astonished by her tale, but encouraged by the fact I could speak with her and maybe together we could make it to the river settlements and my home. No trail existed, so the going was tough. We were to make many moccasins before we finished our journey. We had a ritual. She would fetch firewood and fresh water, and make the meals. I would catch game and fish if there was an opportunity to do so. We always traveled into the rising sun.

She told me there were many small tribes along the way, some friendly, others not so much, and if we came upon them, she would speak for both of us. She made it clear, that if trouble erupted, I must leave her and go on alone as she had a better chance of survival than I. She could always escape after a while, whereas I would not be so lucky.

Her name was Falling Moon. I christened her "Rachel." She said she knew it was a name form the Holy book that spoke the words of her new God and she asked me to teach her to read and write the white man's language. She, in turn, would teach me the Indian ways which were necessary to survive in the forest. A strange relationship developed, to say the least—two strangers taking a journey together, each one seeking something different from the other, yet always for the common good.

She'd offered herself to me not long after we met. She simply appeared at my blanket naked. She was beautiful, with dark skin, coal black hair, and large almond-shaped eyes. She simply laid down with me. The temptation was enormous with her warm soft body pressed against me. I could not bear to look at her, lest I succumb to her obvious attempt at seduction.

With my back to her, I told her of my woman and how I could only sleep with her. She moved over me. In the firelight her beauty was boundless. She was indeed a temptress.

"I find it strange, Eyes Like Mountain Flowers (her name for me), that here in the wilderness, no one can know of our lovemaking. Still, you stay true to your woman? Am I not beautiful? She took my hand and ran it over her body.

"Has she cast a spell over you that you find me ugly?"

I made it a rule never to sleep naked and told her that was one of the rules of my God who was now her God and that she must learn His ways if she was to be happy in her new world.

Of course, I knew that I must teach her about white men. My hope was to meet up with the priest and learn the way to the settlements along the river by our home, but I knew it was a lot to expect as the land was so vast and there were no trails.

* * *

We trekked for many days, always to the east, and met many small tribes, who at one time or another were at war with each other. I explained as best I could that there was more to be gained if they joined forces and then the bigger tribes would not be such a threat to them. I told them of the white man's settlements where all different men came together and were strong, not afraid of the Montagnais or the great Algonquin as together they were just as many and just as strong.

We arrived at a small clearing and the tribal chief explained to Falling Moon that runners from all the tribes we'd passed had arrived with a message from their chiefs that they were eager to sit down in council with Blue Eyes to listen and learn from his wisdom.

"Falling Moon, tell the chiefs I will await them here and will be glad to counsel them on the strength in numbers."

"I will tell them what you have said, Blue Eyes, but I want to be known as 'Rachel' as that is my new Christian name."

"Rachel is a Christian name. It isn't going to be easy to explain to the chiefs. Would they understand you taking a white name if my counsel is so wise?"

Obviously annoyed at my ploy, Rachel just smiled and answered. "Blue Eyes, would they not also find it hard to understand you choose not to sleep with me if this joining is so important?"

Knowing she had obviously won her argument, I told her. "When we are with the chiefs, you will be Falling Moon, but when we are alone, I will call you Rachel. But know this—your Indian name holds more for me in my heart than your Christian name, so some of the time I will still call you Falling Moon."

After we'd eaten and as I laid on my blanket, I realized that my conversation had revealed my feelings for Rachel, more than I would have been willing to admit. I decided to be very careful from then on regarding how we spoke and interacted. I also made a mental note that I would be teaching her to read and write, but never would I teach her to play chess, as the way she had checkmated me over her name proved to me she would make one very unbeatable chess player.

As the winter and cold nights were approaching, I longed to feel the touch of Mary and hear her voice; however, I knew the wise thing was to winter with the tribes and await the snow melt in the spring. From the beginning, I knew I must make a shelter because to stay with the chief, Rachel and I would have to be man and wife.

Their morals being totally founded on what was good for them, they would never be able to accept my morality. Women were made to have babies and above all that was the reason why they were put on this earth and in their present beliefs, I knew they would never understand, especially when Rachel had been quick to see the situation and how it would appear to them.

My approach to home building was of no use whatsoever, so I followed Rachel's direction. First, cut long slender branches, then anchor them in the earth to form a circle, and then tie them together at the top to make a tent-like frame. Next, apply animal hides (which we borrowed) and Rachel tied them together to form a canopy with an opening at the top to allow the smoke from our fire to leave the inside when we built a fire in the evenings to cook and keep warm.

It seemed all too primitive by my standards, but when we took up housekeeping, it amazed me how dry and warm it turned out to be. I was taught to use a bow and arrow for hunting, leaving my powder and lead shot in reserve lest we be attacked. Rachel remained more than able to provide us with fish and until the snow fell, also berries of different descriptions.

I missed my normal diet of Scottish food, but hunger can persuade anyone to develop a liking for other food when necessary and after a while I began to look forward to the meals Rachel prepared for me over a small, insignificant fire in the teepee.

I was amazed at the ability of Indian women to work fourteen hours a day and never complain. Soon, however, talk got around as to why we didn't have children? Rachel was quick to put that blame on me, suggesting that maybe I lacked the ability.

Soon old squaws would bring me the most foul-tasting liquids to drink, which they pointed out to Rachel worked very positively to produce babies when the husband was not quite put together like most men. For my part, I gladly took the horrible drinks knowing when I did, to them it would seem like it was not working, whereby the feeling was that the Great Spirit did not wish it any other way.

The day arrived when the chiefs of all the tribes we'd passed through and some yet to come, arrived for a powwow. I was elected to be the main speaker after all the chiefs made their opening statements, which took at least two days, after which all eyes turned to me. I spoke of the lands across the sea where I came from and the many wars that had ensued until the great chiefs of my land had gathered together and formed a great army, all chiefs having the same amount of power.

"You must select one brave above the rest, who if he fails as a leader will be replaced by another. The word must go out to all the tribes that they feared, that great misery would befall whoever attacked one of their group. The new rule would be "attack one of us means attack all of us in the group."

I found the words easy to say, for this is what would have saved the clans when the English attacked. If all Scotsman had rallied under one banner, the English could never have been successful, but as they were masters of illusion, they had convinced certain powerful chiefs to come to their side and the outcome had been a disaster for the rest.

If I could achieve nothing else, other than uniting the tribes, I felt that I would have enabled them to resist the Crown forces when they came across the Appalachians. Who knew? Maybe together with the rest of us Scots and Irish, we could stand united and make it impossible to subdue us.

As a frontiersman, I vowed to do all that I could to make the day come to pass when all the tribes would unite as one. Hopefully, I should be able to convince my own Gaels to do the same. The first problem was to pick a chief who would be acceptable to all. This proved impossible at first, until I suggested a contest to shoot at a target and the best man would be the first chief.

I constructed a target with a bull's eye and other outer lines which I explained would be worth so many points and then the man with the greatest number of points would win. If there was more than one with the same score, then we would move the target farther away until only one man was the best.

The idea was not too popular, so I added the attraction of a prize. All would put up so many skins and winner take all. The old men suggested that a duel would work, but I was quick to explain if we killed each other to win, then how could we achieve the unity we desired?

The old men agreed, but thought the target was not a man's way. Luckily for me, the winner was the youngest man, maybe not so much a good shot, but he could see farther than the others. I immediately saw a problem and told how in my land over the great sea when a young man was elected chief, he always took the advice of the older chiefs agreeing to go with the majority decision. I was making up rules as I went along, but it was that or chaos, and maybe even bloodshed.

They would unite under one man and swear to the Great Spirit that all would abide by the new laws concerning their brotherhood. Soon the whole meeting was one of ideas and rule-making and they soon forgot my input, other than I had to nod approval every time they reached a decision. Rachel now took on a special place amongst the women. Was she not the women of Blue Eyes, who had brought all the tribes to smoke the peace pipe together?

I could see at a glance, the young braves and maidens would have a greater variety of partners to choose from than before, so the young ones were only to eager to shout out their great admiration for the old wise men, who had the vision from the Great Spirit to bring them all together as brothers and especially their sisters.

I spent the winter cuddling up to Rachel in the cold nights but always managed to resist the temptation to make love, although I felt she did her best to make it harder and harder.

The result of the new treaty meant the Montagnais declared war on one the small tribe, so runners were sent out for all the other tribes to help, which they did and soon the fighting stopped. When I asked for a powwow, I pointed out that if the Montagnais lost, then many more of their enemies might think them weak and attack them. Soon the fighting was forgotten and the tribes resumed peaceful relations.

The winter ended and the snow melted. I made it known I must leave, so Falling Moon and I bade our goodbyes and set off to the east, but not before I was made a blood brother to the tribes, which meant several cuts on my hands to which each chief mingled his blood. If it meant I could return one day and be accepted, maybe it was to worth the pain I had to endure.

* * *

It felt good to be on the move again, every day a new vista and there were many beautiful ones to behold. The sunrises were always magnificent as we always had to be ready before dawn to catch the rising sun and mark our way for that day, then travel until dusk when we would make a fire and eat, and then sleep, ready for the next day's march. If we had to cross a mountain range, the danger was from bears and mountain lions as they were still high in the mountains, steadily moving downhill from their winter lairs.

It resembled what the settlers called a "false spring" as the winter frost began to melt early and the animals that hibernate were now emerging from their dens and lairs, ravenous and most dangerous.

Heading Home

It was on one of those early mornings. We saw the camp by the river we had to cross and wondered what lay in store for us. Rachel decided to go alone and sniff out the danger, if there was any, while I stood back with my pistol and musket, ready to attack if she was in danger. I felt bad at my having to stay behind and have her put herself in harm's way, but I knew she was right to take this approach. It made sense, but I wondered what Rourke would have done. But enough of wondering what might be. What was going to happen was in God's hands.

As I waited for her to come back or at least make some attempt at warning me I had a strange feeling that something was unexpected.

She came walking swiftly, excited and pointing back to a figure trying hard to keep up with her. "He is here! The priest is here, Blue Eyes, the one you seek is here!"

At first I couldn't understand her words, but then it became apparent as he approached she meant the priest who'd lived amongst her people was there in the camp.

He approached me. "Welcome, Brother. Falling Moon has told me all about you and your success with the tribes. I'm impressed." I could tell by his accent he was Irish and he knew Scotland from one end to the other, having been there a good few years.

Yes, the old chief Cameron, he'd visited him on many occasions, but that was before the '45 rebellion. He could only imagine the state of the country since. He'd seen it all before in Ireland, so much death and destruction was nothing new to him.

"So you're trying to get back home, my boy? Well, you're more than halfway there and to be honest, I salute you for your ability to get this far. If I had as much results with my preaching as you have had with your organizing the tribes, I could die a happy man—and that's no lie."

"Well, Father, it's always easy to convert men to a political solution than a religious one. Surely you have seen proof of that in your years of preaching?"

"Very true, but, it's your ability to lead them to making their decisions that I'm jealous of. Truly a gift, you should have been a man of the cloth, my boy."

"Well, Father, I think my mother would agree, but for myself I choose not to turn the other cheek, which I feel eliminates me for a candidate for priesthood."

He laughed and we decided to forget politics and religion for a while and get to know each other. I immediately explained my relationship with Falling Moon was that of fellow traveler and nothing else, lest he think otherwise.

"You're to be commended, Robbie Cameron. Most men I have known would have...well, you know what I'm saying and that gives me great respect for you. These young women see no harm sharing their bodies with a man, particularly if he's attractive. It's their belief that it ensures a good-looking baby and they'll be the envy of the tribe.

"I don't judge them. A carpenter I have read about over a thousand years or so ago said it better than I ever could. 'Judge not less you yourself be judged.' So my conviction is to start with that thought and endeavor to speak about a lot of other things he had to say, in the hopes I might just plant a seed of curiosity amongst the best of them.

"I'm like a dog with a rabbit, I'll shake the thing 'til something gives and by that, I mean, they're willingness to listen to the word of God. And what keeps me going you might ask? Falling Moon, for one. To her, I was like the Baptist, a voice calling in the wilderness."

"Father, you may already know this, but as a good friend would say, 'You, Sir, definitely have a way with words.' Or, to put it in his vernacular, "Man you have a great gift of the gab and no two ways about it."

We sat down and shared a meal and smoked a pipe or two. He and I both stared into the flames licking about the logs, each in his own way deep in thought about our own personal hopes and dreams. A great shower of sparks exploded as logs tumbled in on each other. His face was illuminated by the flames. As the flames died down he began to rake the embers.

"She wants to stay here, with me. She thinks she can help me. I think she can help me win these people over to Christ and for that reason I have persuaded her to stay. Is it a blow to your plans, Robbie? I hope not. In my opinion, she is not ready for the white man's world. Without the likes of men like you, she will be like a lamb led to the slaughter. You can see that, can't you?"

I stood up and put a hand on his shoulder. "Father, you've made it easier for me to go on, I was frantic at the thought of her in the settlements. I couldn't take her home, not straight away. There' already much explaining to do and she'd make it all the harder.

"Just looking at her beauty tells the tale. So I'm glad she's going to stay, but if she ever wants to come later on when I'm back home at my farm with my family, she's welcome to stay. Mary will see to it that she'll go into the white man's world at least prepared to deal with the riffraff we frequently have to call countrymen, even as it sticks in my craw to say so."

* * *

Unless you've seen the magnificence of the forest, its beauty is hard to explain. The trees are tall and their foliage covers the forest like a great parasol allowing the light to filter in, almost like being in a grand cathedral. One feels very close to God. As I walked, I kept thinking,

I wonder how the Garden of Eden must have looked to Adam.

"Of course, like the Garden of Eden, it had its snakes and all kind of wild creatures. I felt their eyes on me at all times of the day and night. My task of finding east became more of a problem, so I took longer to seek my bearings, and it slowed up me up quite a bit.

"It was on one of these morning sightings, I met my next friend and fellow traveler, Pony Who Runs. I christened him "Mac." He was a brave who'd decided to explore the horizons and had to leave his tribe to do so. Indians would go far on hunting trips, but always stayed in much the same location. To meet a young man who obviously was going against the tide, I was interested to hear his story. Of course, it was of course as old as time itself. He'd fallen in love with his brother's wife and she with him.

He and I had much in common, both traveling alone, and I, of course, knew what it was like to lose one's love and also one's country, so we were kindred spirits. We hunted together, fished for food, and in general taught each other more than we already knew about our tribes. As we progressed, I'd mentioned he could come home with me and learn the ways of the white man, growing crops, and having food for the winter when hunting was not always possible.

I haven't mentioned wolves very much as they avoided the white man as much as possible. Being very family oriented, they taught the cubs at an early age the white man was no one to be messed with as he had no regard for them, unlike the Indians, who thought of them as brothers and if not attacked would never think of hunting a wolf for any reason.

The white man had hunted them to near extinction in Europe and would do so wherever he found them in his area in the Americas. I must admit I killed them whenever possible as they looked upon our livestock as game and would attack without provocation, which could wipe out a man's means of milk and butter, not to mention meat when necessary.

In some cases, the Indian regarded them as past relatives and at certain times of the year would have ceremonies which included mentioning the pack as helpful brothers. When the tribes were hunting, they could often lead them to a deer herd, which was the main meat source for winter food. So wolves were not the enemy.

The Shaman or holy man would often wear a wolf's skin and head for the different dances he performed, and he would allude to the possibility he could change himself into a wolf which was regarded as a great sign of his power.

We were making good time as we were both fit and as I was anxious to see my family and he was to learn all about farming. I think in his mind he saw himself return one day to his tribe with all the secrets of the white man's ability to grow crops and always have food to eat. The greatest problem for the Indian was as a warrior, he not happy to do what they considered to be women's work.

So this was the greatest problem facing any tribe that wanted to copy the ways and skills of the white man, to be able to feed his family. It was obvious if he came back with me, he would see the work men did on a farm, and that it was not something we left to women, but to be able to convince his brothers was to me an impossible task.

Prodigal's Return

We at last reached the river, I explained we must first go to the settlement to advise my old friend that I'd returned and explain what had happened and alert him to the press gangs so it would not happen to any other of our townsfolk.

When we arrived at the settlement, Mac was amazed at how big the houses were, how all the people dressed, not to mention the inns and stores. I had to explain you could not just take what you needed it had to be bought. He found this difficult to understand as the Indians had no concept of money. Within the tribe, all things were interchangeable. You help me, I help you, but never did you pay money for anything.

Rourke was furious when I told him how I'd been hijacked. "I told the council these English were not to be trusted and now this." He explained a few men had gone missing and there was genuine anger as the majority blamed Indians for having killed them. The captain who'd taken me would be held and prosecuted should he return to the area and I would be the witness for the settlement. What would be his punishment, I could only imagine. If left to Rourke, he man would be hanged.

We talked and I advised Rourke to take it easy as this could be what the Crown needed to start a problem and have them come to settle it, thereby getting their foot in the door.

"You're right Robbie, that's just what they'd like. Better for us to ban any sea captain who press ganged, which meant he would no longer be able to put into port for trading."

My new friend and I set out for home. He seemed excited to see all I had told him about. I remained nervous, not knowing what I was going to face. Had Mary thought me dead and maybe taken herself another man or would it be like old times and my being gone wouldn't have changed anything?

These were the insane thoughts that raced through my mind as we headed home. I noticed how the settlement had grown. There were new homes and barns and the fenced-in fields made it all look neat and uniform. The wilderness it had been in the beginning was gone. I wondered what my family would think of me as obviously a lot of hard work had gone into the place.

Rourke could not tell me much. When I first disappeared, the men of my family searched the surrounding area, including the swamp, but when they found nothing, they returned home to tend the farm. For the next month, they asked strangers who passed by if they'd seen me, but eventually they stopped looking. Rourke hadn't spoken to anyone from the farm for a while.

He'd been at a loss to know what could have possibly happened. "Robbie, it will be all right. Sure you'll be getting the prodigal son's welcome and they'll be killing the fatted calf, lad. Don't be worrying about anything, just get home and hug that wife of yours and your new son and in a couple of days it will be as if you never left."

"I have a son!"

Rourke simply smiled. He knew that feeling well.

I couldn't help but wonder how true Rourke's view of things be. Would I be greeting as I'd hoped for so long or would I be looked upon with pity because my wife was now in love with another? I couldn't blame her as she has a young son to bring up and only God knew what had become of me. I knew I had to find out for myself one way or the other in all this and face my destiny.

The first man I saw was Dougal. He was sitting on a fence rail, smoking his pipe and eating his lunch. As I approached he peered at me as if in disbelief. So transfixed on the two of us, he fell off the fence and began let loose with a tirade of obscenities as he tried to regain his composure and dust himself off.

I was at immediately at his side and helped him to his feet. Tears were streaming down his face and mine.

"Robbie lad, where have ye been? We gave you up for dead. You'll find things changed some since ye left."

His comment made my heart started pounding. "What things?" I asked.

"Oh, lots of things. Come along and we'll go to the main house. Bring your friend with you. He ran on ahead. I wanted to run, but I was afraid because I didn't know what lay before me was to be a blessing or a curse.

Dougal disappeared into the main house and a moment later Mary came rushing out, wiping her hands on her apron as she ran toward me. She flung open her arms and hugged me, kissed me, all the while crying tears of joy all. All my doubts disappeared. I wrapped my arms around her, hugging and kissing her, never wanting to let go.

She pulled away slightly and smiled at me. "Come along, Robbie."

We walked toward the house hand-in-hand, stopping so that I could introduce her to Mac, who seemed totally confused about what was going on. Mary spoke words of welcome which he couldn't understand, but when she motioned for him to follow, he did. Although Indian ways are quite different than ours, I'm sure he was caught up in the joy of what he saw.

I could see Tom and Anne near the front door, waiting to join in my welcome home. Anne rushed into my arms and embraced me. Tom laid a steady hand on my shoulder. I could see tears in his eyes, as he spoke words of welcome. I left them with Mac as Mary urged me to follow her.

When I finally stepped inside, a feeling of pure joy overcame me. Familiar smells of food cooking, polish and wax assailed my nostrils as Mary guided me through the house. We stopped in front of a bedroom door.

"Shush..." she whispered softly, putting her finger to her lips. She quietly opened the door and we crept forward to peer into a crib. There, lying on a blanket, was a chubby baby. My son!

He had long blonde eyelashes. His blond hair was almost the same color as that of a young page who'd seen service in the army of Charles Stuart. He was beautiful like his mother, which I was glad to see. It would be a blessing if he also had her good nature. I could not have been happier at that moment. For the first time in my life I realized what a lucky man I was to have the love of a woman like Mary, a bonnie bairn, and the love of family and friends. I knew then I was truly home. Here I'd stay, contented for the rest of my life.

* * *

That evening when everyone came in from the fields it resembled New Year's Day, when everyone is celebrating the hopes and promises of good luck it brings. We ate and drank a few drams, smoked our pipes, and danced a few reels to the tune of the pipes. All the while, Mac looked on as if he had fallen in with a bunch of lunatics.

After a few drinks, Mac joined in the festivities and we were just one big happy family. Needless to say, Mary and I spent a very pleasant night and made up for lost time.

The next morning I awoke to a bundle being set beside me on me on the bed and immediately I heard a gurgling sound, together with cooing of a little man speaking in a tongue I could not quite understand. He lay there smiling up at me. I felt like a king knowing this little man was my son and he was happy to be with his daddy.

After breakfast I sat down with Tom and Anne. I told them of my being hijacked and my escape, the Indian girl and the priest, and eventually, Mac. It all seemed too strange to be true. As I recounted my trauma step by step, they began to see a picture of a man torn from his family and but for the grace of God, they might never have seen me again.

I waited until Tom and I were alone and then I asked what Dougal meant about things being changed a bit. Tom looked at me somewhat strained and nodded in agreement.

"Aye, Robbie, and maybe not for the best either. It's our neighbor to the south of us."

"What about him?"

Tom hesitated. "Well, for one thing he's very forceful and I feel if he doesn't get his own way, he can be very dangerous. Already he has been harassing our other neighbors about their land rights. He feels some of their land should be his, even to the point of suggesting that if he doesn't get his way someone might get hurt.

"So far he's been okay with us, but a few weeks ago Dougal caught him cutting down trees on our land and when confronted, he threatened to make trouble for us if we tried to stop him. He argued there had been a mistake with the boundary map and that part of our land was really his."

"Well, maybe I should pay this neighbor of ours a visit and make myself known to him. I'll let him know if it's trouble he wants, then it's trouble he'll be getting."

Tom cautioned, "Robbie, this one is mean man, believe me. I wouldn't put it past him to kill to get what he wants. Be careful, lad. We don't want to lose you over a few trees, now do we?"

"Nevertheless, I'll go and talk to him neighborly like and see what he's up to. Come along if you wish. We'll pay him a visit tomorrow. It's time Mac saw the other kind of white folks. All he's seen until now are the decent ones. He should be made aware that we're not all the same if he's going to settle with us. Don't you agree?"

"Ah well, Robbie, if you must, we'll go tomorrow."

* * *

We arrived at the neighbor's farm at noon next day. I inquired as to where I might find the owner. The lady of the house, his wife, said she'd heard I'd returned and was pleased for my family.

"My husband can be found in the top pasture, along with some farm hands.

We could hear him bellowing long before we saw him. He was shouting orders to his men and cursing them out at the same time. As we approached, he told the men to stop and watch as we came nearer.

"Hello, I'm your neighbor...Tom's son-in-law. I've been gone a while, but I'm back now for good and thought we should get acquainted."

The neighbor was about six-foot-two and obviously a very strong man. He came toward us very fast. Mac was taken by surprise and backed away.

"That's right, Indian, when you see me coming, you back off if you know what's good for you."

Although Mac could speak a little English, he nevertheless showed no sign of understanding.

"As for you, Sir, what do you want with me?" His accent and his belligerent manner brought back the memory of the bridge in Scotland and the soldier who accosted Flora.

"Well, first to say hello and secondly to tell you there are some new rules for you to learn."

"Such as?" he growled, looking at his men with a smirk on his face.

"Well, the first thing...This Indian is my friend and he backs off for no man. I suggest you get used to that fact as soon as possible. Next, there seems to be some problem with you knowing your boundaries and cutting some of my trees down. So, I'm asking you to return them or I will help myself to some of yours."

"Over my dead body." He came face to face with me.

"Well, if that's what you want, I suppose it can be arranged, but for the sake of your wife and family, I suggest you simply do as I ask and that'll put an end to it."

He knew he was losing the argument and tried one more time to play his hand. "I can't return the trees. They're already cut up, so that's an end to it, I say."

I turned to walk away. I looked back and stepped toward him. He backed up. "Then I'll cut down your trees to satisfy my side of this argument. Tomorrow at ten o'clock at your side of land next to mine, I will settle the debt you owe me."

He spat on the ground in front of me. "I owe you nothing." He tried to run after us, but tripped and fell. As he lay there, he hollered after me.

"If you step one foot on my land it will be your last. I've seen your kind when I fought with the King's army in Scotland years ago. We taught them a lesson then and by George I'll teach you another tomorrow."

I took another step in his direction as he tried to get up. "What's your name, may I ask?"

Standing now at attention. "Eric Reid, if you must know, late of His Majesty's Redcoats."

* * *

As we turned to walk away, I remarked to Tom, "He must have been a bairn in the army if he'd fought at Culloden. No mind, we'll see who teaches who a lesson tomorrow."

I shouted back to him, "Remember, Reid, ten o'clock, no later or else you miss my expert tree felling."

He half-turned and saw his men watching the argument. "Get back to work, you swine, or I'll cut your wages. I don't pay you to stand around gawking." He turned away. His face was a red as a sunset. He cupped his hands around his mouth and shouted.

"Be warned, if you come near my trees I'll kill you and all that belong to you."

"So what do you think, Robbie? Do you think he means to kill you, lad?"

"I've met and confronted many men in my life, Tom, and I can assure you he does not fall into the category that I would classify as being the sort who can do what they say. I don't think he's anywhere near that. Tomorrow we'll watch and wait and see what this bully tries to do. I assure you I'll take appropriate action."

"Be careful, Robbie, he has a half-brother and from what I hear they work their mischief in tandem. So it's not one, but two you'll have to contend with."

"Well now, that's about what I would expect from a coward, Tom. Let's go eat a good meal and enjoy a night's sleep. Above all, don't mention this to the women, but I'd like Joshua to come along with us tomorrow. As Rourke would say, 'There's safety in numbers, lad, and never forget it.'"

Tom laughed and we went in for supper.

Although it had been spoken about Robbie going to meet the neighbor, nobody mentioned it. Mary told Anne that all had gone off well and there wasn't going to be trouble. She wistfully remarked, "Robbie has changed when the day has come he'd walk away from a fight, but what worries me is what was it that changed him?"

* * *

The next day we assembled at the house. Tom, Joshua, Dougal, Mac and me. We set off for the place mentioned the previous day and were met not only by Mister Reid and his brother, but a fair amount of neighbors who had heard of the conflict between us. Immediately, Eric suggested a duel to settle the matter rather than cutting down trees. I agreed and almost at once one of the neighbors stepped up and suggested he be the referee as he was totally neutral in this dispute.

Eric immediately produced his pistol to be examined by the judge and I also provided my own for review. When the firearms were approved, we moved onto the meadow where the referee began to organize and set up the seconds.

Just then a scuffle broke out with Mac and Eric's brother whereupon a gun was confiscated from the brother and order restored. It became obvious that Eric now took a different approach, suggesting they settle this amicably and that there was no need for violence.

Eric was surprised when the referee responded, "Because of the apparent eagerness originally shown by you, Eric Reid, it's my decision that if Robbie Cameron is still in agreement, the duel shall be held."

I was determined to finish this problem once and for all, so it was agreed we would continue. We were placed back to back and told to take fifteen paces, turn, cock our muskets, and wait for the command to fire.

The referee counted the paces...one, two, three...'til we'd reached fifteen and then we'd turn and shoot. Before the command was given, Eric discharged his pistol at me and missed. There was uproar, but the referee quickly took command and suggested all stand perfectly still.

"The first man to move, I'll shoot down like a dog. He then announced, "Robbie Cameron, take your shot."

I aimed. Eric dropped to his knees, begging to be spared. At that, I put my pistol into my waistband and turned to leave the field.

Immediately a cry went up as Eric produced another smaller pistol from his pocket and was running toward me when I turned and saw him. I grabbed my pistol, aimed and shot Reid in the forehead. He dropped like a stone.

All at once the crowd surrounded me, slapping me on the back and remarking how this man had terrorized the community for so long, yet he was a coward. Seeing the result, his brother had taken off running and was nowhere to be seen. It was suggested that someone go to

Reid's home and inform his wife what had happened. I said I'd be the one to deliver the news.

Everyone agreed the duel had been a fair one as far as Robbie Cameron's involvement was concerned and that if anyone disputed the outcome, to a man they would stand by me in the matter. Although I was relieved it was over, I couldn't help but wonder what my reception would be at the home of my dead opponent. I could only think how it would've been for Mary had I been killed.

I went as soon as possible, not wanting to have the widow hear the outcome from anyone else. As I approached the house, she came rushing out to meet me. She grabbed both of my hands in hers and began thanking me for killing her husband. "For the first time in my children's lives they will be able to go to bed without worrying what the next day might bring—the beatings he gave them and her, and the cruel treatment of the bonded workers he owned.

I listened to her tell me how terrible their lives had been living with her husband and his brother. Surely the Lord had answered not only her prayers, but also the prayers of her children and the workers. "They will be happy for the first time since they came to our farm."

What was she to do? I wondered. I suggested she throw her lot in with us. We would manage the farm for her 'til her children were old enough to manage on their own and, of course, she would share in the profits.

I felt embarrassed as she grabbed my hand and began to kiss it like I was a bishop or the like. I told her that wasn't necessary as we were all friends and neighbors and only too glad to help each other.

Everyone wanted to hear about Eric's brother, Zachary, but all felt he'd be afraid to return lest the other farmers take retribution on him for the dirty deeds perpetrated by him and his dead brother.

Living on the farm was a joyous time for me and my family. Because of the trials and tribulations I'd experienced in my life, I grew to love the peace and quiet of the farm and the surrounding countryside. As the years went by, we were able to build a school. A neighbor's child went off to a place of higher learning. When she'd earned her degree, she returned to be the school's headmistress.

One day an old friend, the priest I met during my journey home, paid us a visit. It seems the converts were now many and he wanted to get permission to start a school and build his church. We stood talking and I was about to ask him to come into the house, when I saw Rachel standing with the horses. She stood very still, as if in a trance. Her long raven-colored hair fell over her shoulders. The pale yellow buckskin dress enhanced her lean figure and a blue bead necklace hung from her long, sensual neck.

I ran to her. She looked as beautiful as ever. At first I thought better of showing too much affection, lest Mary get the wrong idea, but I felt such joy at seeing her again that I took her in my arms and held her, saying how good it was to see her again after such a long time.

"Robbie, I have so much to thank you for. If not for you, I'd still be with the tribe. Instead I have grown in wisdom and have made a good life for myself with the church."

"Are you going with Father Divers to see the bishop at the settlement?"

"No, I'm hoping I can stay with you until he returns."

"Stay as long as you wish, our home is your home, Rachel. My wife and I bid you welcome."

Mary waited as I talked with the strangers. I motioned for her to join us.

"Mary, I want you to meet Father Pat Divers. He's the priest who showed me the way back to the settlement when I was trying to get home to you. And this is Rachel. She befriended me and brought me most of the way home."

For a minute I wasn't sure how Rachel would be received. When I told the story of my adventure, I never fully described how beautiful she was. Now here she was, standing in front of my wife and I felt a little guilty. Mary took Rachel by the hand and led her into the house, telling her how much she owed her for all that she'd done to return her husband to her and his family.

"I want you to know how much I'm in your debt. From this day forth you must think of this as your home for as long as you wish to stay."

Rachel smiled, kissed Mary on both cheeks, and I knew then my doubts were for naught. They were going to be the best of friends and Rachel found a place in our lives.

* * *

An elderly neighbor stopped and dismounted. "

"Robbie, I bring bad news, laddie. Beatrice has passed and leaves Rourke alone in this world with the children. I wanted you to know as soon as possible as news like that cannot wait my friend."

"How is he reacting? Should I go to him, lest he go berserk and lose all that he has gained these past years?"

"No, Robbie, he's quite calm. Beatrice had that effect on him once the children came. I don't know the man, but his friends tell me after she arrived, he changed from his old ways and became a gentle soul doing whatever was needed in the community, without any care for himself. Truly he was a man beloved by all who know him.

"I spoke with him before we left. First, he wanted to say how sad he was that Tom had passed. He wanted Mary and Anne to know he felt that like himself, Tom had really come to love the new country and was happy to have settled here."

He mounted his horse and then turned to add, "He wants you to know he'll wait 'til the children are over the shock of losing their mother and then he plans to visit you for a time, if you'll have him. I hear there's talk of wanting him in the government, but he's told all concerned that his only wish is to spend what time he has with his children as he knew Beatrice would want it that way."

We had Anne come over in the evening to meet the priest. She immediately explained there was much work for him after he had rested.

"There are marriages to perform." She looked over at Mary. Also, there are christenings and I'm sure not only Catholics, but our Protestant friends will have need of your services too. When she spoke of Rourke, it was with a tinge of sadness.

"That man is surely the best example of what love can do. I always saw the best of him myself, but many thought him arrogant. Father, as my late husband, Tom, would say, 'The love of a good woman can change a man's ways and Rourke is an example for us all. Beatrice and Rourke were meant for each other, of that I have no doubt. Both were lost souls 'til they met and then their lives changed for the better. God rest her soul."

We next saw the romance between Rachel and Mac develop, all the old customs between an Indian man and wife had changed. No more the brave and the squaw who was totally obedient to her man. He found that both he and Rachel had adopted the best ways of the whites and it soon became obvious they would settle down and Mac would build them a home.

And so it was that the years went by and I found that the boys took over much of the running of things so I could spend my time hunting and fishing with my father and Dougal. I was on such a trip then I returned after some weeks away to see many of my friends gathered around the house and immediately thought that maybe Anne was ill, but then I noticed Rourke.

"Robbie, my friend, I have bad news for you this day. It's Mary...she died in her sleep. Anne found her this morning. It must have been a heart attack, as she wasn't ailing."

As I tried to make it into the house, I fell. He helped me up and set me down on a chair.

"Listen, Robbie, you must be brave, I know what you're going through, but remember, Mary, is in a better place now. She would want you to look out for the family."

I tried to comfort Anne, but she was braver than me. Looking into my eyes, she whispered. "Robbie, we mustn't cry now, we'll have time enough for that when this is all over and we can cry together."

After all the commotion of the funeral was over, we sat together by the fireside—Anne on one side and Rourke on the other. I began to reminisce about how after we left the militia, Tom and he asked us to dine with the family. It was then I saw Mary as a grown woman and how I'd acted rather clumsily, but she bade me take her for a walk. That's when she told me she loved me and always had.

That same night I'd told her she was to be my wife and how we would travel through life together. It had been the most wonderful journey, but now it was over and I was afraid to think of living without her by my side.

"Robbie, many years ago, Mary told me she felt she would be the first to leave this world, but she somehow knew it would be your destiny to go on and make a new life when she died. I was to tell you of her prediction and say to you at this time you must go on with your life and fulfill your destiny as God intended."

As Anne spoke, I felt a wave of sadness come over me and I began to sob. Anne cradled me in her arms like my mother used to do when I was a boy. As we sat there together, she whispered, "Now, Robbie, now is our time to cry for Mary. Just three old friends together, who have happy memories to remind us of our love for her. Now is the time we can share our special grief at her loss."

When I gazed through my tears I could see my old friend Rourke was also crying, so I pulled him to us and we wept for my love who was gone from me forever and also for their true loves who had gone before.

The next day things were better and I knew I had to go on for Mary, if nothing else, as she'd wanted it so. The children and I did our best to manage without her to guide us in our everyday lives, as she had done for so long. Alas, I felt Anne never got over Mary's death. From time to time she'd say how parents should never have to bury their children—that it was not God's way.

One morning we found her at the graves of Mary and Tom. I felt she'd died of a broken heart. I knew she would be happy to be with them for eternity.

John, my brother-in-law, became a prominent member of society. He married a free bond girl. They had two boys—Tom, the eldest and Robert, who every time I saw him looked just like the big man I had first met during the Indian wars, all those years ago.

Rourke would visit often and sometimes when the mood struck us we'd venture into the swamp to hunt gators as their skins were becoming valuable, just like the beaver had been all those years ago when the gentile classes in Europe would wear top hats made of beaver pelts so as not to be spoiled by the rain.

Occasionally, we'd spend nights camped out in the forest with a jug of whiskey and some cigars. There we would think back on those times we'd spent together in the Prince's service. From what we'd been told by others, the poor man drank himself to death...truly a sad figure in history.

We'd often talk about how it would have been if he'd not came back in '45, but as Rourke always said, "Robbie, we have nothing to be sorry for, lad. We did our duty and his failures must be left at his feet. That's probably what made the man an alcoholic. You and me, we went onto bigger and better things, thank the Lord, and if not for him, would we have met Beatrice and Mary? I think not."

Destiny Takes a Hand

I was sitting on my porch one day, looking out on my prosperous farm when a tinker came by mending pots and selling needles, and all kinds of haberdashery. I asked him. "How's the world treating you, my man?"

He laid down his basket, looked at me, and replied, "Good morning to you. How am I, do you say? Well, I've been worse off many a time, but if I had money, which I doubt I ever will..." He rubbed the stubble on his week-old beard, re-lit his clay pipe, and sat down on the step of my porch before he continued. "I would take my leave of this country and travel back to the land of my birth."

He rubbed a tear from his eye. "Just once more I want to hear the birds chirping in the glens and the soft gurgling of the streams as they rush down from the mountains, the gentle rain on my face as I tramped a mile or so down the glen to buy a dram at the inn and sit by a friendly fireside.

"I would sit and listen to the old men talk of the uprising and the brave men who fought in it. Men like Robbie Cameron of Locheill and Rourke, the Irishman, God rest their souls. They must be dead these many years."

As I sat there, he gave me a wave of his hand and went on his way. Dead these many years, I must remember to let Rourke know the next time I see him. He'll be surprised to hear of it. I began to think on what the tinker had said and as I looked around me, it was as if I no longer belonged there. The family was all business-like and I felt more and more in the way.

My ideas on how things should be done no longer made any sense in the scheme of things and although no one would say so, I think sometimes I was more of a hindrance than a help. I walked down to the patch where Mary and her parents lay, and sat down. Not meaning to, I soon fell asleep. When I awoke, it was as if I had heard Mary's voice.

Robbie Cameron, what's become of you? If you don't watch out you'll become an old man, so you will. I'm surprised at you moping around the way you do. Why don't you and that rascal Rourke take yourselves off to Scotland for a visit before it's too late and you're crippled with rheumatism? Go on now, when you're still fit and able. Maybe it'll give you a new lease on life, if nothing else.

I hesitated to talk to Rourke. He had his family to think about and as for me, what would the family say about my wild scheme. They were not in favor, all except my granddaughter, who pulled me to her and kissed me.

"Granddad, I think it's a grand idea and although I don't remember Grandma, though I'm named after her, I think she would say, 'Go my love and may the angels take care of you on your journey'. It was as if Mary herself was standing there in front of me and I knew I must go.

Within a few days I'd taken the bull by the horns and told Rourke of my plan.

"Robbie, I was just the other day thinking the same thing, but was afraid to mention it lest you might think me an old fool. I know we're not as young as we once were, but we don't have a foot in the grave yet, do we?"

I was sorely tempted to recall my conversation with the tinker, but was afraid to as I know Rourke too well. Without a doubt, he's the most superstitious man I ever met. One word about us being dead would put an end to any traveling to Scotland and that's for sure.

"Well then, it's settled. We can leave as soon as the next ship for Scotland arrives and who knows, maybe you will meet up with some of those married ladies you were so cozy with when you were on the run after Culloden?"

"Well now, Robbie, I have a feeling they're a bit long in the tooth for me, but never mind, maybe I'll be bumping into a daughter or maybe a granddaughter of one of those lovely women if I'm lucky."

"It will be more like they'll be giving an old fool like you a shove out of the way, than a bump, I'm thinking, Rourke. But where you're concerned, I'd never bet on it, that's for sure."

I informed the family of my intention to travel and between them they should decide who would take over from me a soon as possible. "But where will you go, Father?" my daughter asked.

"Scotland will certainly be my first choice."

"But Father, surely there are too many sad memories in Scotland for you to go back?"

I hesitated. "Well, that's true. There will be some sad memories and I'm sure a lot of good ones will come to mind when I get there. Now don't be too annoyed with me, girl, you must admit I never interfere with your lives, so I feel it's only fair you let me have my way in this matter."

Scotland

We sailed from the settlement on a clipper ship, a new fast type of vessel whose accommodation was much better than the last time I'd sailed for Scotland.

When Rourke and I had last stayed in Edinburgh, all kind of refuse used to be thrown out from the windows onto the street and the smell in summer was sickening. Now they were cobbled for the many coaches they had to accommodate. We stayed at a grand hotel and were treated like royalty, as the figured anyone coming from America must be rich beyond their wildest imagination.

But we soon tired of the city. I longed for the moors and the rivers of my youth, so we set out up the Great Highland Way, which runs all the way from south of the Loch Lomond to Inverness and beyond.

Along the length of the Loch, we could see herds of highland cattle with their shaggy coats and long horns being driven to the various markets. There were soldiers, mostly Scottish soldiers, not too many Redcoats to be seen.

Rourke remarked, "We're now so respectable they treat us like gentlemen. Quite a change, eh Robbie?"

* * *

When we arrived at the home of the Duke of Argyll, the new chief was as slippery as a wet eel, just like his great-grandfather and he was very interested in what profits could be made in the Carolinas if one were to invest some money there.

There had been a wild scheme to invest in the Indies, growing bread fruit—a cheap way to feed the many slaves housed on plantations. Many Scots had lost all their money in what was to be known as the South Sea Bubble.

The scheme had collapsed in financial ruin. Being a canny Scot, the Duke appeared apprehensive, but interested in the American economy just the same. I stayed only long enough to observe the proper ritual of visiting a Clan Chief and soon headed to the home of my ancestors—the house of Cameron.

We were told there wasn't a male heir still alive to lead the clan. The youngest of his daughters was in residence, her husband having died of blood poisoning. She had no children, so there was no heir take up the challenge of heading up the Cameron clan all over the world.

What I expected to see was not what I'd imagined. The lady was beautiful and I wondered how such a fine buxom woman had not remarried again after her husband had died. I surmised she must have had many suitors visiting her after the demise of her man.

She embraced me warmly and said she was very pleased to meet a Cameron from the New World. She was interested as to how many there were in my branch of the Clan.

I explained, "The country is vast and we Camerons are scattered over thousands of miles apart."

She could only wonder at the thought of it all. She made me welcome and insisted I stay at the castle.

At dinner in the great hall that evening, she recalled how her great-grandfather, with her sitting on his knee, would tell the story of the day his man came down with the pox and was not able to fight for the Clan against Argyll's man, a German no less.

"Young Robbie Cameron, a friendly lad, had agreed to stand in and had thrashed the Duke's man to within an inch of his life. He'd preserved the honor of the Clan and made them some gold coins in the bargain.

"Now that this lad is here in the ancestral home, Robbie, you'll be getting visits from far and near to shake your hand." She also added, "And to eat your food and drink your whiskey, so I hope you have enough money to have all this happen and save face?"

Not wishing to be outdone by her dry Scottish humor, I suggested I could have a grand gathering in the great hall and feed and supply drink for them all at once.

* * *

She'd agreed, the plans were made, invitations sent, and the night of the ball arrived.

I was summoned to her quarters and she inquired, "Do you have a kilt, Robert Cameron?"

"The last time I was in Scotland, Ma'am, it was not all that healthy to be caught wearing a kilt, so the answer is 'No, I'm afraid I don't have one."

"I can easily have you fitted into my late husband's. He and you were about the same size, although he was not as trim and as fit as you are, but I think it could work just the same."

True to her word, I was given the kilt and sporran and plaid socks and shoes, all the way down to the *sgian dubh* which is always worn in the stocking in case of trouble.

The night was a roaring success and when it was over, we sat by a great log fire, talking about my life and how it all happened.

"You, sir, are a most extraordinary man."

"How do you come to that conclusion, Ma'am?"

"My name is Nora. Now, let's see." She sat back counting on her fingers. "A pageboy to the pretender, Charles Stuart, a sailor, a pirate of sorts, an Indian fighter, a frontiersman, an adventurer, and also a farmer. My, what a grand life you've led, Robert! I've lived here in this great house all my life while you've seen a goodly part of the world."

"That may be true, but then you were born into this life and could not have changed it if you had wanted,

Nora. Now me, I'm a simple man. Fate took me from a humdrum life and showed me how to live...not forgetting my true friend Rourke, who is my mentor and father and brother, all things rolled up into one."

"I feel like I've known that handsome Irishman for years. Where is he? I've missed the rascal these last few days. I hope he enjoyed the month he spent here at the castle. At least the housemaids will miss the occasional nip at their buttocks as they passed him by. The man's a lovable rogue, so he is and that's a fact." She feigned a cough and smiled. "I have to admit I felt left out as he stayed well clear of my derriere."

"He's gone to visit his relatives in Ireland and sends his regrets that he could not be with all of us here tonight."

"Well, Robbie, please let him know we all had a grand time tonight and I danced for the first time since my husband passed away. So, let him know...if nothing else, Nora Cameron had a very happy night indeed."

She rose and filled my whiskey glass, pouring a sherry for herself. She settled down looking into the flames licking up the chimney as she spoke.

"What's to become of you now, Robbie? Will you go back to the Carolinas or stay in Europe? Have you remarried since your Mary died?"

"I haven't. I would find her hard to replace and once you've truly loved someone, it's hard. Don't you agree?"

"I would have agreed with you if you had asked me that question a month ago, but now I'm not so sure. She sipped her sherry. "You see, God help me, I think I've fallen in love with you, Robbie Cameron." She blessed herself. "I don't know what I can do about it. Tell me to stop jabbering and leave you at peace with your love for Mary and I will say no more."

It was as if I was dreaming. This beautiful woman had just told me she was in love with me and here I was standing here like I was a rainy Friday, as my mother used to say, when I would be in a trance while reading a book. I awakened from my dream and sat down beside her.

She looked into my eyes. "Robbie Cameron, why did you have to come here with those sparkling blue eyes? They're so vibrant and clear...it's as if they can see into my very soul. Why did you have to make me think of being in love for the first time in my life? My marriage was arranged for me, I never knew 'til this minute what being in love felt like—not that it's so great. I can't wait to see you and then if you don't say the right thing, I think you're getting bored with me and I panic. Then when you're gone, I can't wait to see you again. Oh Robbie, what am I to do? Tell me, what am I to do?"

I took her in my arms and kissed a strange woman for the first time since Mary died. I didn't feel guilty about being here with Nora for I knew that I too had fallen in love with her the first minute I saw her, but to know that she loved me too was wonderful. We kissed again and caressed each other, not caring about anything or anyone. Whatever the morrow held for us was not important. All we wanted was tonight and each other.

* * *

She lit a bedside candle. As we laid in her bed, she ran her fingers through my hair and she kissed me. "I can't go to the Carolinas, Robbie. My duty is here. You can see that, can't you? I love you more than life itself, but I have the clan to think about. Could you possibly stay here in Scotland and help me with my duties as my husband? Tell me you can, Robbie. Oh God, please tell me you can! I can't think that fate would send you to me, only to take you away again. Fate couldn't be so cruel, could she? I think I'll die of a broken heart if you say you must go back."

"Nora, my life is easily changed around, but there's the Clan. I would guess they would never agree to such a marriage. In any case, I'm only a commoner. You're as near to royalty as one can get in Scotland. Who of the other clan chiefs would sanction such a marriage?"

"Robbie, my Robbie, times have changed, my darling. The chiefs don't have the same power they used to in the old days. As far as the clan is concerned, I watched you meet with them. They liked you because you're so easy to like. You have a way about you, as my grandfather used to say. 'Thon young Robbie Cameron has a way with him. It's as if his blue eyes can look into a man's thoughts and capture them for himself. He could charm the birds out of the trees thon lad could.'

"So, have no fear of the Clan, only one man can put an end to this idea and that's you. Tell me? Do I become the happiest woman in all Scotland or do I spend the rest of my days like a hermit shut out from the world 'til I die?"

I took her in my arms and looked into her eyes. "No, my darling, you won't have to endure such a fate. If you want me for your husband, nothing in this world can keep it from happening."

The news went out that Robbie and Nora were to wed in a month's time and all would be welcome. The clan chiefs were also sent invitations and a great wedding was planned. It was to be the greatest event since "forty-five" when all the Clan had been together to raise the standard of the pretender to the Scottish throne.

No one refused the invitation which meant Robbie Cameron was everybody's favorite and a great event took place. There were people from all over Scotland, even Rourke was there and when the priest had finished the ceremony, we kissed and the great feast began.

After a while we decided to leave the merry-making to the youngsters. As we drove off in the coach, we each looked out a window and waved our goodbyes. Nora turned and looked at me.

"You know, Robbie, the old chief told me before he died, that one day your seed would be the head of the clan. I never did understand what he meant."

I tried to answer, but the tears welled up in my eyes and all I could do was turn and look at Nora's face. She cried too. After I held her for a minute, I thought, Someday, when we're long gone, maybe a seed of my seed will come to Scotland from the Americas and he will be chief. Maybe that's what the old Cameron meant.

Just to be there with Nora and feel the love she had for me was all I wanted for this moment in time. I thought, 'Who knows? Maybe someday in the future a descendent of mine will come to Scotland, he will find his love here in the Scottish highlands just as I had done. He will stay and help rule the clan for many a year.'

* * *

As I lay down my pen and the ink on the page dries, I realize that I have come full circle from a boy, daydreaming in the hay loft, to an old man sitting here in the great hall with a fire burning in the fireplace and a dram of whiskey in my hand, enjoying a host of memories. I'm reminded of all my dear departed friends as they madly dash into my thoughts, as if to be sure they're not forgotten.

Maybe at my age I should feel sad, having outlived most of the friends of my youth, but strange as it seems, I feel my story is not ending, but somehow just beginning anew. If I were to be asked by a stranger 'What are your happiest memories?' I would have to say, Rourke, Mary McHugh, and Nora Cameron.

The clock is striking five and the dawn is breaking over the loch, as a covey of grouse, startled by a magnificent buck with tall antlers, wing over the calm water. As the sun rises, it floods the room with rays of pale golden sunlight. I must find a spot in the huge bookcase in which to hide my story. Who knows, maybe someday it will be found by a kindly soul who will dust it off and spend a few quiet hours reading of my life and adventures.

Destiny

The train from London was cold and crowded. Being from North Carolina, the English weather had Robbie Cameron freezing. "Do you think Scotland is even colder than here?" Robbie asked.

"From what I heard of it, you're damn right it's colder and they don't have central heating either. So, how the hell did we get stuck with this assignment? Tell me if you can?"

The tall, lean Texan stood smoking a Pall Mall. I thought better of saying what my friend didn't need to know. I'd asked for the assignment when it came up on the squadron notice board.

Wanted. Two fliers to move to Scotland to work with British pilots, teaching them to fly our fighter jets. I immediately sought out the Colonel.

"Me and my buddy are eager to go and besides, my family came from there hundreds of years ago. I've read in the family bible of a great house and land which belonged to our Clan."

The Colonel looked up from his desk as he shuffled files. "The Clan you came from, Cameron, was probably sheep stealers or as legend has it...sheep somethings," he added, smiling.

I laughed. "Maybe a bit of both, Sir, but let's face it, who else is willing to go to Scotland in the spring? It's 1944. When there's a chance, the second front will open up any day now in Europe."

"That being so, what makes you so gung-ho, Captain Cameron?"

"Well Sir, I just thought since I'm over here and all the folks back home would get a kick out of seeing the old place. I can maybe pay a visit, take a few pictures and send them home. Cheer them up a bit, don't you see?"

"Cameron, for all you know it's probably fallen down in a heap of rubble, so what then? Oh, I get it. You take a picture outside some big glitzy castle then *shazam*, that's the old homestead. Yes, Dad, things are still looking good for our sheep stealer relatives, believe it or not."

I looked longingly. "Okay," the Colonel relented. "I don't want you causing me any trouble up there on those moors. Especially, I don't want any trouble with the locals from you, Cameron, and that Texas longhorn friend of yours.

Remember what we were told, 'Don't make fun of the way they talk, how they cook, and stay away from those gals whose husbands have been gone overseas for five years. And if I get one complaint from their bobbies about you two, you're outta there pronto. Get it?'"

Now it didn't seem like such a good idea when the weather was factored in, what with the lousy food and the rationing. Heck, even the scotch was rationed. At least back in camp they could still get the odd bottle of liquor and cigarettes. The Colonel told them he'd send stuff from time to time, so maybe it wouldn't be so bad.

* * *

When the train stopped, the whole carriage shook and both woke up at the same time. They'd been dreaming about home and boy was it ever a letdown. They picked up their gear and headed for the transport office on the platform.

"So you two heroes are over here to teach our boys how to fly, are ye?"

"Not exactly, it's a new plane...and well, it's different than the ones your pilots have at the moment. So our job is to let them know what to expect."

"Well, I'm sure we'll all sleep a bit easier tonight, knowing you have arrived here in Scotland right enough."

Tex got kinda pissed. "Listen, laddie, we didn't start this war and we sure as hell could be doing something else back home if you don't want us here?

The clerk looked up and stamped their orders .He glanced up at Tex. "I'm sorry, lad, don't fly off the handle. It's the way we Scots are. We don't mean anything by our jibes. God only knows, we'd probably be speaking German if it wasn't for you and a lot just like you. Don't mind me.

"It's just I'm an old soldier and I was in the last one. Somehow, I feel those blokes in the League of Nations should have done a better job and we'd all be a lot better off. It's not you, lads, it's this blooming war that's getting us down. We've been at it now for five years and it's getting a bit hard to take. So please, don't mind me.

"Anyway, you'll find the lassies are crazy to go out with you Yanks, with your perfume and cigarettes and all that money to spend. My son remarked just the other night at dinner. 'You know what's wrong with the Yanks, Dad?'"

"No," I said. "What, son?"

He looked up from his plate of fish and chips. 'They're overpaid, oversexed, and over here.' Of course he was only joking."

Tex rubbed his hands together and remarked as two women passed by and gave him the eye.

"Well now, the thought of all those women makes me think this was not such a bad idea I had after all. Just think, we're probably gonna be the only two American flyboys in the area. Man, we are gonna have a ball, old buddy, just you wait and see."

* * *

The camp was near the sea in a place called Ayrshire. Hard as it was to believe, the locals told us the weather was the best in the country, as the Mexican Gulf Stream came near to making landfall and made the climate warmer. Tex couldn't quite understand about the Gulf Stream.

He'd figured if his mom put a parcel of tamales and peppers and maybe even a hamburger patty or two made from prime Texas longhorn beef into a box and let it go adrift that it would eventually end up on our beach."

I scratched my arms as I lifted the window shade and looked out on a wild, rainy day. "The only problem is, Tex. The damn war will be over before that day ever dawns."

I was lucky. One of the pilots was getting married and needed money, so being the nice guy I am, I bought his two-seater sports car. The steering wheel was on the wrong side, but that was okay, because these crazy Scots drove on the wrong side of the road all the time.

Now, to get back to the car. It was called an "Austin Healey." It was painted deep green and had a hood you pulled up when it rained, which was all the time. It wasn't much bigger than a high class baby stroller, but what the hell, the roads were real narrow and nobody had any gas to run a car anyhow. Everything was rationed, but maybe I could get a pass and look for my ancestral home.

I'd just roll up, knock on the door and say, "Hi cousins! I just dropped in from the Colonies to say hello and maybe have a spot of tea. What do you think?"

My daydream of superiority was over when the squadron leader asked me to go up with him and put the plane through its paces. Well, talk about egg on my face. This guy could fly anything he got his hands on. He was an artiste. He explained that in the Battle for Britain, if you were good you lasted a week and if you were excellent, maybe two weeks, but if you were lucky, you lived to tell about it.

However, he explained in about a month they were expecting all new pilots, just out of flight school, so we should take life easy for now and see a bit of the country.

"Sir, do you think I could get a pass to go visit my Clan headquarters? I could take Tex with me and we'd stay out of trouble, I promise."

"Where is this clan estate, Captain Cameron?"

Our commanding officer was tall and sported a great ginger mustache. "I don't rightly know, Sir, but the name being Cameron, does that give you a clue?"

"Well, the Camerons are situated in Argyll, not too far from here on the northeast side of Glasgow and that's about seven hours from here over very narrow roads. So, I'd say, maybe a day's drive. Do you have enough petrol coupons?"

* * *

We started on our way, but when Tex reached Glasgow and saw all the pretty girls, he said that it was more like his kind of town. He wanted to spend his time there rather than looking up my family ghosts, so I dropped him off at the nearest hotel and went on alone.

I knew the estate was in the vicinity. Maps were nonexistent as the War Department had confiscated all maps of the British Isles when the threat of an invasion from the Germans had been expected earlier in the war.

So here I was, driving in a country with little or no road maps or signposts. I mistakenly complained to an old man who I stopped to ask for directions. He listened very carefully and when I'd finished speaking, he replied.

"What would we want with road signs, laddie? Sure we all know where we are and where we're going without any maps or signposts.

* * *

The inevitable happened. The car ran out of gas. Stranded by the roadside, God only knew where, I saw what turned out to be a Rolls Royce coming toward me. At first I worried about this monster hitting my little sporty car, but the driver stopped and pulled in behind.

"Having car trouble, are we?"

She was something—not too tall, with auburn hair, green eyes, and a marvelous set of gams. She was dressed in a kilt and a silk blouse with ruffles covering her breasts. I tried to look pleasant. I offered a cigarette.

"Oh, American, I've never tried one before. Ours are rationed...for the troops mostly."

I closed in to light her cigarette and smelled her delicious cologne.

"Well, yeah, as a matter of fact I've run out of gas."

"Run out of...oh, you mean petrol. Well, I can give you a lift, but sorry, I can't help with petrol, I'm afraid." She tipped some ash and took a drag.

"That's okay, I'm probably miles from where I should be anyway."

"And where would that be, pray tell?"

"Well, for starters, my name is Robert Cameron and I'm looking for the home of my ancestors, Come to think of it, I'm possibly on a wild goose chase. Still, what the heck, I tried."

"Are you one of the Camerons from Northern Virginia, by any chance?"

I was completely taken aback. "Have we met?"

"No, no," she stammered. "I was just looking at a rather old book I found quite by accident in our library the other day and I saw we had...or have relatives in Virginia. So naturally I wondered if by chance you were one of them."

"Not only am I one of them...heck, my ancestor came back to Scotland and married the daughter of the clan chief, I'll have you know."

"Well, good for you. Does that mean we have to genuflect when we meet you?" she said, smiling.

"No, don't bother. Just kiss my ring and that'll satisfy protocol," I said, laughing.

"My name is Nora Cameron. I was named for that lady your ancestor married."

"Well, how about that! Hey, we might be cousins or something. Where do you get all this information? Is there a book I can buy to take home to my dad? He'll go crazy over this...crazy!"

"I'm studying the family history for my doctorate at St. Andrews University. Maybe you've heard of it?"

"No, I just got here last week and all I know is Ayrshire, Glasgow, and wherever the heck I am now. Tell me, where is this place? Not Brigadoon, by any chance?"

"You should be that lucky. If I remember correctly, they had lots of good food, dancing maidens, and whiskey by the barrel. This is no make-believe glen, I'm afraid. Here we have little to spare and although it's coming down misty, we're not about to disappear any time soon."

She slid over the seat and unlocked the car door. "What's up, are you frightened to drive on this lonely road by yourself?"

I'm being careful. It's not the first time a German pilot, newly shot down, has tried to steal a car and make a break for it.

"Hop in and I'll take you home. We're only about a mile from your ancestral castle. How would you like to come with me and spend the night in the bed your ancestor slept in all those years ago? I mean by yourself, of course. So don't be getting any funny ideas, Yank."

She smiled, put the car in gear, and we took off. It took only minutes to reach the estate. Was I ever overwhelmed! I thought for sure the place would be in ruins, like those stories you read by that guy...what's his name? Oh yeah, Robert Louis Stevenson, I believe, the one about being the Laird of Shaw's.

I always liked that story. It reminded me of the yarns I heard about my ancestor when the family organized the big annual meeting of Camerons from all over. It was a blast and the stories they told were the greatest. Of course, I guess it was all make believe?"

"Not necessarily, Robert, why don't you go down to the library and read an old record of much that happened. It's written in diary form. You may get a surprise or two Believe me, it's not all fairy tales, that's for sure."

* * *

Nora and I ate dinner at a great oak table. As she filled my wine glass she told me about my ancestor and how he'd married the clan chief and stayed on. "This is the table he'd sit in the library reading or writing his memoirs."

She served a brandy and a cigar while I settled down to read an account of my ancestor's return to the Clan ancestral home, marrying Nora, and how they lived for years the happiest couple in the county, so it was written.

A short note in the diary margin noted when Nora died. Robbie lived only a few months after her death. It was said he died from a broken heart after losing his love. I talked out loud without realizing. "Do you think it's possible to die from a broken heart?"

Nora was stoking up the fire as she turned and stood there with a hand on the mantle shelf. "Oh, I think it's possible, Robbie." When two people love each other that much and one dies, the other has nothing left to live for. If you believe in life after death, then they're together again in the next world."

"You Scots are sure a romantic lot, that's for sure. In the States, hell most people get divorced at least once, so not much chance of broken hearts there."

"Aye, well we're not in the States, are we, Robert Cameron? She walked over and re-filled my brandy snifter.

"Personally, when I marry, it will be for one time only and that will be it—no divorce in my life, that's for sure."

"Well, I think you've got something there, Nora. I too would like to think it will be a once-in-a-lifetime deal for me, but who knows what my other half will do?"

"Well then..." She placed the poker back on the hearth.

"Why don't you find yourself a wife here in Scotland and take her back with you when the war's over? There's plenty who would jump at a chance to live there, that's for sure."

I noticed she began to blush so hard it looked like her cheeks were on fire. Fortunately, I pretended to be deeply engrossed in the diary of my relative and hadn't noticed.

I wondered how she could have been so affected by her own remark. It wasn't as if she knew me all that well. As a matter of fact, she probably didn't even give me a second look. So why was she being so foolish? I thought about it for a moment and then went back to reading.

I was having a hard time sleeping. Was it all the information in the diaries? I couldn't be sure. Then I thought, it couldn't be that young, Nora had gotten to me. After all, I hardly knew her and she seemed the type who was going to marry some professor of Laird or whatever, so wasn't too interested in a flyboy like me.

* * *

When I awoke in the morning, the birds were chirping and for a moment I was scared to look out the window in case I'd somehow been transported back in time. It was strange feeling, but I really could imagine it. Just think what would the guys back home say if they could see me now, all tucked in a bed that was at least a few hundred years old. Man, who would have thought it? My pass was over and Nora made sure I had enough petrol to get me back to base. I thanked her for all that she'd done to make me feel welcome in our ancestral home. As I turned to leave, I kissed her on the cheek and then drove off with a strange feeling I'd be back some day. I remembered we'd talked one time about me returning on my next pass.

* * *

The war changed with June 6,, 1944. The Allies attacked the German Atlantic wall and soon had the German army on the run. I never did have a chance to visit Nora again. The war was over, I shipped back to Virginia, enrolled in a university, dated a few girls, and eventually obtained my degree. It was at a party being given in my honor that a friend of my father's asked what my plans were now. Having survived the war, I would be getting on with life and now had a degree to my name. Strangely, I began to think about making a wrong decision and hating the rest of my life. I shrugged off the feeling and went to get another beer and dance with a family friend.

* * *

The next day the feeling was back and I spent several miserable weeks deep in thought. One morning at breakfast I announced that I was going back to Scotland to get away, to clear my mind and figure out what to do with the rest of my life.

"Are you sure it's to clear your mind? Maybe it's that girl, Nora, we've all heard about since your return?"

"What do you mean, Mother?"

"Robert, it's just that you're ready to talk about her at the least opportunity, do realize that?"

I didn't answer at first, but thought about what she said. Then, as if experiencing a revelation, I said, "I guess you could be right, Mother, but it's only right now that I am beginning to admit it."

"Robert, nobody knows you like your mother and I think one way or the other it's something you have to do before you can settle down."

* * *

The flight into Prestwick Airport brought back all the memories of my time in the Air Force. I took the long train ride up the side of Loch Lomond into Argyll and then a rickety bus trip right up the road to the estate, where it dropped me off. I was traveling light. I slung my knapsack over one shoulder and walked boldly up to the great oak doors with the clan crest carved into the sturdy oak panels. I used the great brass knocker and waited. After a few minutes a pretty young lass with fiery red hair and emerald green eyes, dressed in a maid's uniform, opened the door.

"What business do you have with the Cameron house today, Sir?" she asked with a smile.

"I wish to see..." My voice seemed a bit squeaky, so I started again, I wish to speak with Miss Nora. Is she at home?"

"I'll see if she is receiving today, Sir. Please, may I know your name?"

"Just say Robert Cameron from Virginia wishes to speak with her, if he may."

She showed me into the great library and I stood looking out the huge windows down the road as far as the eye could see. How old is that grass? I wondered. Hundreds of years at least. How many men have cut it over the centuries?

My thoughts were interrupted with the sound of running feet on the polished oak floor. The door burst open and Nora came rushing in, grabbed me and hugged me. In turn, I hugged her tightly.

After a minute, she pulled back a bit and held me by the shoulders as she gazed into my eyes.

"Well, Robbie, you look good, but don't take so long between visits. We missed you, don't you know? We want to see a bit more of you from now on."

She looked wonderful. Her eyes flashed as she spoke. Her voice was like music to my ears as she took my arm and guided me to the sofa.

"Now, sit down. I'll ring for tea and scones, your favorites. Tell me, what happened in your life since we met last? I was sure you had married a lovely southern belle and had a family." The maid appeared.

"Please bring us tea and scones," Nora requested.

After the maid was gone, I replied, "Not yet." I told her of all that had happened to me since last we met.

"And you, Lady Cameron, have you a fiancé or maybe a boyfriend, or have you gotten married since I saw you last?"

"No, Robert. I'm still an old maid," she said, resting her hand on mine. "Who would want to have anything to do with a redhead like me? But, I'm still hopeful. As my old nanny tells me, 'If I don't hurry up, I'll die in despair.'"

We both laughed and for some reason neither could take our eyes off the other. The conversation was definitely electric. Before I realized it, the buttered scones and tea were finished, heavy velvet drapes were being drawn, and the knurled oak logs in the great fireplace were lighted. The end table lamps were switched on and the room took on a warm glow.

I wondered about the soot-covered black iron cauldron and desperately wanted to try pushing it to one side to see if there was a door open in the hearth.

"Does that blackened pot actually conceal a hidden passageway?"

"I'm not sure, Robbie, but when the fire's gone down we can try it and see. Or, if you're feeling adventurous, we can try it now."

She took a log poker with a hooked end and slowly pushed the bracket. At first nothing, then all at once the stones in back of the hearth began to open. They made a sort of crunching sound and flecks of mortar fell into the fire, causing crackling noises. The draft from the opening forced the flames out into the room, Nora jumped back and I caught her in my arms.

She stretched her arm to grab a lighted candelabra. I picked it up and as I did she kissed me again, but this time with real passion. I just stood there holding the candelabra while the flicker of candlelight illuminated her face.

"Well, that's better. I wasn't sure you'd respond at first, but I take it you have feelings for me too, Robbie Cameron. So, let's go exploring and see if there's a tunnel and where it leads.

We entered a small lobby with great spider webs hanging from the ceiling. I went first, holding the candelabra in front of me, occasionally brushing away a spider web so that Nora could follow. She gripped my free hand tightly, almost as if she expected to see a bearded clansmen charge at us from the darkened tunnel.

I stopped at a stone bench and set the candelabra down. I blew away the dust of centuries and pulled her down next to me. I began exploring her anatomy as we kissed. My hand felt for her breast. She stopped me.

She held her wrist up to the candlelight. "Oh my, look at the time. We must dress for dinner. I have guests coming this evening."

"Nora, I'm sorry. I was too forward. I apologize."

She gave me a friendly tap on my chin. "I'm not complaining, Robbie. I was beginning to think it would never happen between you and me, but we have guests coming and here we are making out in this tunnel of love means we're running late."

I held the candelabra to light our way back as I answered. "I'm traveling light—no dinner jacket, not even a sport coat, so I guess I'll pass and go find a room in the village. Do you have a car or someone who can give me a lift? I'm sure not going to try finding my way by myself in the dark. It's like black velvet out there and possibly haunted by many of your overzealous ancestors."

"Robbie," I have a surprise for you. We exited the tunnel and Nora led me upstairs to my bedroom. She opened one of the heavy oak doors. In the cedar-lined closet hung a highland dress kilt.

"This was last worn by your ancestor, Robert Cameron. We had it restored last year and tonight it won't be out of place if you wear it, as we're all dressing for dinner. So put away any thought of leaving here. You're a guest for as long as you wish to stay."

I was a little skeptical of how I'd look, but when I donned his bonnet complete with a pheasant feather and glanced in the mirror, to my surprise I liked what I saw.

* * *

When I came downstairs, the folks had already arrived. I walked into the room, everyone turned, and then silence. Nora took my arm and announced, "Ladies and gentlemen, may I introduce Robert Cameron from America...the Virginia Camerons. Robert, my guests..."

Introductions followed. I'd never remember all those names, so I just smiled a lot. "This is my favorite," Nora whispered in my ear as she introduced an elderly gent dressed in a kilt, holding a good-sized glass filled with an amber elixir.

"Professor, how are you? Robbie, he knows where all the bodies are buried. Callum, this is an American Cameron, Robbie by name."

He stood looking at me with his head to one side, as if sizing me up. "At first I felt we'd met, Robbie, and then I looked above the mantle shelve and saw the portrait hanging there, you could have sat for the artist. It's uncanny."

"My Lord, you're right, Callum. Robbie, it's quite unbelievable, look at it."

I looked at the portrait of a handsome man in highland dress. I could see the uncanny likeness.

* * *

The evening was a huge success and by the early hours all were gone, save two people who wanted to be together more than anything else. We remained sitting at the huge fireplace, sipping a brandy and watching the flames. We made love in front of the fireplace on a tiger skin rug, possibly killed by a distant relative on a hunt in India. Nora sat nursing her brandy with both hands as she looked over at me, but she gazed into the liqueur as she spoke.

"You know I canna leave the home of our Clan, don't you Robbie? I was tied to this house and this land even before I was born. It's my heritage, just like yours is in Virginia—only this is different; the rules are different. You belong to the new world, while my loyalty is to the old. I know it sounds odd to you, but that's the way it is here in Scotland with the old families.

"I could feel different, but too much depends on this house and this Clan. Now the war is over and plane travel is for everyone, I feel Scots from over the globe will dream of someday visiting Scotland and getting close to their heritage. I must be here like a beacon in a lighthouse to say welcome. 'Welcome, all you Camerons!' It makes no difference of circumstance. You are a Cameron and as long as Scotland stands for truth and loyalty, so will you be made welcome when you visit this home, which is and for always be your heritage. That is my purpose, Robbie. That is my destiny."

I could see the tears in her eyes. I leaned over. "I understand, Nora...believe me, I understand. When I decided to visit this home again, I had but one thought and that is to ask you to marry me. Oh, I told others it was a sentimental journey, but I knew in my heart that you were the reason for my coming once again to this ancient house with its ghosts and memories, both good and bad, with deeds done which no man can speak of, but always and forever, for the good of the Clan.

"I know now you could never be happy away from this beautiful old house and its grounds cared for by both my ancestors and yours for all those centuries. Now, especially with the world changing, there is a need for this place and others like it, for without them Scotland's heritage will surely be lost in the coming years."

I knelt down before my love. "If you'll marry me, I'd be willing to spend the rest of my days in this old fortress with you, my love, and be content to do so."

* * *

The clan consented to the union. Nora and I were married. People came from all walks of life to witness the marriage and to wish Robbie and Nora Cameron long life and happiness. It was a grand wedding and the sounds of bagpipes were to be heard for miles. Most in attendance wore the clan tartan and the ceremony evoked memories of days long since passed.

When all the toasts were complete and the last glass smashed to smithereens, we started off on our honeymoon. Driving away in the classic Rolls Royce that Nora was driving when I first set eyes on her, I thought about all that had taken place. We smiled and waved out the car window at the folks lining both sides of the driveway to bid us "God speed."

Deep in thought, Nora spoke first. "Robbie, I wonder, when your relatives and mine were married all those hundreds of years ago, do you think they also drove away from the house in their carriage waving to the well-wishers?

"Did they ever imagine that one day a man from America named Robert Cameron and a Scotswoman named Nora Cameron would take the same road to happiness as they'd taken? Could she have thought that someday the love she felt for her Virginian would be matched by one of her descendants? Is another endearing love, just as strong for another Robert Cameron from Virginia and a Scot lass called Nora possible? I like to think it is."

As she spoke, a small rain shower began as it does only in Scotland. Without warning, it soon engulfed us in a whirling mist which significantly reduced our visibility. I peered out into the mist and as the wipers cleared away the condensation, for just an instant, I thought I saw a handsome couple dressed in their finest wedding clothes—she in a silken gown and he in his highland dress, smiling and waving.

I belatedly answered. "Yes, my love, I really think she did have such a thought."

* * *

POSTSCRIPT
Argyll 1953

Please indulge my vanity, but having found my ancestor's diary, with tales of his many exploits, I felt no harm could be done in bringing his story of the Cameron family up to date.

There are now two heirs to the Cameron clan. One is a bonnie blue-eyed lad named Robbie and fiery red-headed lass named Mary, after the wife of Robbie Cameron, a well-known duelist for Cameron of Locheill in those long ago days of chivalry.

D. N. Curran

ABOUT THE AUTHOR

D. N. Curran was born in Cupar, a small town near St. Andrews, Scotland. He emigrated to the United States when he was a young man and successfully ran his own custom homes construction business. When he retired, he relocated to Las Vegas, where he's enjoying a budding career as a writer of fiction.

6944262R00153

Printed in Great Britain
by Amazon.co.uk, Ltd.,
Marston Gate.